THE SEEKING

A MONSTROUS CREATURES NOVEL
BOOK ONE

MARLENA FRANK

For those who dare to dream,
Who fight for truth,
And resist.

For those who dare to dream,
Who fight for truth,
And resist.

PREFACE

I used to be haunted by nightmares. For several months when I was young, I would dream the same nightmare again and again every night. It made me afraid to go to sleep. It made me exhausted when I was awake. I thought there was something wrong with me because I had never heard of anyone else having nightmares like that. I didn't want to talk about them with friends and family because I was embarrassed. Part of me feared that discussing them gave the dreams power.

Dreams have a strange, uncanny hold over us. When we are locked within them, we know truths that are lost to our waking minds. They can be resplendent or terrifying from one breath to the next, and sometimes they can even change our lives.

These days I've made peace with my nightmares. Instead of fearing them, I look forward to them. I use them for story ideas and to brainstorm plots to frighten readers. This story, I admit, was born from one of those nightmares. Kudos if you can guess the scene.

I hope you enjoy this shared nightmare as much as I enjoyed crafting it. May it strengthen you to face your monsters during the day.

Marlena Frank
5/11/2020

PART ONE
APPLE PIE

CHAPTER I
THE EXALTED

The scent of freshly baked apple pie filled the cold morning air... I hated it. It was a tradition of Carra, baked throughout the town at the end of October every year. Most thought it was a lovely treat, a warm and sweet way to step into fall, but it made my stomach clench.

It was a holiday favorite for The Seeking, and today almost every home in town had a pie.

I took a deep breath, allowing the scent to flow through me, allowing my hands to tremble before willing them to be still. It was only morning, I reminded myself. There were many hours before the clock struck midnight and The Seeking began. The hunt wasn't on yet; besides, I still had people to see.

Wrapping my scarf tighter around my neck, I headed down the hill, away from the Exalted House. The dirt path felt solid under my feet even as my heart fluttered like a hummingbird in flight.

While the sun had only just peeked over the horizon, all of Carra was bustling. They were celebrating, of course; the Great Feast would take place tonight, where they would make sure the hunters and dogs were well fed. I felt their eyes on me as I walked down the street, faces turning toward me, eyes peering out through windows. If I wasn't careful tonight, any of them might catch me.

A blast of wind scattered a pile of leaves and I started, clutching my hat over my braids as my boots sank slightly into a muddy patch on the dirt road.

Whenever they caught me looking at them, their intense gazes would turn into cheerful smiles.

All of them were deceivers.

There was no polite, understood rivalry this year.

No, this year, there was outright anger towards me and my family. I could feel it in the air but couldn't pinpoint it exactly. Was it because we had been in power for so long? Five years didn't seem that long, but I couldn't deny how the resentment had grown over time.

A young woman, who had auburn hair and pale skin, looked to be a few years older than me, walked towards me on the path. She was smiling, but when she glanced up and saw me, her smile hardened, and she turned quickly down a side road. She was hardly an exception to the rule.

Every year I watched their pleasantries grow thin. As the months passed, I noticed how they stared up at the Exalted House with undeniable envy in their eyes as their bitterness grew. Many were biding their time

CHAPTER 1
THE EXALTED

until tonight, when they had the power to make a change.

At midnight the bell tower would toll and The Seeking would begin. Their smiles would no longer need to be masked. At midnight their true hatred would come out to play.

"Good morning, Dahlia," a frail old woman with wispy white hair and watery eyes said as she folded linens and dropped them into a basket.

I nodded, returning her smile even though I hadn't the slightest idea who she was.

That was the problem with being part of the Exalted. Everybody knew who I was even if I didn't know them. Some I got to know if I had to work a court case or investigate a situation, but generally they were unknown faces with unknown names. At least I was used to going through the pleasantries without even thinking about it.

Another cold wind blew past me and already I could tell it would be a rough night. I picked up the pace, wanting to be away from so many prying eyes. I wanted this Seeking to be over, for the hunt and the cruelty and the hatred to be done with. But I had to follow the rules of Carra. We all had to, even if The Seeking brought out the worst in people.

"Running about causing trouble, Little Mouse?" Mr. Broskow asked, his booming voice sending a cold chill down my spine. I was hoping I was out early enough to avoid him, but he, too, was up early this morning.

I turned to see him lingering in the doorway of his shop, a bloody axe at his feet as he tied the legs of a pig carcass to a hook, the blood pouring down into a bucket below. I wondered if he had waited for me to walk by just so he could try to intimidate me by bleeding out a pig. That was the sort of tactic he liked to use - brutal viciousness to throw me off guard.

Broskow was a big man with a sallow complexion, a thick beard, and bright red cheeks. He lived for The Seeking. He relished the hunt and he saw me, one of the smallest of my family, as easy prey.

I stopped and grimaced as the scent of blood momentarily overwhelmed me, but then glared as I called out, "My family has the day off to prepare, as you well know."

He leaned against the doorway, the pig's carcass swinging slowly in the wind beside him. Its eyes were closed, its mouth open, likely from delivering its final scream – I held back a wince.

"Come here a moment."

Part of me wanted to ignore him. There was no law stating that I had to talk to people who heckled me, but I knew I was still being watched. I glanced around and could see several faces peering out through their shutters. How I handled Broskow might determine how many of them would decide to chase me down when the moon was high.

So, I gathered my strength and stepped towards him. "What is it?"

The first thing I noticed was that Broskow's gloves glinted in the morning light because they were wet. When he picked up his bloodied axe, I felt my heart skip a beat; he winked before hoisting it above his head. I gasped as he brought it down on one of the pig's legs, and shuddered as he dropped its pale limb with a thump into the bucket below.

I took a shaky step back, my body trembling as a crowd formed around us. He grinned, malice clear in his eyes as he stepped forward and dropped a hand on my shoulder; it smelled like old meat and I swallowed hard.

His grip was painful, but I refused to wince. I had already shown weakness and could see how much he enjoyed it, but I wouldn't do it again.

"Say hello to your parents for me," he said with eyes like a dead fish. "Tell them that I'll be the one to return you tonight." He gave me a little shake, probably just to show how much smaller than him I was for the audience that had gathered.

My hands fisted at my sides. "Strong words for someone who has never been able to catch any Exalted children."

Broskow's eyes narrowed and his fingers tightened on my shoulder, where pain started pulsing outward. "You had best hope that you do elude me this year, Little Mouse. When Pearl and I become the new Exalted, we'll send you out to test the Boundary Line every night for the rest of your short little life." He dragged a bloody finger across my cheek. "I don't think you would last a single night."

I grimaced. My family had been part of the Exalted for five years and my brothers and I had survived four Seekings, but I knew how organized Broskow's hunting parties could be and how vile his intimidation tactics were becoming.

He made my little brother cry last year as he poured blood over him on the street, in front of the town to witness. Come midnight, he would put together at least ten men with promises of high positions after their victory and round up his trusted troop of hunting dogs. This was just the precursor to the ruthlessness of tonight.

I pulled away from his grip. "We'll see about that."

He leaned down, his maddened grin fading. "Four years is a long time to elude me, Dahlia. I won't let you make it to five." His voice lowered, "You come from a bad seed. Your father cheated so he could live in the Exalted House, and his reign will not last much longer." He paused, our eyes locking. "None of you deserve to be our leaders."

I stepped away from him. "My father didn't cheat; he followed the rules the same as everyone else!" By now several people had stopped to watch us. The old woman with the laundry basket wore a smirk. A middle-aged man passed us on the street before he stopped to lean against the building on the opposite end of the trail, laughing in a drunken haze.

Broskow adored it; he loved having an audience. He stood up straighter, easily towering over me, and spoke to the people around us. "Bribery is for cowards who are too weak to hunt their prey on their own." He pointed at me. "Her family does not deserve to be our Exalted. Who here will help me hunt down Dahlia Priest tonight and drag her to Town Hall?"

A small cheer erupted from the onlookers.

"Together, we'll make sure the Priests have seen their final dawn as the Exalted!"

I felt the blood drain from my face. This time the cheer was more heartfelt, and some of the people cheering – some of them I knew.

My wrist was grabbed in a claw-like grip and I jerked back to see the old woman with the laundry basket, her eyes watering with anger.

"Perhaps we ought to hold onto her now, and bring her when the bell tolls," she said with a cracked voice. "That would be easier."

"No, no," Broskow chided with a wide, toothy grin. "We must follow the rules. Carra would fall without her traditions." Again, his eyes met mine. "Don't worry, she won't escape us tonight."

In my heart I knew he was right. Every year the hunting parties grew more and more determined and I had to push myself to be smarter and faster than every person in town.

I turned from them and ran.

I no longer cared what they thought.

"That's right, run!" Broskow's laughter taunted me from behind. "Run, Little Mouse, back to hide in your hole! It won't save you!"

I pictured Bisa's face in my mind: her warm smile, her easy laugh, her mischievous eyes.

I wiped at my face, at the blood on my cheek. I hated

the warm blood that was seeping into my leather tunic and growing colder by the second. I hated the way I smelled. I hated that I had let Broskow get to me, and I knew that word of what happened would spread quickly.

Why couldn't I have just left him alone? Why did I always have to try and prove them wrong? If I just didn't care, it would have been so much easier.

I took a few deep breaths as I turned down the next street. I didn't want Bisa to see how shaken I was. She would fret and want me to stay, but I had to be strong for tonight, didn't I?

Dappled morning sunlight streamed down through the pines. Leaves rustled and swirled past my feet, and in the distance a crow cawed. Earlier, before I ran into Broskow, I had felt like I had plenty of time, but now I felt like every minute before midnight was fleeting. Only mere hours of daylight were left before the terror of The Seeking began.

All I wanted to do was to sink into Bisa's arms and forget all of it.

I STEPPED inside Mr. Eddington's restaurant and immediately appreciated the heat from the fireplace in the corner. The room was filled with pine tables and matching chairs on a well-worn wooden floor. Everything in Carra was made of pine because those were the only trees within the Boundary Line.

"We're closed!" Mr. Eddington called from behind

the swinging doors of the kitchen. "Come back for lunch." When my boot squeaked against the floor, he stuck his head out with a suspicious look. He was a short man, bald on top save for a handful of wispy white hair that stuck out against his golden brown skin.

"I'm just heading up," I said, hoping for a quick exchange so he wouldn't see the shape I was in.

His eyes went wide. "Dahlia! By the Grays, what happened to you?"

I shrugged. "Just Broskow being an asshole again. Nothing I can't handle."

His face clouded over with disgust as he approached, but I knew it wasn't aimed at me. "No matter what they say, remember they can't do a damn thing until midnight. This is your time, not theirs."

It was hard to look him in the eye as I nodded. Mr. Eddington had always had a piercing gaze, though I'd never seen him really angry. Even when the restaurant was packed with people, he was able to keep calm.

"They don't seem to care much about rules."

"You've had to hide for too many years if you ask me." He pulled a white cloth from where it was tucked behind his belt, the same he normally used to wipe down the tables. "Here, hold still." He wiped the pig's blood off my cheek then did his best to wipe it off my shoulder.

I thought I had done a decent job of it myself, on my cheek at least, but the cloth came away with more blood than I realized. The leather tunic I wore was normally easy to clean, but some must have gotten into the seams. That could be a problem, as even the Exalted family only had so many outfits. Clothes in Carra were rarely replaced because materials were always scarce.

He sighed. "That's going to need a good washing to get out."

I thought back to the old woman with the watery eyes and her basket of laundry. "No, that's okay. I'll see if Bisa can work on it."

"Ah, that's one of Bisa's, isn't it?"

"It's from a few years back, but yeah. She insisted on making one herself since my last one fell part." I gave a small smile and he nodded, stepping back. I was trying to lighten the mood, but his anger lingered.

"Bisa's upstairs. Remind her that she and her little brother are welcome to come down and enjoy some apple pie tonight. She may be my only tenant, but that doesn't mean she needs to hole herself away all day." He balled up the bloodstained cloth in his hands. "Tell her if she needs anything from me today...or tonight, let me know." His eyes gleamed as he said this, and I understood this offer was for more than just Bisa.

"Thanks, I'll let her know." I made to head upstairs, but Mr. Eddington lowered himself into a chair, and the tone of his voice told me that I wasn't yet permitted to leave.

"You're a strong girl, you know that?"

His bluntness took me off guard and I wasn't sure how to respond. I turned toward him and watched as he dragged a hand over his head.

"My boy Ray, I used to call him my little ray of sunshine. He was insightful for his age, just didn't know how to keep his tongue. He meant well but he wasn't strong like you."

I cocked my head to the side, "I forgot you had a son."

"Oh yeah, little Ray was a ball of energy." A grin spread across Mr. Eddington's face as he looked down to the bloody cloth in his hands.

For a moment I could imagine what he looked like ten years younger and dealing with backtalk from a gregarious son. Then the smile faded, and the years fell hard on his features again.

He twisted the bloody cloth into a tight rope. "His mouth, though. That's what got him in trouble. One day he said the wrong things to the wrong people and, well, he didn't last long monitoring the Boundary Line."

"I'm so sorry," I whispered, my mind slowly wrapping around his words after the run-in with Broskow.

Mr. Eddington spread out the cloth, as if he only just realized it was stained completely with blood, and used the back of his arm to dab at his forehead. His expression softened again. "Your family are good people, Dahlia. Don't let anyone tell you differently. When Ray got killed out there, your mother and father were the first to visit. They did everything they could to help. I'm grateful for that." He cleared his throat and looked down to the worn boards beneath his feet. "I'll do anything to keep them as the Exalted."

I nodded, trying to understand. "But that's what the Exalted do; we help people."

"No, they don't," he said, slamming a fist down on the table and making me jump. "The Exalted was why my boy was out there to begin with. Your folks weren't part of them then. They were just concerned friends; people who understood the value of a life. That's what good, decent people do."

"I don't understand," I admitted, stepping towards him. "I thought that was the whole point of the Exalted Family: to help people and lead them. If the children can keep their family safe, then The Seeking proves—"

"The Seeking doesn't prove a damn thing! All it does is lead to fewer children, which means more food and resources for the ones that survive it."

I clamped my mouth shut. Never in my four years of being in the Exalted Family had I ever heard anyone talk like that. I didn't even know what to say.

He pointed a finger at me. "Your family made the Exalted worth something. You all actually cared and didn't send anyone out to monitor the Boundary Line. Before your parents came along, the Exalted were crooks. If you couldn't promise a week of free meals, or room and board for one of their brats, then you might be sent to the Boundary Line, too."

He nodded toward the door. "That's why there are so many out there hunting you every Seeking. They want that power. Some of them live for that chance. That's why whatever happens tonight, you and your brothers cannot be caught."

My mouth went dry as I stared at him, and it took me a moment to find the right words. "I thought they just wanted to be the Exalted."

He choked on a laugh. "Of course they do! They want

it to get back at their enemies, to force people out on the streets, or to have some poor child be used as an example to the other families."

My wrist tingled, and I rubbed it, trying to dispel the memory of that woman's grip. What would happen if any of them became the next Exalted? If I was sent to monitor the Boundary Line, how long would I last? Would my brothers be killed as an example, too?

For the first time, Mr. Eddington's support of my family made sense, and I felt like a fool for not talking to him sooner. I wanted to say as much, but the words wouldn't come. The most I could muster was a weak, "I'm sorry."

He waved a hand indifferently then pushed himself up from his chair. I could hear the cracking in his knees. "Good luck tonight, Dahlia. To you and your family." He turned back to the kitchen and didn't give me a second glance.

I noticed the way he favored his right leg and the defeated set of his shoulders. He walked as though he was disappointed, as though his advice had once again fallen on deaf ears as it always had, though this was the first time he had ever really spoken to me outside of a kind greeting or asking if I wanted any food.

My father was the one who spoke highly of Mr. Eddington, who always mentioned how he put in a good word or supported their decisions during town discussions. I never knew why, though, until now. Why did it take me getting pig blood splashed on me to get me to talk to him?

Laughter from outside the building pulled me back to my senses. It could have been Broskow's laugh, but I couldn't tell. Even if it wasn't, I needed to see Bisa. She always helped me think straight.

I returned to the stairs and climbed the steps two at a time, wishing I had said more to Mr. Eddington, but unsure of what I could have said. All I knew was that my fear for tonight was even worse than before, and my mind was filled with a storm of questions.

As I CLIMBED the next flight of stairs, I kept seeing Broskow's grinning face and hearing the excited cries from his crowd of supporters. I suddenly had not only my life to consider tonight, but many others as well. If we lost the Exalted House, who would take our place? Someone like Broskow? He'd send me straight to the Boundary Line, and probably others with me. Bisa? My little brother, Dameon? My heart leapt into my throat; I couldn't let that happen.

I shook my head, I couldn't think of everyone, even though I wanted to. I had to focus on myself today. Even Mr. Eddington knew that. He had promised his support for me, so I might be able to take some bread or other food with me later. Any sustenance I could find on The Seeking was a gift.

I reached the top of the stairs. It dead-ended into the attic's simple wooden door, where Mr. Eddington had been kind enough to let Bisa stay. I caught the scent of pig's blood still on my tunic as I knocked on the door. I couldn't shake the feeling that the blood had marked me somehow.

Bisa pulled the door back, and any worries I had were forgotten. She had put her long hair up in a loose bun, highlighting her round cheeks. I loved that hairstyle on her, and I couldn't help but wonder if she fixed it that way on purpose. She also wore one of her flattering dresses that accented her wide hips, trimmed with spare red fabric around her wrists and along the hem of her skirt. It was definitely on purpose, I decided. Her warm brown eyes lit up with excitement as soon as she saw me.

"Oh, you came!" She went to wrap her arms around me, but I stopped her by stepping out of reach. A frown pulled at the corners of her full lips.

"Broskow got pig's blood all over me. You really don't want to hug me right now."

Her hurt melted into frustration. "He does know The Seeking doesn't start until tonight, right?"

She wrapped her warm hand in mine and pulled me inside before I could reply. I sighed and felt the remaining tension melt out of me just from being in her presence. She had that effect on me even after more than a year of dating.

Bisa removed my scarf and dropped it into a basket by the door, examining the blood on my shoulder. "It smells awful!"

"He smelled worse," I retorted with a smirk. She laughed and met my eyes as my heart skipped a beat.

"Come on back and I'll draw you a bath." She took my hand again, and I followed.

Most of her small apartment was filled with scraps of fabric, spare wool, baskets of sewing supplies filled with notions, and half-finished garments hanging in each room. We passed by Marcus's room and I frowned. It was empty. I'm so used to seeing the six-year-old playing with his toys on the floor that I was confused.

"Where's Marcus?"

"At school. Already at that age. Dad would be so happy." Bisa didn't mention her mother; she hardly did anymore. I squeezed her hand and she gave me a brief smile.

We slipped through the tiny bathroom doorway and I couldn't help myself – I reached down to grab her large rear. She squealed and laughed as she moved away.

"Not until you're cleaned up! Keep those exploring hands to yourself."

I obeyed with some reluctance and stripped, my eyes tracking her movements as Bisa not only drew me a hot bath and demanded I climb in, but also took my soiled tunic.

"What are you going to do with that?" I asked, settling down into the tepid water. At least it wasn't cold. I winced, realizing I'd gotten spoiled by the hot baths at the Exalted House.

"Getting it cleaned for you." She held up a hand when I frowned. "Don't ask me how, I've got my ways. You just relax. Gather yourself. I need you to be ready tonight, sugar." For the first time her genuine smile faltered, and I could see the familiar panic that swam under the surface when The Seeking came around.

I rolled my head against the back of the tub and closed my eyes. There was moisture on my cheeks, but I couldn't tell if it was from the tub or my tears. "It's going to be so hard tonight, Bisa. Broskow is already riling people up and it's not even noon yet."

I heard her footsteps approach before I opened my eyes to see her sitting down on the edge of the tub. She reached out and rubbed my shoulder, as though trying to massage away any memory of Broskow.

"It'll be okay, you hear me? You have friends. We'll help you out."

I nodded, suddenly unable to speak and averted my eyes.

"No, don't you look away from me." She took my chin and I looked up to her, this time feeling the hot tears spill down my cheeks. "I love you and I refuse to lose you over this stupidity, do you hear me? If you let them beat you now, then you won't have a chance tonight. You have to be strong for me, Dahlia."

I sniffed and nodded. "Mr. Eddington thinks I'm strong enough, but I don't know if I am."

She returned to massaging my shoulder, my arm, and finally settled on rubbing the back of my neck.

"I hate The Seeking," she said. "I hate that you have to deal with it year after year. It's barbaric." She huffed. "I've never met a Gray Person mind you but they must be monsters to require it."

"Don't say that," I said, my voice coming out weaker

than I'd like. "They can hear you. The Gray People hear all, or so they say."

"I don't care if they do! They know we suffer, and they don't give a damn. Sometimes I wonder if their so-called protection is really worth it."

I was quiet. I knew where this conversation was going; I had heard it many times before. Bisa was thinking of her father, who died when Marcus was born.

"What's the point of their help if it comes at such a cruel cost? It's not even reliable either! My dad never went over that Boundary Line, but he was still killed. He was drunk, sure, but his son was just born. He had a good reason to celebrate. He stepped outside to get some fresh air and he never came back." She took a shaky breath. "I still remember staring out that damn window, shivering in the cold, and waiting for him to return. There wasn't a single Gray Person around to help him. What's the point of The Seeking if they choose not to help us? We're animals trapped in a cage," she growled, climbing to her feet. "We're making the best of it, but we all know that's what it is."

"Don't think such dark thoughts. I need you to be strong, too."

She gave me a sad smile. "I know. It's just hard."

I reached up and grabbed her hand with my wrinkled fingers, her russet brown skin just a few shades lighter than mine. People who looked like us made up about half of Carra, but sometimes if felt like less on The Seeking. "That's why we have each other. We're stronger together, you and I."

She smiled then and kissed the top of my hand, her lips soft and cool. "You and Marcus are the only reasons I'll survive this ugly place." I frowned, unsure of what to say, but she let go and walked to the door. "I'll let you relax a bit then come check on you."

"I love you," I whispered not really wanting her to leave. I knew too well the long day ahead of me and how much I would miss her warmth, her smile, her presence.

She kissed her fingers then held them up to me as she shut the door.

CHAPTER 2
THE GRAY PEOPLE

I was a child again, curled up in the chilly bedroom of my youth. It used to be my big brother's room, but once he moved out, it became mine.

It always felt empty and barren, even with friends over. I didn't have enough to make the walls not echo: just my bed, a chest of drawers, and a small bookshelf. I was happy to not be sharing a room with my younger brother, Dameon, though, so I tried to make the most of it.

I shivered despite the four blankets stacked on top of me. The shutters never closed right, always letting in the cold night air.

Through the crack in the shutters, I saw movement: a pale body amid the dark trees, gleaming in the light of a full moon. It was one of the Gray People. They were patrolling the Boundary Line, I told myself. They were making sure the monsters wouldn't get me.

The pale body appeared again through the crack in the shutters. I held my breath. It was watching me.

She was a woman with dark hair and eyes like pits. Her skin gleamed the grayish blue of her kind, the color of a birch tree in the light of a full moon. Fear crept into my veins, but then I thought of Grandma's dry laughter and reassurance.

"There's nothing to fear from them," she had said as her face crinkled into a smile. "They're our protectors. Anytime you see one, know that you're a little safer than you were before."

Still, I couldn't deny the fear I felt as I stared into this Gray Person's empty eyes, only for her to vanish when I blinked.

I don't know why, but I needed to see where she went. I needed to see if she was still outside.

Climbing out of bed, I threw off all my blankets and shivered when my feet hit the cold wood of the floor. But still, I wrapped my arms around my stomach and padded over to the window.

The cold wind howled, whistling through the gap in the shutters. I looked around, but all I saw were the shadows of the forest in the distance. I decided to try closing the shutters once more and reached out for the latch that was hanging on the inside.

Something cold and gray touched my hand instead. I gasped and dropped to the floor, backing into the corner of the room near the window's ledge.

The shutter pulled fully open, the hinges squeaking

against the wind's resistance, and the Gray Woman leaned her head inside.

Her neck was long, and her black hair hung around her face. Her hands clutched the windowsill like spider legs. She turned to look at me, her expression stony and emotionless, and I saw that her eyes were actually empty sockets.

Then she smiled.

It was such a cruel thing that it terrified me.

She reached a bony hand in through the window, her fingers tipped with long, black talons.

I buried my face into the lace of my nightgown as I heard one bare foot hit the floorboard, then another. My heart was pounding in my temples.

Maybe Grandma was wrong, I thought to myself. *Maybe they aren't really our protectors.*

It grabbed hold of my shoulder, its fingers like dead, rotten wood left out in the snow. I felt cold breath on my ear as it hissed in a raspy voice, "Dahlia...Dahlia, time to wake up."

I woke with a gasp and nearly sank underwater in the tub.

Bisa was stroking my hair, saying soothingly, "It's okay! It was just a dream."

I stared at her for a long moment as the cold shivers from my dream faded. The water in the tub was cold, but I was covered in a sheen of sweat.

"Sugar, are you alright?" Bisa asked with concern.

I shook my head, the memory of my bedroom still bleeding into my vision. "The Gray People." That's all I could say at first, but Bisa was patient with me like always and waited. "I always seem to dream about them when The Seeking comes, but this wasn't just a dream. This happened."

Bisa narrowed her eyes and soon the scene spilled out between my rambling lips. When I described the woman with the long black hair crawling in through my window, she pursed her lips.

Once I fell silent, she gave a slow nod. "You sure that actually happened to you?" I could hear the fear in her voice. "I've never seen their hands, but I've never heard of them climbing into houses either."

"It did," I whispered, finally getting my trembling under control. "I must have forgotten about it, but I don't know how I could have. It scared me so badly at the time. I must have been only six years old." I looked up at her, needing to see her eyes. "You don't think I'm lying, do you?"

"No." She squeezed my arm. "I've just never heard of that happening is all." We sat there a second, with Bisa biting her lips before she grabbed me a towel. "I hate to ask, but what happened after?"

"I woke up."

"No, I know that. But what really happened?"

I turned away and stared into the still water of the tub. I tried to reach for the memory, tried to recall what *had* happened.

The Gray Person reached out to me, and her hand was colder than I imagined as it wrapped around my shoulder. Her breath was like frost; I remembered that because it gave me goosebumps. But I couldn't recall what she said, or even what happened after. The memory was cut short like a frayed rope.

"I don't know," I whispered. "I don't remember."

Bisa stilled, then gave me a nervous smile as she handed me the towel she had been nervously twisting in her hands. "I don't know if I could forget something that bad. Surely your parents knew about it, right?"

"I mean, I guess. If any of my family knew that I had encountered a Gray Person, none of them talked about it."

"Come on," Bisa said, turning away after the silence went on for too long. "I heated up some stew for you. I need to make sure you're fed for tonight."

I got up, drained the tub, and toweled off. I was still shaky, but I tried not to focus on that. Bisa was right, I was losing daylight and didn't have the luxury to lie around unearthing old memories.

Bisa was about to leave but then stopped and cocked her head to the side. "Oh, not again," she sighed and stepped around me to bend over the tub. "This damn thing cracked again." She pointed to a fresh break in the wood on the far side.

"That was my fault, I'm sorry. I didn't mean to fall asleep," I said, frowning.

She got to her feet, giving me a familiar smile. "No

worries. That poor tub has already cracked twice. It was old when Marcus and I moved in last year."

I pulled on the temporary clothes Bisa had left near the tub for me, a simple gown that came down to my knees. "Was that only last year?"

She nodded and kissed my cheek, her lips cracked from her nervous biting. "If you hadn't spoken up for us, Marcus would still be living under Mom's roof. I can't imagine what that would be like."

I smiled and took her hand, the disturbing dream fading like fog. Last year Bisa put in a request with the Exalted Family to have her mother's home investigated for negligence. Marcus was still living there at the time, even though Bisa was living on her own, and she was concerned for her little brother's health and safety. She'd watched Marcus grow more frail and sickly, month after month, before finally claiming negligence against her mother. As a representative of the Exalted, it was up to me to investigate.

I'd heard the rumors of Zola Figg's downward spiral after her husband's death. From the reports, I knew she had shuttered up all her windows, only went out shopping for supplies at night, and complained that even candlelight hurt her eyes. Still, I wasn't prepared for the squalor I saw little Marcus living in when I arrived. The place reeked of rotting food and overflowing chamber pots.

It was during the process of liberating Marcus from his mother's home and speaking to my father and mother on Bisa's behalf that Bisa and I grew close. The whole investigation took six months, and even though she and I had known of each other, we never got the chance to really talk until then.

She was the bright light amid all that mess.

After it was all settled, we started dating. One day I was paying her to mend my pile of old clothes, and a few weeks later we were making out in her kitchen. I think it helped that Marcus liked me, too.

Lost in thought, I let Bisa lead me towards the kitchen. "It was hard watching you stand up there representing me and Marcus," Bisa said with a smirk. "You were so damn fine I lost track of what you were saying sometimes and almost missed my lines."

"Father had asked me how you were doing at one point. He mentioned that you sounded distant and distracted when you had to voice your consent. He thought you were just very upset. If he only knew, right?"

Bisa glanced over her shoulder as I sat down in the kitchen. "Marcus wanted to join us for lunch, so make sure you behave, okay?" Her smile betrayed the sternness of her words.

I nodded, making a point to sit on my hands. She just shook her head.

Bisa got me a big bowl of stew that tasted almost like Mr. Eddington's house special downstairs. She wanted to copy it without having to ask him for the recipe.

Marcus joined us for lunch, emerging from his room with barely a glance at me. We tried to keep the conversation light and upbeat. Bisa hated getting the boy wrapped up in the troubles of The Seeking, especially after all he had been through.

Marcus seemed oblivious enough at first as we ate and joked around, but before he headed back to his room to play, he came over and wrapped his arms around me. His curly brown hair hid his eyes, but I could feel his tears through the cloth gown Bisa had given me.

"Marcus..."

He held me tight and I shared a look with Bisa, who had come to stand beside me. A hand covered her mouth and her eyes widened. I ruffled his hair, trying to keep myself composed.

"Be safe, Dahlia." His voice squeaked from his tears. "Don't let the bad guys get you."

"I won't," I promised quietly.

He let go of me abruptly and darted to his bedroom, closing the door behind him. I only got a look at his face briefly, but I saw his cheeks were wet with tears.

Bisa and I exchanged bittersweet smiles before she sighed. "Maybe that boy knows more than I like to admit."

"I think he knows enough," I leaned back in my chair. "We can do our best to protect him, but he still lives in Carra, doesn't he? He understands what's going on. I don't know if I like him referring to his own townspeople as 'bad'."

Bisa caught my eye. "Aren't they, though? Once midnight strikes tonight, this town will be full of 'bad' people."

Bisa cleared the plates and then brought me to her bedroom to get out of earshot from Marcus. She pulled me down to the edge of the bed and wrapped her arm around mine as we sat side by side.

"So..." Bisa squeezed my hand. There was determination in her eyes; all jokes and smiles were gone. "What are your plans for tonight?"

A year ago, when Bisa first asked me to share my plans for The Seeking, I was reluctant. The general consensus is to not trust anyone if you are in the Exalted Family. Even siblings don't share their plans for fear of letting it slip beforehand.

A year ago, I struggled with trusting Bisa with such dangerous information. But now she was an integral part of my preparations. She was my confidant and was almost better at planning for potential problems than I was.

"There's an old farmhouse out near the Boundary Line that got hit hard by the storm this summer and is still in ruins. Mr. Mackeral only used it to keep his sheep before then, but it's got an old, broken trough where the pigs used to be kept. I'll be hiding beneath it. I've already cleaned it out and stored supplies there."

Bisa's eyes narrowed. "You don't think that'll be a bit obvious? There aren't that many abandoned buildings in Carra."

"It's near the Boundary Line and people don't like going that far out, especially on The Seeking. There's also a nice supply of mud that will help throw off Broskow's dogs. He's already been bragging about them."

She arched an eyebrow. "He might be trying to throw you off the trail. You know he throws threats around like honey just to see if it will stick."

I sighed heavily. "Broskow is known for his dogs. He always has at least one."

Bisa shrugged and I could tell she didn't like the idea, but honestly no hiding place was perfect. Each of them had weaknesses. "So, if your primary hiding place gets found out, what then? What else is out there?"

"If that happens, I head to the woods. Remember that hollowed-out tree I showed you that one day?"

She smiled and a gleam entered her eye. "That's where you used to hide from your brothers, wasn't it? But you're not a little girl anymore, sugar. You can't really fit in there, can you? What kind of hiding place would that be?"

"It'll be a tight fit, but it's better than being out in the open. At night, they won't be able to see me that far away."

"Far away," her eyes went wide. "Wait. Dahlia, that's not just near the Boundary Line - that's past it. You literally have to step over the dandelions to get there."

"Yes, but—"

"No, that's not an option. I don't like that at all."

"I used to hide there for hours as a kid and nothing attacked me. I really don't think it's a big problem."

She unlaced her arm from mine, turned to face me, and took my shoulders, squeezing tight. "Look, Dahlia. I just want you to be safe. You're more important than the damned Exalted, okay?"

I thought of Mr. Eddington downstairs. I thought of a young man walking the Boundary Line with nothing more than maybe a wooden dagger and a torch. I looked down at the floor.

"I want to be safe, too, but I also have to think of my family. I don't know what's going to happen to us if someone like Broskow gets to live in the Exalted House. I don't know what might happen to our friends or anyone who supported us."

"If you're worried about me, you really don't have to be. I'm not afraid of—"

"It's not just you. It's Mr. Eddington downstairs. It's anyone who has spoken up for us in the past. It's anyone we've helped. For all the people out hunting me down, there are lots of people hoping I make it."

She was silent for a moment before eventually nodding. "Only as a last resort, you understand?"

I nodded.

Satisfied, she let go of my shoulders and shook her head. "I swear I don't like the mind games involved in this. There are just too many angles to consider."

"You mean you don't think being a member of the Exalted is as glamorous as it's cracked up to be?"

She laughed. "Glamorous is the last word that comes to mind. It's like you're a solitary militia."

"You just have to learn to be one step ahead of everyone else."

CHAPTER 3
HUNTED ANIMALS

It was almost dusk when I headed out, a small satchel of food hidden under my cloak: emergency supplies, as Bisa told me, though I could tell by the smell of them that they were Mr. Eddington's pastries. Bisa was an excellent cook, but even she couldn't replicate those.

The cold wind hit my cheeks as I stepped outside, but I didn't mind. Marcus had gone downstairs to see Mr. Eddington for a little while, giving Bisa and me a sweet couple of hours together. My body still tingled, and my cheeks felt flushed; in contrast, the cold breeze felt good.

That was her way of wishing me good luck for The Seeking. Neither of us spoke about it, but we both knew the risk was very real and that I may not live to see her again. She wanted to make our last moments memorable, and I certainly wasn't going to complain.

The sun was beginning to set, and I knew that my day of freedom was quickly waning.

The streets of Carra were alive with activity and the thick scent of apple pie seemed to clog my nostrils. As I headed back toward the Exalted House, almost everyone I passed had the familiar scent cloaking them.

When I was little, Grandma said that The Seeking had its roots in an old holiday that used to be celebrated in the Old Days, sometimes called All Hallows' Eve or Halloween. At one point, whenever Carra was created, it was decided that Halloween would instead be known as the day of The Seeking.

She had also mentioned a plant called a pumpkin, something big and orange, but all Carra had were apple trees, so that's what we used instead. I liked to think that pumpkin pie smelled way better than apple pie, but I probably would have still been sick of it after so many years.

One woman passed by me with four dogs following behind, and I stepped aside to keep the pack from being able to catch my scent. It didn't really matter, but I didn't want to give them an early start.

A boy carrying about ten unlit torches, followed his father who carried a lit one, drew near me, but he was too focused on where he was going to even notice me as I hurried by.

Next, I weaved around some of the children who were play fighting with sticks.

"This Priest is mine!" One of the boys shouted to his attacker and I couldn't help but stiffen. The Priest child, who I assumed was supposed to be me or one of my siblings, was a toddler, likely a sister of one of the boys. I shook my head and kept moving.

There was an excitement and a buzz in the air that made my stomach sink. It filled me with dread.

I was grateful that I hadn't chosen to wear the colors of the Exalted today. In the daylight, people like Broskow could identify me, but here as twilight approached, it was harder to spot faces. I pulled my cloak closer around me as I approached the shops.

Apples, cinnamon, nutmeg: the scent of apple pie was overwhelming here, and I saw stacks of them cooling on shelves and windows. As daylight faded, shops would only sell dozens of types of apple pie to prepare for The Seeking.

I noticed Broskow's butcher shop was closed and the darkness in the windows made my chest tighten.

Where was he? Normally he would be out enjoying the festivities, selling pies like many of the other vendors, but his absence worried me. Was he trying to start The Seeking early?

I heard a raucous burst of laughter from one of the nearby buildings; there were lights on inside, but it appeared closed to the general public. With my heartbeat pounding in my temples, I made my way to one of the windows and peeked inside.

There was Broskow, as well as the old woman with the laundry basket. I could only see their backs, but they, along with about a dozen others, formed a ring. At first, I thought they were talking in a circle, but then I saw snippets of a person between the gaps - they had surrounded someone.

Suddenly, the old woman's hand shot forward and shoved hard enough to make whoever it was fall to the ground. I heard a familiar cry and my mouth went dry. I hurried to another window, trying to get a clearer view.

"Let me go!" a young boy called out, clearly in tears. My breath caught. It was my younger brother Dameon, who was only nine. I gripped the collar of my cloak in a fist as I caught glimpses of his round face, his cheeks wet with tears. The group around him laughed.

I saw red. What Broskow and his followers were doing was illegal. Tormenting a member of the Exalted was punishable by the harshest laws of Carra, but as The Seeking drew closer, the normal rules and regulations of the town fell apart.

Dameon got to his feet, only to be pushed over again. I heard the skid of his arm sliding across the wooden floor right before he cried out again. I was so furious I felt like I could breathe fire, but storming inside wouldn't help anything, especially not with so many of them. I wasn't very tall, and Dameon was even shorter than I was - we would have no chance.

I looked around, desperate for any distraction I could provide, and picked up a rock. I flung it as hard as I could through the window.

The muddy rock flew through the air. It would've hit the old woman square in the shoulder, but she ducked, and it continued past and then slammed into Broskow's right forearm.

The burly man gave a cry of shock and I quickly ducked before stalking around the building.

I stopped and looked back in time to see Broskow and the others examining the window. With a smirk, I stepped around the corner.

Dameon was already taking advantage; I saw him halfway out of one of the other windows to my left, his fingers barely holding onto the ledge. He fell onto his side in the dirt and I bit back a gasp at the thud his body made. He winced, scampered to his feet, then ran.

I wanted to call out to him, but the others would hear; instead, I ran after him. It was colder now, and I could see my breath as I pushed myself to run faster. He was surprisingly fast, and it took me the length of a couple of buildings to catch up to him. Reaching out, I looped my fingers around his sleeve.

"No!" he gasped out between harsh breaths.

"Hush, it's me!"

His eyes were wide, scared at first, but then with a grateful groan he crumpled against me. His panting gasps turned to crying and I pulled him closer, feeling his hot tears against my stomach.

I stared up at the twilight sky. The stars were just beginning to emerge through the purple veil, and darkness was already stretching toward the sun. Only a few precious hours before the start of The Seeking, and I was glad I had found my brother in time.

"I know, I know," I whispered, swallowing down the dryness in my throat. "But we need to keep moving. They'll be looking for both of us soon."

Eventually Dameon pulled away, his eyes downcast. "That was you with the rock, wasn't it?"

I nodded and he gave a heavy sigh. "I'm glad you found me."

"Me, too." I clenched my jaw to keep from saying too much. Dameon didn't need to hear my complaints again. He heard them every damn year.

We walked together, Dameon clutching my hand so hard that it was throbbing, but I didn't pull away. He was only nine and deserved to have a good cry after that.

We moved away from downtown Carra, leaving behind the buildings with pies on their windowsills and growing crowds of drunks and hunters.

"I didn't mean to get caught already. I just wanted a piece of pie." Dameon stared miserably at the ground. "They said they were selling them inside, and I was dumb enough to believe them. How could I be so stupid?"

"Broskow's a snake. You can't believe anything he says this time of year." I looked around to make sure we were alone before speaking in a whisper, "Has Mother gotten you a hiding place this year?"

He nodded, also keeping his voice low, when he replied with, "Yeah. I told her I could've hidden myself, but I guess she did know better after all." His face scrunched up again, tears already swimming in his eyes.

I wrapped an arm around him and gave him an awkward side hug. "It's okay, kiddo, trust me when I say you're not missing anything fun. I wish I had a cushy place like you."

He nodded and wiped at his tears but said nothing more. We had gotten so used to keeping secrets from each other that it was hard to remember a time when we didn't.

Every year, Mother saved as much as she could to ensure she could pay the high fee of a trusted family to keep her youngest son hidden from the hunting groups. According to our parents, he wasn't permitted to hide himself until he turned thirteen, thank goodness.

I was pretty certain our parents would pay the family as long as they could to ensure that their youngest was completely safe. They simply couldn't afford it for all of us. I still remembered that first year when I found Mother crying over the dining table, her entire savings laid out before her. She just rocked back and forth saying, *"It's not enough."*

Father tried to distract me by leading me upstairs, but I knew the truth. It was at that moment I realized that being part of the Exalted Family didn't mean you had any guarantee of money or safety. When Darik, my older brother, and I spoke about it, we both decided it was best if that money was spent on Dameon rather than us.

By the time we reached the Exalted House, the sky was a dark purple with only a hint of light along the horizon. At five stories, it was the tallest structure in all of Carra. No building was permitted to be any taller, and from the rooftop, you could see the entire town sprawled out around you.

We started uphill, up the dirt path that led to the

front door. I nodded to our two guards, Kaleb and Marissa, positioned farther up the hill.

Kaleb nodded back as Marissa smiled, saying, "You two are back late."

"Dameon was —"

"I got caught up looking at all the pies," Dameon lied, cutting me off.

I pursed my lips and noticed the flash of concern in Marissa's eyes. If Dameon didn't want to talk about it in front of them, even if it was illegal, I wasn't going to push him.

"You two have plans for tonight?" I asked, eager to change the subject.

"My bed," Kaleb groaned. "I'm looking forward to getting to sleep in tomorrow."

I grinned, turning to Marissa. "What about you?"

"I'll wait for Mary to get home, then turn in. I'm sure she'll give up after a couple of hours anyway." Marissa looked to the ground.

I nodded, unable to keep from clenching my teeth. Mary was Marissa's wife, and I knew they had an adopted daughter Dameon's age. I couldn't help myself and said, "I didn't know Mary was interested."

"She's not normally," Marissa admitted with a sigh. "But this year..." She trailed off, and I understood what she meant. This year was different. This year felt off. Everyone wanted to take part, except for Kaleb apparently.

"Good luck, I guess," Dameon muttered and dragged

me up to the front door of the Exalted House. I was grateful for the excuse to get away. No one was required to work during The Seeking, even the Exalted Guard, but it still felt wrong for Marissa's wife to be taking part in it.

"Even they're in on it," Dameon snapped a tad too loudly.

"They're allowed to. Everyone is," I said, knowing it wouldn't help. He pulled the front door open with a huff.

Inside we were greeted with silence and the finest wooden craftsmanship Carra had to offer, everything polished to perfection with rectangular, decorative rugs running along the walkways throughout the building. They were more to prevent the wood from being damaged than to provide actual decoration.

Normally, the house would be bustling with activity from people getting the final approval for the day's case, to workers polishing the handrails of the staircases, to the chef and her team getting dinner prepared, but not tonight. The house was empty save for our family. The silence felt heavy and wrong.

It was hard to call this place home when we first moved in, but over the years it got easier: a few scratched floorboards from the three of us racing around the house, a bannister that was snapped off when Darik tried to show off to his friends, and the familiar carpet by the door that Dameon had used to hide his painted mess back when he was only five. Those moments helped to make the Exalted House feel like home, but on these nights, it felt like I was trespassing.

Dameon stepped away to wash himself up for dinner, still covered in mud, so I headed into the dining room where Mother was likely waiting.

The dining table was laid out with a pair of candelabras, which made the room far darker than what I was used to. Each of the places had been set, a tradition that Mother insisted she be permitted to continue on the night before The Seeking despite how taboo it was.

She was standing at the fireplace, her back to me and her long shadow stretching and dancing across the gleaming table.

Mother wore a plain, cream colored gown, which was the traditional color of The Seeking. It was to remind the Exalted Family that on this day we were no more than commoners. It was intended to humble and maybe even insult us.

My mother was a defiant woman, though, and had added her own touch to the gown. A black petticoat peeked out just above her flat shoes; her hands were enclosed in matching black gloves, and a netted black shawl hung over her shoulders. If not for the gown itself, she might have been going to a funeral. She had worn the same outfit last year, too, and claimed it was for warmth, but I didn't believe her. She liked to launch small rebellions against rigid expectations.

I shifted and she turned when a floorboard creaked beneath my foot; her smile was reminiscent of the one she wore at dinner parties that we hosted on a regular basis. It felt false. "Dahlia, you made it! I was beginning to—" she blinked, refocused, and then gestured to the table, "I was afraid the food would get cold."

I sat down and started spooning beans onto my plate. It was a simple meal of cornbread and vegetables, reminiscent of the meals we used to have before we became the Exalted. I tried not to notice that she had clearly been crying.

"Dameon is with me. He's cleaning up."

She put a hand to her chest and gave a genuine smile before coming over behind me, placing her hands on my shoulders, and planting a kiss on top of my head.

"Blessed be those that watch over us," she said before pausing. "He was supposed to be home an hour ago, but when he didn't show I got worried."

I nodded, digging into a boiled potato I'd just placed on my plate. I couldn't help how good it made me feel to hear her praise. I always felt like I had to work double to earn it, compared to my two brothers.

"Have you heard anything from Darik yet?"

She pursed her lips. "He came by for lunch, but I got the impression he wasn't interested in joining us for dinner."

I shook my head then downed a glass of water, appreciating that the well water no longer had that weird aftertaste it got in the summertime when the rains were heavy and the days were hot.

Truthfully, I wasn't terribly surprised that Darik had once again refused to spend time with us around The Seeking, but it still made me angry. At least he had the decency to drop by for lunch this time. Last year, he was gone a full week and laughed at our relief when he emerged the day after The Seeking.

His antics always weighed on Mother the most, and each year I saw how it aged her. It had to be difficult not knowing where we were for a full day, or whether we were safe. Some of the Exalted before us had died trying to find hiding spots for The Seeking, and some had died under more suspicious circumstances.

I reached out and placed a hand on hers, feeling the delicately stitched embroidery beneath my palm. She felt cold despite having stood in front of the fireplace moments before.

"We'll come back, okay? We'll be safe."

She let out a wavering sigh and a tear slid down her cheek. "I don't worry about you, Dahlia. I know you will. Of all my babies, you're the one I worry about the least."

I blinked. "Really?"

She laughed as she wiped the tear away. "You take after me - clever and determined no matter the obstacle. Just make sure it doesn't lead you into danger." She clasped my hand tightly in hers. "Sometimes I wish we had never become the Exalted."

I nodded, understanding her more than she probably knew. "People say we're one of the best families that have ever had the title. We've done so much good... Look at Bisa and her little brother. He would still be shut up in the filth of their mother's house if we hadn't helped."

"That was all you, Dahlia. You're the one who led

that investigation and the one who got that little boy to safety." She looked away. "Besides, I don't put much stock in what people say anymore. They'll tell every Exalted Family they're the best. It's how they treat us on The Seeking that really matters. Either way, it's my children that are put in danger every year, my children that have to suffer. I hate it." Her lips trembled as she said the words and she turned her head, almost ashamed of herself.

I stared at her in shock. I had never heard her say such things before. Even as difficult as it was the first Seeking, she never voiced such thoughts.

I suddenly thought of what it must have been like for her and Father, trying to decide if they should attempt to become the Exalted Family. Father had bribed someone at the clock to run it forward an hour. When one of the then Exalted Family's sons had come back, believing The Seeking was over, Father nabbed him. I often wondered if he and Mother decided to do it together, or if it was just him. Did they ever realize the sacrifices they would all have to make?

"I'm sorry," I said, not knowing what else I could say.

She shuddered. "It's not your fault. Don't worry about me and my many fears. I want you to be safe tonight, and I expect you to come back to me, you hear me?" She stroked my hair.

"I plan to, Mother. Don't worry."

She smiled and I thought she might cry but the tears didn't fall.

"Is everything okay?" Dameon asked, and I turned to see him stepping into the dining room uncertainly.

"Of course it is!" Mother said and gestured for him to sit.

We shared a glance before I went back to eating.

For the next hour or so, Mother spoke of what all Dameon would be doing the following day. Despite his fears and embarrassment earlier, Dameon seemed excited about the games he would be playing. Neither of them spoke of where Dameon would be staying, which, while I understood why, was always uncomfortable.

"Hm, Darik's not here again?" Father's deep voice reverberated on the wooden floors and walls as he stepped into the room. He, too, was dressed in a cream shirt and pants, though I noticed this year he was wearing a black overcoat and black gloves that matched Mother's. He frowned as he sat down beside Mother and put an arm around her waist to give her a squeeze. "I wonder where that boy hides all the time."

"I don't know," Dameon said around a mouthful of food, "but it must be a pretty good hiding spot if it works every year and he doesn't have to pay for it."

Father sighed and turned to me. "You have your plans all sorted out then, Dahlia?"

"Of course," I said, not hearing the confidence in my voice that I had with Bisa earlier. "I'll be fine, I've got plans and backup plans."

He nodded, apparently satisfied, and turned to Dameon. "I heard Broskow was giving you trouble earlier."

Dameon had been drinking water, but slowly put his cup down, his eyes downcast as he gave a short nod.

Father clenched his jaw. "Did they hurt you?"

He shrugged, still not meeting our father's eyes. Mother looked like she wanted to go hug him, but Father shook his head.

"It's not your fault that they pick on you," he tried to reassure in an awkward voice.

"I know," Dameon muttered. "I just wish they would at least wait until The Seeking began. I want to be able to hide like Darik and Dahlia do. I'm sick of being picked on every year when The Seeking gets close."

"Oh, Dameon," Mother said and I could hear the sorrow in her voice.

"Do you think I don't get picked on every year?" I asked. "Or that Darik doesn't?"

Dameon looked at me, his cheeks streaked with tears.

"It happens every year, especially once October hits. I can't even walk to Bisa's without getting insults from people like Broskow. These people aren't going to go away, and the longer we're part of the Exalted Family, the worse it's going to get."

"That's enough," Father said, drumming his fingers on the table. "There's no need to scare him like that, Dahlia."

"It's true though. All it takes is one misstep. All it takes is one person seeing him through a window, and he's on the run like us, if he's not captured or killed first. I know you all don't like to talk about what it's like, but he needs to be ready for anything. Even if it feels safe, it might not be." I locked eyes with Dameon, feeling my throat clenching as tears threatened. "I just don't want anything to happen to you, kiddo."

Mother dabbed at the corner of her eye with a napkin, unable to look at me.

"This isn't the time," Father emphasized, glaring at me.

A silence fell over us as the clock chimed. It had a low tone for a bell, but it was loud enough to be heard at every end of the town.

One, two, three.

I suddenly worried that I had lost track of time. It was only getting dark when I went to help Dameon, but that must have been eight o'clock at least. The walk back, dinner: how much time had it taken?

Seven, eight, nine.

My chest grew tight, waiting for the additional bells. It couldn't be much later, they would have heard the chimes, wouldn't they?

Ten, Eleven.

At once we all got to our feet. I grabbed rolls and stuffed them into my pockets. Mother's voice was shrill and panicked, "Jamel, how is it so late? It couldn't possibly be midnight already!"

Twelve, Thirteen, Fourteen.

"Is somebody drunk?" I asked as I pulled on my cloak.

"No." Father stared out the window toward the

center of Carra. "Apparently The Seeking starts early this year."

I hugged Mother as tightly as I could. Her face was wet with tears; I hated that our last moments were cut short.

I hated that I had snapped at Dameon for no good reason.

I hated that I had started an argument when I should have been enjoying what could have been our last minutes together.

Eighteen, Nineteen, Twenty.

"They can't do that, can they?" she asked as I let go and turned to hug Dameon. "We're still the Exalted Family until midnight. They can't take that away from us, not yet!"

"I'm sorry," I said in Dameon's ear, blocking out Mother's cries. "Be safe. Don't take any chances. If things look suspicious you run, okay?"

His voice broke as he whispered back, "I love you, Dahlia. Please be careful!"

Twenty-one, Twenty-two.

As I pulled away, Father grabbed me for a quick hug and said, "Go, and stay to the woods as much as you can. There's no telling who will try to take advantage of the extra time. Don't let them catch you off guard."

I nodded to show him I understood and kissed him on his cheek, his beard scratchy on my lips.

"Stay safe, sweetheart."

I headed out the front door and into the night, my pockets overflowing with biscuits. Already I felt like a hunted animal as I took a hard left and headed for the darkness and safety of the trees.

This year The Seeking would be longer than any other.

The bell mocked us all as its chimes continued.

Twenty-three, twenty-four, twenty-five.

PART TWO
HIDING PLACES

CHAPTER 4
THE HOLLOW

I must have walked a hundred feet or so by the time I saw the villagers stomping down the dirt road toward the Exalted House. There were at least twenty of them holding their torches high, the light making their smug grins easily visible despite the distance between us. I ducked back further into the woods, until I could only catch glimpses of them. Who had been paid off to make the clock chimes meaningless?

It was obviously supposed to be a jab at Father. He had bribed them the first year to chime the bells an hour early. That was what got our family into the Exalted House to begin with, but it wasn't even close to midnight yet.

It felt like something Broskow would try, especially after Dameon escaped from them earlier. I scanned the faces as best I could, but there was no sign of him. I couldn't even hear his dogs barking, and he brought those with him every Seeking. His absence only made me more eager to get to my hiding place as quickly as possible. If Broskow was behind fixing the clock, but wasn't heading for the Exalted House, where exactly was he?

A cold wind swept through the trees and I shivered. The sooner I was hidden, the better I would feel.

I WALKED CAREFULLY through the woods, stepping around piles of dried leaves and navigating through tall grass and thick foliage. October was perhaps the worst time of the year to try to sneak through the woods. Many of the trees were already bare, but some of them still had their leaves, and those were the ones I tried to stay near. I needed whatever coverage I could find.

Down a short hill, I came across a pile of dead leaves that had collected against a deep trench, completely obscuring the ground. The wind was stronger here and I could see more leaves settle against the mound while I stood. Going through it would make a ton of noise.

I took a few moments to look for an alternate path, but couldn't see one. This section of leaves was actually smaller than other areas of the embankment, at least the parts that weren't overgrown with trees and undergrowth. Likely this used to mark the boundary of someone's land, and the trench was supposed to help with drainage, but it was also very good at collecting leaves.

I took a breath to steady my nerves. Every second I wasted, I could feel Broskow's dogs getting closer to me as I lost ground. Normally I might try climbing a tree and leaping across to avoid the leaf pile, but there were only saplings here, nothing that could hold my weight. The only path was through.

With my heartbeat pounding in my ears, I took my first slow step, ready to run at the slightest sound of pursuit. A few leaves crunched under my foot and I froze, expecting one of those torches to appear through the dark and the bare branches.

After a few seconds, I built up enough courage to continue. I lifted my other foot and slowly lowered it down into a gap. I was pleased with how quiet I was until I put weight on it. My foot slipped and I had to latch onto one of the saplings to keep from falling on my face. That was when something moved past my foot.

Even through my leather pants I could feel each scale as it dragged across my calf in bursts. A line of leaves began to move and settle, and I guessed that whatever snake I had disturbed was slowly unfurling itself from its slumber. I stood there, barely breathing.

I racked my brain, recalling lessons Father taught me when I was little. Don't run from a snake. It might get even more startled and strike, and I had no idea if it was poisonous or not. I couldn't even see it.

I bit my bottom lip so hard that I tasted blood. I slowly lifted my back leg and brought it forward, hearing the leaves crinkle around me and knowing that if anybody found me now, they would have me for certain, especially if I got bit in the process.

Plus, there was no rule that the prey had to be brought back alive. A corpse was all that was needed as proof for The Seeking.

I brought my foot down on solid ground and wanted to scream for joy but couldn't. Oh no, I couldn't make a single sound.

Then slowly, so slowly that the muscles in my legs began to shake, I brought the other one forward and onto solid ground. I glanced back to see if the snake was moving toward me and spotted the cat-like slits of its eyes. Its body was well hidden underneath the leaves, but I knew it was definitely poisonous, probably a rattlesnake from the glimpse I caught of its scales as its head poked out.

Feeling sweat start to pour down my back, I slowly took another step, then another. I heard no rattle, or the sound of leaves moving, but I didn't break into a run until at least five more steps away.

Then I ran as hard as I could.

I don't know how long I ran, but I only stopped when I started seeing stars burst across my vision. I stopped at a clearing and crouched down beside a large, old oak. My hands were shaking, my legs ached, and if Mother had been there, I might have just sat down on the ground and cried my eyes out.

I shook my head. No, there would be time for that later. There would be time to curl up in Bisa's arms and cry until my body was completely spent. I had to last that long, though.

Leaning my head against the cold pine's bark, I tried my hardest not to think about how close I had come to dying. I hadn't even made it to my hiding place yet and had already almost gotten killed.

"You've got this," I whispered to myself even as my throat constricted. "You'll be okay, you just have to make it to the barn."

I breathed in the crisp scent of decayed leaves and found my bearings. The barn was still a good fifteen-minute walk away, if I avoided the roads, and I had no idea if there would be camps of people waiting along the path.

A gleam of yellow made me jump as I stood up. I assumed it was a torch and prepared myself to run, when I realized that it wasn't flickering like fire should. It glowed with its own internal light, pulsating to a strange rhythm. It was one of the yellow dandelions that marked the Boundary Line.

Suddenly the cold wind wasn't so invigorating and pleasing; the tree that I had used to rest against was strange and untrustworthy.

It was never a good idea to be near the Boundary Line. Creatures from the woods crossed over all the time into Carra, and if a Gray Person wasn't around to kill them, you were as good as dead.

Sure, I had a knife in my boot in case I needed it, but the beasts out here were different. Some said they were impervious to blades, others said they could be as big as a horse with teeth the size of knives. They were supposedly drawn to the scent of fear, and I had plenty of that pumping through my veins.

I walked briskly toward the barn, internally counting my steps as I tried to put distance between myself and the Boundary Line.

One, two, three, four, five...

I breathed a sigh of relief, though I was not quite able to regain that exhilaration I had felt earlier after moving deeper into the woods.

~

THE OLD BURNED out barn belonged to Mr. Mackeral, and at one time it had thrived – that is until he had gotten drunk one night watching his flock of sheep and left his campfire unattended. He awoke to find the whole building in flames. He said he didn't remember starting the fire to begin with, but nobody believed him.

No longer trusted to watch any of the livestock, he was relegated to the streets. This happened the first year my family lived in the Exalted House. I offered to investigate, but Father said it wasn't needed. He said Mr. Mackeral was too drunk to watch where he peed, let alone watch sheep.

Before leaving the safety of the tree line, I looked around the empty field that separated me from the barn. Nothing, not even the distant howls of dogs, only the cold wind and the constant rustle of leaves. Hunching down, I made my way through the knee-high grass, grateful as the long blades sprung back in place behind me. Hardly anybody came out this way anymore, which made it an ideal spot.

I went around to the back, to the long wooden feeding troughs that sat beside the only remaining wall of the building, blackened and angled as it now was. The troughs had indeed survived, all four of them, and I crouched down in front of the one that I had prepared.

Underneath it was what looked like an old slab of wood; it appeared worn and partially rotted away. I pulled it back to reveal the ditch I had dug for myself.

It had taken months to prepare, making sure that I had space not only to lie down, but also to sit up. I had wanted to make it deep enough to stand in, but had run out of time - plus removing the excess dirt would look suspicious, and then making my way back into town without anyone noticing my dirty clothing had been difficult and exhausting. I also had to space out my visits so that nobody questioned my absence or wondered where I was spending my time.

The ditch was lined with blankets, with a spare one to use for myself, and a small basket of dried goods, along with the fresh fruit I had added yesterday, sat in one of the corners. The food would hopefully keep my energy up. I just wished I had water, but hadn't felt I could trust any water I'd put down there to stay good for long and didn't want to risk it.

Yesterday I had thought the hole was miserably small and that it wasn't nearly the underground bunker I had envisioned it to be. However, looking at it with the cold wind running a chill along my spine, it looked like a perfect place to sleep.

Shivering, I moved the blankets around to make sure I didn't have any unexpected guests, like the snake from earlier, then climbed inside. I reached out to pull the old slab of wood over me and then pulled the spare blanket up to my nose. Of the many years I had spent hiding and running from people during The Seeking, this was the best outdoor hiding spot I had ever chosen.

Exhausted, my eyelids drooped as I stared up at the stars through the cracks in the wood and listened to the wind whistling. Perhaps in a few hours I would slip out to relieve myself just before dawn, that way I wouldn't have to worry about that as the sun emerged.

The wooden slab over me wobbled with the next strong gust of wind. I jerked, tangling myself further in the blanket. There was a chance it might draw someone's eye, but considering how remote the place was and how tired I felt, I just didn't care.

The sound of the wind and the cocoon of the ditch soon lulled me to sleep.

HONESTLY, I don't know how long I slept; without the chimes of the clock there was no way to tell the passage of time. I probably could have slept the entire night and been able to forget for a little while that I was a target of The Seeking.

The dogs, however, had other plans.

THERE'S something primal about the sound of barking dogs, especially ones that you know are out to attack you. They were still a good distance away, but the sound carried far on the night air. The barks jerked me awake as panic gripped my heart and my breathing turned into gasps. There were a lot of them, and to have that many hunting dogs out tonight... I knew who they belonged to.

Those were Broskow's dogs.

Wide-eyed, I realized then that I had made a terrible mistake. I had led them directly to me when I left the Exalted House and then came straight here. Usually, I would have ducked into a shop or two to throw them off, or maybe taken a longer path, but this Seeking was anything but normal. With the clock chimes being rigged and the scare with the rattlesnake, I had completely forgotten my normal precautions.

"Plan and prepare," Father had told me, but I was so focused on my newest hiding place that I had forgotten.

The barking was getting closer and I pulled one of the blankets up that had been in the ditch for at least a week. It smelled like earth and I felt pieces of what I hoped was just dirt spray across my face as I pulled it over me. The dogs stopped barking and I heard the footfalls of horses, but I couldn't tell how many there were.

I stayed still, listening for what I couldn't see with my eyes. My body was shaking, and I had to force myself to take deep breaths to keep calm.

"This has to be the place." My heart skipped a beat. That was definitely Broskow. Of course he would be the one find me.

"Are you sure?" It was a woman's voice that I didn't recognize. "I don't like the feel of this place one bit, Alex."

Weird, I had never heard Broskow be called by his

first name, even by his closest friends. Who was this woman?

"Oh, quit your griping. The dogs know what they're doing, just let them do their job. If you ever want to share a bed in the Exalted House again, then stick with the plan. These dogs can sniff out a rabid squirrel clear on the other side of Carra if I asked them to. They'll sniff out the girl, you wait and see."

I shivered. I wish it was just bravado talking, but Broskow was known for his hunting dogs. He trained them almost from the day they were born, and they were about as dear to him as his own children. Other villagers said he even slept out in the kennel with his favorite dog when it got sick because Broskow had been so worried for him.

Hiding underneath a trough wouldn't be enough to escape him or his dogs. I would need another plan – now. Otherwise, when they did finally spot me, I would be at their whim, and Broskow had a *lot* of dogs.

I reached down and pulled out the knife in my boot. It wasn't very long, and the blade wasn't terribly straight, but I had taken very good care of it over the years. The handle was what showed its age. It was rusted around the bottom and had been replaced with wood a long time ago. It was once retractable with a small button, or so I was told. The blade was probably made years before even my great-great-grandparents were born.

I had never seen metal before until Darik gave it to me on our first Seeking. He said it had saved his life before we had become the Exalted Family, and he wanted me to have something to defend myself with, especially on The Seeking. He never said where he got it, and I never asked.

Sometimes it was better not to know.

The sound of the horses grew louder as they moved around to the back of the barn. I could make out their voices easier now, and I gripped the knife tightly to my chest.

The ditch turned painfully claustrophobic as I berated myself. Instead of being so focused on digging downward, I should have dug more outward so I could have more room to fight if I needed to. For some reason I hadn't even considered it.

"It's just an old barn anyway," Broskow said. "What are you so worked up about?"

The woman sighed. "Did you ever talk with Mackeral about what happened here, or did you just accept the gossip like everyone else?"

"I didn't just accept it, there wasn't anything else to know about it. Mackeral was drunk, he fell asleep, and his campfire burned the barn to the ground. He was lucky the sheep didn't run into the woods and get themselves killed."

"I suppose that's a nice explanation, simple and stupid," the woman retorted. "Mackeral certainly isn't known for his brains. But I've spoken with him often since it happened. When nobody else would give him even a scrap of food, I offered him rolls from the bakery. When he was forced to sleep out on the streets, I gave him a blanket to stay warm. I'm pretty sure I was the only person in the world who cared that he still existed."

"Alright," Broskow huffed out. "What's your point then?"

"Mackeral swore to me on his life that he never started that fire, and worse yet, he saw what had. It was a pair of Gray People - a man and a woman. He saw them sitting in the tall grass watching the place burn to the ground. And the sheep were sent back into town, walking in a single file, without a sound. He supposedly told Jamel Priest about the whole thing, but we all know how reliable Jamel is."

"The whole Priest family are a bunch of cowards if you ask me." Broskow raised his voice. "You hear me? Cowards!"

I bit my lip. I wanted to leap out and run. I wanted to get as far away as I could.

I also knew I didn't have a chance, not with his dogs so close.

A dog's brown tail wagged past and I held my breath. I could hear his nose working overtime and I gripped the knife tighter. They would find me soon. What would I do? Where would I go? The barn was a lost cause, even after months of preparation. What was I supposed to do?

Then I remembered the place I had mentioned to Bisa. The place where I wasn't even sure I would fit. The place I wasn't supposed to ever go. Sure, it was incredibly dangerous, but compared to being cornered, what other choice did I have?

The view of the night sky suddenly became obscured

as a dog's snout pressed into the gap between the trough and the wooden slab that covered me. The brown eye of a big, muscular dog locked onto me. Then he started growling. My pulse was pounding in my temples. No, I couldn't move, not yet.

"Wait," the woman whispered, "it sounds like—"

"We've got her!" Broskow shouted with glee. The sound of hooves drew closer and I heard someone dismount. The dog was digging beside the wooden slab, still growling.

I was shaking from head to toe, waiting for the right moment, waiting for one of them to act. If I lunged out at the dog, I could get swarmed by the pack.

I had to wait. I had to rely on causing confusion.

My fingers trembled against the handle of the knife.

"Come on, come here, boy," Broskow ordered.

A woman's face came into perspective. She had taupe white skin with pink, pinched lips and peered down at me with absolute disgust. "Is that..." she started as she crouched down on hands and knees to get a better look - and that's when I moved.

I shoved the wooden panel upwards, smacking her in the chin. Her head flung back; she cried out in shock.

I climbed out as fast as I could and scrambled to my feet. The woman reached out and gripped my forearm with strong fingers when I jerked forward to run.

"Don't you dare, you little brat!"

I screamed and lunged with the knife, ripping up her forearm. Her eyes went wide as her grip fell away and I took off into the tall grass. That's when I realized Broskow was screaming, "Pearl! Pearl, are you okay?"

"Don't worry about me - get her!"

The dogs started howling, drowning out Broskow's shouts of rage.

I pumped my legs hard, tasting coppery blood in the back of my throat from where I'd accidentally bitten my tongue at some point.

The dogs were gaining on me and I choked on a sob. I could hear them cutting through the grass and I changed direction, now running for the trees. In my haste, I leapt over the underbrush and nearly got my foot tangled on a hidden vine.

I saw one of the dogs in my peripheral vision, a black shape lunging at me in the darkness. I didn't stop. I kept running until I spotted the golden markers at the edge of Carra: the glowing Boundary Line. I hoped this worked.

With a whine of fear, I leaped over the barrier. The dandelions swayed slightly as I flew past. I knew the way to my tree. I knew it when I was a child, and the memory was still there. I had passed this area so many times recently to prepare my hiding place, and I knew this would be my backup. I'd just hoped I wouldn't have to use it.

I climbed into the hollow of the tree. It was the only hiding place where Darik could never find me when we were children. He was too terrified of crossing the barrier – like I hoped the dogs and Broskow would be.

As soon as I crawled into it, I knew it was a bad idea. I was far bigger than I had been when we played hide and seek, and while the hollow had seemed so big and empty in my memory, now I barely fit. Bisa had warned me about this, I just thought I knew better. I was so very wrong.

I had to crouch down and hug my knees in order to squeeze back inside of it. I was lucky I was so short - if I had been any taller, I wouldn't have fit.

Broskow's dogs slowed to a stop as they approached the Boundary Line, howling and barking because they knew exactly where I had fled. There were seven of them in all, and they formed an angry line, their eyes locked onto me.

The woman, Pearl, approached first. Unlike the dogs, she didn't see me and was clearly afraid, looking along the Boundary Line like a woman facing a firing squad. She dismounted her horse and walked over to the dogs, who grew quiet as she approached. She was a tall woman with short white hair that gleamed blue in the moonlight. I recognized her then; she was Broskow's new wife.

"Where did that brat go?" she asked and fiddled with a cloth wrapped around the gouge I had made along her arm.

One of the dogs whined but she pushed it aside with her leg. She drew closer to the Boundary Line, but couldn't quite bring herself to step over it.

The dandelions glowed eerily in the still night as another cold breeze blew.

Just walk away, I pleaded with her in my mind. *Just walk away and give up. Please.* But she didn't. Instead she began to pace up and down the Boundary Line like a sentinel. As I watched her, I tried to recall what I knew about her.

She was a quiet woman, and everyone was shocked when she and her previous husband won that Seeking. They had dragged in a boy, scrawny Tom Farrier, kicking and screaming. He had been tied up with rope that cut into his wrists. Tom still had red marks on his wrists from that night almost ten years ago. He had been so energetic and playful before, but now he was shy and quiet, working on his father's horse farm while drinking his nights away and trying to forget the past.

Either way, Pearl and her husband had only lasted a year as the Exalted. Their daughter was killed the following Seeking, and many thought it was in vengeance, for the girl's body was found alongside a creek, her face wet while the rest of her body was dry. The murderer was never found.

In one night, Pearl and her husband had lost their only child and their position of power. Her husband died shortly after. They said it was because he was so stricken from losing his daughter, but now I knew that Broskow had shared a bed in the Exalted House before. Had they been seeing each other then?

When I had heard Broskow had gotten married again a few years back, after his wife died during childbirth, I didn't realize she was the Pearl everyone spoke of.

If working in the courts had taught me anything, it was that someone who has tasted power can become even more desperate for it.

Pearl's long plain skirt swished back and forth, her gaze intense as she stared into the woods. Her arm was still bleeding, but there was a keen anger in her face. Broskow had arrived and was squatting down with his dogs, searching the tree line for me, but was thankfully unable to see me without walking over the Boundary Line. As determined as they were, neither of them were that brave.

My legs were already cramping. Could I make a run for it? Broskow was distracting some of his dogs, but so many of them were wandering up and down with Pearl as she paced. I wished they would give up already. I was watching them all so intently that it took me a moment to register the noise coming from up above me.

Even though I had spent hours of my childhood hidden in this hollow tree, aware that I was breaking the biggest rule in all of Carra, somehow I had been lucky enough to never have seen a creature of the woods. I don't know why; perhaps it was dumb luck, or perhaps there were more Gray People around when I was younger.

When I saw a long, spindly leg come down from the top of the tree and latch onto a corner of the hole I was in, I very nearly screamed. Instead I jammed the back of my hand against my mouth to stifle the sound.

It took me a moment to recognize what it belonged to. There were tiny rigid hairs all over the leg, and it was bent in two places. Then another one came down and reached in on the other side of the hole, inches away from my leg. They were spider legs, but far larger than any I had ever seen.

I swallowed harshly and gripped the knife in both hands as tight as I could. That was when its face slowly lowered down and came into view of a beam of moonlight. The body itself was oblong and covered in long, coarse hair, but then the front of its body bent forward, and I realized that was its head – a head that was attached to a long, snakelike neck. Its flat face was made up of two large, yellow orbs, but its circular mouth jutted forward. Inside were rows and rows of teeth.

Two more legs came down as I stared at it, dumbfounded and horrified.

Then it struck.

It was as fast as a snake. The eyes had stunned me, but somehow my instincts kicked in and I brought the knife up just in time to jab at the underside of its mouth. I heard a *ting* as the knife struck the hairs, yet the creature seemed unfazed.

This is how I die, I thought to myself. The knife could have possibly saved me from Broskow or his dogs, but there was no fighting this thing.

"Any luck?" Broskow said in the distance, and the creature's snake-like neck swerved back toward them, like a finger that could bend perfectly in the opposite direction. Then it bobbed its head up a few times and I realized it was sniffing the air.

I looked to see the cloth on Pearl's arm was completely soaked with blood.

The creature began to descend, and I realized where

it was headed. I took the knife and struck at its hairy belly again and again, but it was like trying to cut at a rock. It didn't even turn to look at me, and instead crawled down the length of the tree, its spider legs moving with barely a sound.

"Not a sign of her," Pearl said. "It's like she just vanished."

The dogs were backing away from the Boundary Line now, whimpering and whining; the horses stamped at the ground, but neither Broskow nor Pearl noticed.

I wanted to scream a warning, to do something, but I felt cold and nauseous. My hands were trembling and wouldn't stop. My arm throbbed from where I had tried to cut at the creature. All I could do was watch as it scurried from tree to tree, using the long shadows to hide itself.

I followed its yellow eyes as it got closer to them.

There was a beat of silence...

Then it dropped down from the branch of a tree that hung over the Boundary Line and landed on Pearl. Its legs skittered down her shoulders and its head looped forward to attach directly to her face. She only had a moment to scream before the sound was muffled by the wiggling creature.

"Pearl!" Broskow yelled, nearly falling to the ground as he scrambled back. He picked up a crossbow he had strapped to his arm and shot off several bolts at the monster, but they bounced off like toys.

Pearl had grabbed onto its legs and tried to pull it off, but it wouldn't budge. Her hands fell away with blood trailing down her palms. Broskow picked up a tree limb and tried to pry it off, but the wood bent and snapped in his hands.

With a muffled cry, Pearl fell to her knees, her movements more frantic now. I couldn't tell if it was suffocating her, or if it was eating her. Its yellow eyes just stared blankly outward, barely acknowledging that she was struggling at all, and hardly noticing that Broskow was even there.

I bit back a sob when she fell fully to the ground and the creature, unfazed, put a pair of legs out to keep from falling off. Its mouth was still in perfect alignment where it had first latched on.

Broskow was screaming and sobbing, bashing at it fruitlessly with the broken tree limb still in his hands. He tried to call his dogs to help, but they had fled along with the horses as soon as the creature had appeared.

My eyes grew wide, my hand coming back to cover my mouth, as it unlatched itself, and pieces of Pearl's face came with it. She was liquefied and no longer discernible as the woman she once had been. White bone protruded around the eye sockets where her eyeballs should have been. Her face was now a mixture of shredded muscle, deep shadows, and bone.

My breaths came in hot and quick pants against my palm.

The creature turned lazy yellow eyes onto Broskow. He looked down at the broken stick in his hands and dropped it, like a guilty child being found out for some wrongdoing. He backed away, holding his hands out as it stepped towards him.

It leaped.

I hadn't realized that it could leap so high or so quickly, and I gasped as I watched its legs land on Broskow's shoulders, its mouth inching toward his face, but this time it didn't get the chance to latch on. Something had grabbed one of its legs and flung it to the ground.

Blinking, I saw a Gray Person, a man by the looks of him, standing almost directly beside Broskow, with skin gleaming that ghostly gray blue in the moonlight and his eyes gaping black holes. What terrified me the most was that he wore a wide, amused smile.

Broskow fell to the ground and crawled over to a tree trunk, sobbing. The Gray Person looked at him with utter enjoyment, before ripping a leg off of the spider creature. Black blood spewed everywhere, and the creature began skittering and jumping, trying to escape. It started to shriek in such a high pitch that it made my ears hurt.

Apparently, the Gray Person didn't like it much either, because it picked up the torch that Pearl had been carrying and shoved the entire flame into the creature's mouth. More black blood erupted; the screaming soon stopped.

I watched the creature roll back and forth right before the Gray Person slammed it against a tree trunk, and black blood stained the wood and splashed onto the ground. Its yellow orbs were empty and dim; its thrashing ceased completely.

The Gray Person smiled and dropped the creature onto the ground before heading over to Broskow and crouching down in front of him. I could hear Broskow scream as he tried to back away, but the Gray Person grabbed hold of his chin and forced him to look at him.

As Broskow stared into those empty eyes, his screaming slowly stopped, and his jaw went slack. His eyes widened, and his body twitched occasionally as though he was being shocked. When his eyes were half-lidded, the Gray Person picked him up gingerly, like a child who was out past his bedtime.

I shook my head, not wanting the Gray Person to take him away, but not knowing what I could possibly do. I wanted to scream but couldn't even do that.

All I could do was watch.

The Gray Person approached the Boundary Line but stopped and turned.

He looked directly at me and smiled.

My breath caught in my throat as my stomach dropped. I looked away, not wanting it to entrance me like it had Broskow.

When I looked up again, the Gray Person was gone and so was Broskow. I took a deep breath and closed my eyes for a moment, trying to get my breathing under control and my heart to stop racing.

When I looked back, I startled. The Gray Person had returned, but this time without Broskow. He grabbed one of Pearl's legs and one of the legs of the spider creature and dragged them off into the woods. All that remained of the horrific scene were the pools of black blood everywhere.

As the minutes passed and daybreak approached, I realized I could no longer feel my legs, yet still I sat despite the cold. Sunlight brought the gory scene before me to life.

Guilt washed over me.

If I hadn't cut Pearl's arm, it wouldn't have gone after her. If I hadn't chosen this tree to hide in, I wouldn't have awoken it. It would have left all of us alone.

Now someone was dead.

Was my family losing power really that bad compared to Pearl getting her face eaten off?

I leaned my head back, letting the hot tears roll down my cheeks.

CHAPTER 5
A COLD DAWN

I don't know when I fell asleep, but by the time I managed to open my eyes, the sun was clear over the horizon. My back and shoulders hurt, my legs had no feeling left, and I knew I needed to leave that tree hollow.

I was terrified.

What if I climbed out and woke up another one of those spider creatures? What if the Gray Person came back and killed me for being on their side of the Boundary Line?

I shivered, realizing how cold I was; both the ground and I were covered in frost. I needed to get someplace warm – quickly - but was it safe to go back to the barn with my stockpile and blankets? The only people who knew about it were Broskow and Pearl, and one of them was dead.

I felt the burn of tears but pushed them back. I needed to get out of the woods, to get back to relative safety, and I needed to find a way to wait out the rest of the day.

Stretching out my legs was harder than I expected; they had fallen completely asleep. I had to pull them out with my hands and let them flop to the ground as the blood returned to them. It took a few minutes for the pins and needles feeling to go away before I felt I was ready to actually walk on them.

I carefully dropped down and landed on the frost covered leaves, then gingerly stretched my legs, back and shoulders while suppressing another shiver. Everything popped and hurt at the same time. I was still trembling from head to toe, so I wrapped my arms around myself to keep warm.

Carefully scanning the trees as I walked, I stepped over the Boundary Line and started back toward the barn. The wind was blowing harder this morning and my teeth rattled. I thought about running to the barn, but I was afraid: of the creatures of the woods, of the townspeople, of everybody.

The barn looked empty when I reached it. No horses were tacked out front, and there were no dogs roaming about. I sighed and my eyes burned a little, but I couldn't tell if it was from the cold or from crying so much. I looked forward to burying myself in my little blanket-lined ditch.

As I moved around the back of the barn, I jerked to a stop. There sat Broskow on the ground beside my hiding place, smoking a pipe. I bit back a frightened cry when our eyes locked and he scrambled to his feet.

I took off again for the woods. Once I was out of sight, I would reach down for my knife. Somehow I had remembered to push it back down into my shoe last night.

"Wait!" he called from behind me. "Wait, I don't want to capture you!"

There was urgency in his voice, a fear that I'd never heard from him before. I stopped and turned to face him, shivering so badly my teeth chattered. It could end up being a trick like the clock chimes.

He stood at the edge of the barn's boundary, a woolen shawl over his shoulders and his pipe now in his hands. His face was all pink and his eyes were red-rimmed, like he'd been crying.

I thought of Pearl, of the gash I'd made on her arm, of the spider creature I had awoken, and before I knew it, I was walking back to him. I stopped ten feet away, not quite trusting him, but the guilt was eating at me again.

All my fault.

"What do you want?" I asked around my chattering teeth.

Broskow said nothing, just looked me up and down. I probably looked like a person who had spent the night in a damn tree, disheveled and dirty. "I want to help you."

I shook my head. "If this is a trick—"

"No trick," he said and held up his hands. "I promise. I just," he blinked quickly and swallowed, "I want to talk... about what happened."

I pursed my lips against the guilt and fear churning in my stomach. The words fell out before I realized I was speaking. "I'm sorry." I shook my head. "I didn't mean for her to get hurt."

Broskow stepped forward slowly and pulled off his shawl. He kept his hands in my line of sight. When he got close enough, he lifted the shawl up and tried to wrap it around me, but I pushed his hands away.

"Don't be stupid, you're going to freeze."

I gripped my elbows. "How do I know this isn't a trick? This could be just another clever tactic to lock me up somewhere."

"I told you I'm not—"

"I know what you said. But I also saw what you and your friends did to Dameon yesterday. I saw you laugh while he cried."

There was a helplessness in his eyes that took me off guard. "I remember that. I remember what that felt like. Please, I don't want to capture you or hurt you or whatever you think I want to do to you, I just... I need to talk to someone." His eyes were glassy, and he was swallowing as though trying to keep from bawling his eyes out.

"You want me to trust you?"

"Please," he whispered, holding the shawl up again. "I don't have anyone else to talk to. You're the only person who saw what happened."

I stiffened. Every muscle in my body was tight from the cold, and I was exhausted. There was truth to his words, and oddly enough, a truthful look in his gaze. I pursed my lips and then nodded, allowing him to wrap his shawl around my shoulders and put an arm around me.

I tried not to flinch as he said, "Let's get you warm and then we can talk more, okay?"

I nodded again, clutching the warm shawl tighter around my shoulders.

Against probably everything I had ever been taught to do during The Seeking, I followed his lead back toward town. The shawl was warm enough to at least stop my teeth from chattering.

WHEN WE WERE ALMOST within sight of town, Broskow grabbed my arm and pulled me to a stop.

"What are you doing?" I asked suspiciously.

"Disguising you." He wrapped me in his huge coat and put his own hat on my head. The hat was far too big for me; the earflaps came down to my shoulders and I could barely see out from under the rim of fur.

"You think this is really going to work?"

"Sure," he said with a small smile. "You'll be my daughter Maryann. She's about your age anyway." He grinned at my snort, his teeth holding his pipe in place. He stepped forward, but I pushed him back and his amusement melted. "What's wrong?"

"Do I look like a fool? You're taking me to your house, where you'll lock me up. Then you'll tell everybody about how clever you were to lure me into your own home."

He sighed. "I guess it does look that way, but that's

not it. I just want to talk, preferably in a place that's warm. I want to know what you saw and," he lowered his voice, that pained expression coming back as his gaze shifted to the ground. "I need to know what happened to me."

The desperation in his voice swayed me more than any of his promises could. Having spent years handling court cases for Carra, I knew that tone. His eyes held the same look that a wild animal's did, and a terror I had never seen on his face before. Suddenly I, too, wondered what happened to him when the Gray Person took him away.

"Okay," I whispered. "But it's still never going to work."

"Why not?"

I pointed to my cheek. "I look nothing like Maryann."

He nodded. "Okay, let's see..."

He stuffed my braids up into my hat. Then he wrapped his scarf around my mouth and my neck until there was only a gap left for my eyes. He pulled his gloves off and slipped them onto my hands. They were too big for me, so I had to keep my fingers curled for fear of them falling off. By the time Broskow finished with me, the only way you could see even a patch of my skin was by looking under my fur hood.

"Just stay calm," he said before taking my hand and leading me, as though it was that easy.

It was the morning of The Seeking, and most hunters used daytime to recuperate from the night before. We were also lucky it was so cold out; otherwise we might have been caught while we were talking before.

I stared at the ground and at people's feet as he led me through town, but even that felt dangerous. I had never attempted walking through downtown Carra in the middle of The Seeking before, even on such a cold morning. Most people would probably consider that giving up.

Fortunately, I knew the roads of Carra well and was able to guess generally where we were as we walked. I caught the scent of horse manure as we passed the horse farm on the edge of town, and then heard the scouring of clothes, meaning we were close to Broskow's butcher shop.

That was odd, since his home was on the other side of town. Maybe his children were at home still, waiting for news, and he wasn't ready to tell them what happened to their stepmother. For them, this would be the second mother they had lost.

Broskow's grip on my hand tightened and soon we were heading downtown, where the scent of apple pie was the strongest. It set my heart beating faster as we approached his butcher shop. By the number of shoes I could see, the number of people still in town was down-right astonishing. I thought more of them would be staying out of the cold or out hunting for me and my brothers, but I heard music playing at the bars and laughter on the wind. Most of them were enjoying their day off rather than hunting for children.

We passed Eddington's restaurant and I spotted

Bisa's shoes by the door. I knew they were hers because she always liked to personalize her shoes, and these had cute blue bows stitched in on the sides.

I reached out and brushed her coat, not daring to say a word as we passed. I heard her footsteps come to a stop as we kept moving, and I hoped that she understood that it wasn't just Maryann grabbing at her. She didn't say anything, though, and while it was probably because Broskow was at my side, it still hurt.

An hour ago, if anyone had told me I would be trusting Broskow not to capture me on The Seeking, I would have laughed in their face.

I hoped Bisa would somehow know it was me, even though that was ridiculous.

Disheartened, my shoulders tensed as we passed crowds of people gathered in the street, and at one point I heard someone run up beside us. I held my breath.

"How goes the hunt, Alex?"

Broskow gave a hearty chuckle to cover my startled sound as I jerked to a stop, "It goes, it goes."

Did they hear the bitterness in his voice like I did? Did they hear the terror hidden behind his words? He didn't slow down but pulled me until my feet shuffled forward again.

As we made a final turn through town, I knew we had to be close to the butcher shop. Was he taking the long way around?

Broskow came to a sudden stop, and I heard him gasp lowly before tightly squeezing my hand. I lowered my head further.

"Hey, Dad!" Stefan Broskow, the eldest of his children at nineteen, said. "Hey, what's up with you, Maryann?" I saw his pale hand reach for my hood, but I smacked it away. "Ouch! That hurt!"

"Leave her be, Stefan," Broskow ordered. "She's not feeling well. I think she's come down with something." Stefan gagged and took a big step back. "Anyway, I need you to go out and round up the dogs. They were so intent on their hunt, they got away from me."

"Oh wow! Yeah, they must have picked up the scent of one of those brats."

"Who knows..." His voice was filled with discomfort as it trailed off. Broskow led me over to the front door of his shop and I peeked out just enough to see him pull out his ring of keys.

"Hey, what do I do if they're like eating on one of them when I find them? Should I just bring back their remains?"

Broskow slammed a fist on the door and Stefan took a couple of steps back in surprise. "Do as I say and gather them up. I don't care what they're doing. If they're not back in the kennels by noon, I'm going to tan your hide."

"Y-yessir," Stefan stammered before turning and running off.

Broskow opened the door of his shop with a grunt and let go of my hand. I hurried inside. He had a large fire going in the hearth and I breathed a sigh of relief. I hadn't realized how cold I was until I felt that wall of heat. The door closed behind me and I could hear the key get inserted into the lock.

"Don't!" I cried, pulling the hood down. "If you lock that, then The Seeking is over."

He arched a gray, bushy eyebrow at me and removed the key, replacing it back in his pocket. "I hadn't realized the rules were that specific."

I pulled the scarf off from around my neck and went to the hearth, soaking in the warmth as Broskow closed the shutters. "There are a lot of rules. I guess most people don't know them as well as we do."

"Sorry about my boy," he said as he shuttered up the last window. "He gets carried away."

"He doesn't sound that different from how you usually are."

Broskow looked uncomfortable at that. "Look, I don't want any trouble with you. I just want to talk." He stiffened. "Last night, I don't know what happened, and I just need someone to talk with." He pulled a wrapped bunch of jerky out from one of the cabinets. "Here, take whatever you like."

I briefly considered that they may be poisoned, but my stomach insisted otherwise. I grabbed at least three slices from the bunch - each slice was about half the width of my hand, and about as long - and started eating them all at once.

Broskow chuckled before he emptied out his pipe over the fireplace. He fetched us both drinks and let me eat in silence for a few more minutes while he packed fresh leaves into his pipe and stared into the fire.

I sat on the floor in front of the flames but kept him in my line of sight as he settled down in his armchair nearby. It was the first we had ever been in each other's company where we weren't fighting or taunting each other. It was strange, as though I was seeing him – the real him - for the first time, and he wasn't the monster I had made him out to be.

Don't get me wrong, he was hardly a good person, but now that I had seen real monsters, I realized he wasn't one. He was just really good at pretending to be one.

"I can't remember much of it," he said finally. "I remember...something coming out of the trees and killing Pearl. I remember beating on it, trying to get it to let go of her, but then Pearl fell and I..." he trailed off. "I don't remember what happened after that. I woke up in bed at my house. I thought I had dreamed all of it."

I stared, noticing the way the firelight accented his cheekbones and wild eyes. His face was turning pink from the heat, but he didn't seem to mind. He just stared, hands shaking. Something had to have happened to him when the Gray Person took him into the woods. I remembered the expression he had - like he had been stunned into silence.

A shiver went down my spine.

"I need you to fill in the details," he admitted finally, glancing in my direction. "I need you to tell me what happened after she died. I need to know how I got from those woods to my house without remembering a single step."

The heat from the fire felt like it was baking my fingers as I shifted closer to the flames. I considered being honest with him, but then what happened once he got the information he wanted? What would he do with me?

"You're not going to like what I have to say." He didn't respond so I continued, "Some things you're better off not knowing. That's what my mother tells me."

"I don't give a stinking carcass what kind of ridiculous advice Ivory Priest has to give." He slammed his fist on the arm of his chair. "Tell me what happened to my wife's body!"

I shrunk back on instinct, suddenly not sure if being in this shop was any safer than being in the woods. "I don't have to tell you a damn thing if you act like that."

He got to his feet and I hopped up as he approached, putting the opposite chair between the two of us. If I had to, I thought I could lift the chair to throw at him, but I wasn't sure how heavy it was. The knife was in my shoe, but reaching down to grab for it would give him an advantage. The chair at least gave me some protection.

He looked like he wanted to grab hold of me, but then seemed to second-guess his decision. He looked at me, then the chair, and stepped back.

"Look, this isn't what I planned to do. I don't want to bring you in or kill you. I don't want any of that anymore. I just want to know what happened."

"And like I said, I don't have to tell you anything if you're going to demand it out of me."

He shook his head with a snarl reminiscent of his dogs and slammed a fist against the wall. I winced.

He sat back down in his chair and picked up his pipe

from where he had dropped it. "I'm not trying to bring up old blood, I just honestly want to know what happened. I still don't want to believe it, but I know she really is dead. I went back and looked for her, but all I saw was the black blood on the ground. She disappeared." He swallowed thickly. "I can't even bury her!"

I studied him, fighting my knee-jerk reaction to flee. It had always been easier to flee from Broskow's anger than to deal with it, but for the first time I saw true sorrow on his face, and I pitied him. Not only that, but I was the cause. I made Pearl bleed. I felt that now familiar guilt resurface.

But, if it hadn't been Pearl, then I would be the one missing a face.

"Tell me," he requested again, this time gripping the arm of the chair instead of slamming fists into walls. Against everything my instincts told me to do, I sat down in the chair opposite him and started to speak.

"I was in my dugout waiting for one of you to get close enough..."

I TOLD BROSKOW EVERYTHING, from the slash on Pearl's arm, to how I had awoken the spider creature slumbering in the tree, to the way it had scurried from the shadows to reach his wife. Trying to be as kind as possible, I spoke briefly of the attack on Pearl and his own ferocious, but ultimately fruitless attempt to protect her. Then I spoke of the Gray Person.

"Wait, so he's the one that killed it?" he asked, looking like a child listening to a tale before bedtime.

"He put a torch down its throat. There was hardly anything left by the time he was done with it."

Broskow had been silent before this, so I gave him a moment to elaborate, but he just cleared his throat and motioned for me to continue.

The part that I explained in detail was his apparent hypnosis by the Gray Person, how at first he had been scared but then seemed to relax into a state of shock. He watched me with his mouth open and his fingertips trembling on his pipe.

"You said it took me *into the woods*?"

I nodded, sharing his concern.

"But I don't remember any of that. I woke up at home, in my bed!"

"Maybe he wanted to make sure you were safe. You were really upset."

Broskow got to his feet and began pacing in front of the fireplace. "No, no, I mean obviously it didn't want me to tell anyone. I saw it rip that thing apart. I had forgotten that somehow, but it's coming back to me. Then it looked me in the eyes and—"

There was a knock on the door. I jumped to my feet; Broskow and I looked at each other in mutual surprise.

"Who is it?" I whispered after another knock came.

Broskow shrugged. "Stefan maybe? I don't know, but get your hood up."

I wrapped the scarf tighter around my mouth and pulled the hood up as he got the door. I was expecting

Stefan or one of Broskow's many friends; any would love an excuse to find me trapped in a building with a single exit.

"Turn around and get inside," a woman's voice demanded. Intrigued, I leaned to the side to peek around Broskow. In the doorway stood a woman with a lovely, curvaceous figure. I pushed the hood up and stepped to the side. It was Bisa, standing with a full-sized crossbow aimed at Broskow's stomach.

"Do I need to repeat myself?" she asked with an expression so intense it made my heart soar. I couldn't imagine where in the world she had found a crossbow, let alone figured out a way to hide it under her skirts the entire walk here.

Broskow stood in the doorway in a state of disbelief before he turned to look at me as though I could somehow account for all of this.

I shrugged.

Having the pointy end of an arrow pushed against his flabby midsection finally put some energy into his steps and he backed quickly into the shop, allowing Bisa to follow him in. She closed the door with her foot, never taking her eyes off of him.

"Dahlia, honey, are you okay?"

I blinked, feeling dazed as I slowly unwrapped the scarf and pulled off the hat. I had to stop admiring how beautiful she was and actually keep her from killing Broskow in his own butcher's shop — the irony wasn't lost on me.

"It's okay, Bisa, he's not hunting me anymore."

She glanced at me with wide eyes. "What?"

I walked around to her, holding my hands out. "He's not hunting me, it's okay."

Bisa glanced from me to Broskow then back to me. "Is this some kind of a trick?"

"I'm so glad to see you!" I wrapped my arms around her, forcing her to lower the crossbow in the process. She was hesitant until I kissed her and that seemed to show her that I was indeed not being held against my will.

"Damn," Broskow muttered, leaning heavily against his countertop. "I swear, that was the last thing I expected."

Bisa glared at him. "Dahlia, I hope you have a good reason for making me lose the advantage here."

"I do, I promise." I took her hand and drew her over to the fireplace.

IN A MATTER OF MINUTES, I brought her up to speed, this time with Broskow's help. He was right; just talking about it was helping him remember what all had happened. There were occasional gaps that I had to fill in, usually around where the Gray Person had come to help, but at least now he was able to talk about it without sounding disjointed and crazy.

"And then when the Gray Person looked at me — well if you can call it looking since it had damn holes for eyes – it told me to be calm and to shut up," Broskow recalled.

I opened my mouth to interrupt, but paused when I realized how fully he was in the memory now and didn't want him to lose it completely.

"I—" Bisa began, but I nudged her. I could see by this point that she was just as intrigued and disturbed as we were, perhaps more so since she had all of it dumped on her shoulders without any interaction with the creature or Gray Person.

"So, I did," Broskow continued. "I didn't even consider not obeying, I just suddenly felt calmer than I had ever been in my life, but I was still scared. I didn't know what was going on, but I wasn't even interested in talking anymore. It felt as if I had never even known how to speak." He took a deep draught on his pipe; Bisa and I watched and waited.

"Now, this is going to sound crazy, but when it put me down in the woods, I was still completely out of it." He dragged a hand through his thin, gray hair. "I was calmer, though - it looked me in the eyes and told me to *be* calm - so I was." He shook his head. "But when it put me on the ground, it crouched down and looked into my eyes again. This time was different."

He cleared his throat and took a deep puff of his pipe. "It's hard to find the right words. I can picture it, but it's hard to explain. I felt like it opened up somehow. It was like a door opened up to somewhere way bigger on the other side. It felt massive and more than anything else, empty, just painfully empty.

"There was a sadness to how empty it was, but as I looked at it, I heard this ringing sound in my ears and my head started hurting something terrible. And suddenly the place wasn't empty anymore. The Gray Person backed away with a smile and told me to not remember him."

Bisa and I exchanged glances.

"What?" she mouthed to me.

I shook my head, then turned to Broskow. "They can do that?"

Broskow ignored me. "The first time, I was scared of what was happening to me, but this time was different, too. I felt scared back when I saw him throwing that spider around, but now I felt this overwhelming desire to scream. I couldn't even open my mouth to try. I knew something had happened to my mind, something wrong." He shuddered.

"I realized that the empty room he had showed me was like his stomach and when he filled it, he did it with my mind, my thoughts, my feelings. He filled it with parts of me like stuffing a sausage before he walked away full, and I walked away..." His words faded as he looked at us, the firelight glittering in his hollow, terrified eyes. "...empty."

Bisa stared at him, her face scrunched up in confusion. "What do you mean?"

Broskow shook his head and I could see he was still trying to make sense of what sounded like madness when he tried to put it into words. "I don't know. I just felt like I lost a bit of myself. I don't mean physically, not like an arm or something, but a piece of myself." He groaned in frustration, tears in his eyes. "Just thinking about it makes my head hurt."

I felt terrible for him, for Pearl, and for what the Gray Person did to him afterwards. I kept getting stuck on the image of his frozen expression after looking into its empty eyes, and suddenly a few of the pieces started falling in place. "Maybe that's a side effect," I said slowly, thinking out loud. "It told you not to remember it, right?"

Broskow nodded, wiping his eyes and his nose on his sleeve.

Bisa blinked at me with wide eyes and mouthed, "Is he crying?"

I nodded to her then said, "The whole reason he came looking for me to begin with was because he couldn't remember what happened to Pearl after the attack. He couldn't remember anything except waking up here. Now that he's remembering, I wonder if that's where the headaches are coming from, because he's fighting against it."

Broskow bit his lip, looking doubtful, but Bisa was quick to jump on board.

"But we've never heard of the Gray People doing this sort of thing before. Why is he the first to mention it?" She glanced at Broskow with thinly veiled disdain.

"I don't know, maybe it worked before."

We both turned to him, and Broskow gave an awkward chuckle. "You mean I'm smarter than they expected?"

"I wouldn't go that far," I said, dryly. "Maybe you

were just too shaken after what happened to Pearl to forget it completely."

He glanced to the floor as his humor died away. "I still don't know what it did with her body."

"Well that's obvious, isn't it?" Bisa said. "They don't want us to have a body to examine. They don't want us to know anything about the creatures that live in the woods; they want us to stay ignorant. It's easier to control us if we don't know what we're up against. They keep us scared and they keep us distracted with all this Seeking nonsense."

I looked at her in surprise and she shrugged. "You have to admit it works. Most of Carra is out there hunting for you and your siblings right now, not investigating what happened to Pearl."

"But what about that crazy thing they did to my mind, taking parts of me like that." Broskow shuddered. "What was that about? That had nothing to do with that spider creature or with keeping us distracted. What was that for?"

"Maybe," I said, almost afraid to say it aloud. "Maybe that's how they feed."

I KNEW AS SOON as I said it, it might be too much for Broskow. His mind was already in a bad state and that knowledge might just push him over completely. He worked as a butcher, hacking up sheep and pigs for everyone in Carra's consumption. Just mentioning the connection could lead to a breakdown, but instead he stood there transfixed.

"Is he okay?" Bisa whispered after a minute of silence.

"I have no idea." I stood up and approached him. "Broskow...uh, Alex? Are you alright?"

"Yes," he said, "I'm fine."

He headed to his countertop and pulled out some butcher paper and a piece of charcoal. "Feeding, yes, they have to be feeding on us somehow." He started etching out a large oblong circle on the table, and Bisa and I both approached somewhat nervously.

"This is the Boundary Line of Carra," he told us, tapping the rough sketch.

"Sure," Bisa agreed, glancing at me. "More or less anyway."

"Now, all along it we have those bright dandelions that glow, who knows why anymore, but everybody respects it. Nobody wants to go across that line. Not normally anyway - except you."

He pointed the piece of charcoal at me and I felt my stomach tighten. Bisa turned to me with judgmental eyes and I looked away quickly to avoid her gaze.

Broskow cleared his throat. "Don't worry about it, it doesn't matter." He drew a much smaller circle off to the side of Carra. When it was finished, he flipped the paper around. "Okay, so this smaller circle isn't Carra. This is the boundary we keep when we're watching a flock of sheep. Now this one," he paused and marked an X outside of that small circle, "this one represents you,

Dahlia. You're a straggler that likes to wander outside of formation."

Bisa laughed. "She sure is." I gave her a look and she just shrugged. "What? It's true!"

"Now normally with sheep we'll walk alongside them for a bit to get them to calm down, then slowly steer them back to the herd. The Gray People can't do that of course, nobody would want that, so they just let the Boundary Line do its job." He tapped on the circle of Carra. "This is a two-part system. This barrier works as a way to keep us in, sure, but it also seems to do the opposite of what a normal fence would. It's not built to keep out predators; it's made to let them in."

"What are you talking about?" I asked.

He grinned; eyes wild. "Stay with me here. This fence doesn't keep out predators like you would think. No, this fence seems to act as a signal to the Gray People, like the way I'll whistle to tell my dogs to hold back. They don't seem to care much if a few of us get injured or killed, they just don't want the flock as a whole to be put in danger."

"I was always told the Gray People protected us," I argued. "My grandmother always told me not to be afraid of them."

"Of course they wouldn't want us to fear them," Bisa said, shaking her head. "It's easier to take an animal down when it trusts you."

I put my head into my hands and stared down at the stained countertop. Countless pieces of meat had been handed over this countertop to paying customers, without a single person realizing that they were no better off than sheep or pigs.

Were we all really just livestock, or was Broskow redirecting his fear into some crazy conclusion to make himself feel better about what happened last night?

Bisa rubbed my back and I leaned into her, glad to have her with me again. Everything felt a little less hopeless when she was at my side.

"I don't know about all this. Do you think we're jumping to conclusions? You said it yourself that your memories weren't complete. Maybe you're filling in the blanks and seeing a motive that isn't there?"

He laughed at me and folded his arms. "I think I would know what I experienced, Dahlia."

"Not necessarily. I've seen it happen in court before. People are good at creating a narrative when there isn't one, or filling in gaps when they can't recall what really happened - especially when they're nervous or distressed."

"I know what I saw," Broskow said firmly, and I could see how convinced he was.

Bisa bit her lips and looked between the two of us as though she could smell a fight about to break out. "Look, it sounds like you've both had a long evening. Why don't you rest up before anyone says something they might regret?" She looked at me with warm, pleading eyes.

"I guess I am tired," I said. "I slept in the hollow of that tree for a good chunk of the night."

Bisa pursed her lips and I just knew we would be discussing all the thousand ways that was a bad idea at some point, but she kept her thoughts to herself for the moment. She turned to Broskow, who sighed and tossed the charcoal onto the table with a clatter.

"Fine. But we'll need someone to keep watch. Unless you or I want to become the new Exalted, we need to keep that front door unlocked. That means that if anybody comes through, we keep Dahlia's presence a secret."

The tension lifted from my shoulders for the first time in weeks. A safe, warm place to sleep on The Seeking? At Broskow's butcher shop of all places? How was this even possible?

"I'm not too keen on the job, to be honest. Being part of the Exalted Family seems like a bit too much stress for me," Bisa said with a wink at me. "Plus, I have no intention of ever having children."

Broskow saw our exchange and I saw him turn away as though in physical pain. "Yeah, I have no intention of living in that house without Pearl. It would feel...wrong."

He shuffled toward the back of the building, where I saw he had a big pile of hay and a blanket, probably a makeshift bed for whenever his work kept him late. He kicked it around to split it into two piles.

"I'm sorry about your wife," I said softly, my apology sounding small and useless.

"Don't be. She and I both decided to hunt you down together." Broskow flopped down on the closest pile of hay, sending pieces of it into the air. "She and I were going to get to the top together, or not at all. I loved that about her. She was cunning and determined, no matter the odds. I told her she didn't have to come with me and the dogs, but she insisted. Said she enjoyed the hunt as much as I did," he said, his voice growing strained. "It seems ridiculous now. Maybe if we hadn't been so determined, so ambitious, she would still be alive."

Bisa took my hand and squeezed it; we exchanged a look. I had villainized Broskow and anyone associated with him for so long that I wasn't sure what to do when he needed reassurance, and neither did Bisa it seemed.

"I'm sorry, too, Mr. Broskow," Bisa offered when I remained silent.

He shrugged and pointed to the haystack opposite his. "You can take that one, Dahlia. It's smaller than mine, but, well, it ought to work for you."

"Thank you," I whispered as I made my way over. I had expected to sleep on the floor.

I spread the hay out for my own bed as Broskow was trying to get comfortable on his pile of hay, his long legs splayed out across the floor.

I couldn't help but smile as a piece of hay stuck to my hand, remembering how my brothers and I had to change out the hay for our beds so often when I was a kid. The smell of it brought back all the old memories of getting into hay battles with my brothers.

Broskow tossed his blanket at me, pulling me from my thoughts when it almost hit me in the face.

"Wait, are you sure?" I asked.

He nodded. "I don't need it. It's hot in here anyway with that fireplace going."

I disagreed; the corner of the room where we were

was chilly by comparison. But, I took the blanket anyway. It was smaller than I expected, and I wondered if he normally used it as a pillow because it wasn't big enough to cover even my small hay pile, and my ankles were itchy against it.

Restless, I breathed in the scent of it, allowing my thoughts to take me back to my smiling grandmother, and of a time when my parents weren't dealing with the political turmoil of Carra on a daily basis. It made me think of a younger me hiding in that hollow tree, waiting for hours on end for Darik to find me.

Bisa waited until I got settled before she brought her cloak over to cover me.

"I'm okay, I don't need it."

"It's more than just for warmth, sugar, it's to keep anyone from seeing you if they step inside."

I bit back any commentary and pouted, letting her cover up my feet. "Bisa..."

She leaned down and kissed me, her lips warm and soft against mine. I wrapped my arms around her shoulders, wanting to pull her down with me into the pile of hay, but she resisted when I gave her shoulders a tug. When we finally broke free from each other, she was smiling.

"I've got a job to do. Quit trying to distract me!"

"But you're so pretty when you're distracted."

We held each other for a long moment before she stole a second kiss and whispered, "Sweet dreams, sugar. I'll make sure nobody finds you, I promise."

She pulled away and walked back to the front of the

shop. I found myself watching her hips as she left and wishing once again that The Seeking was over so I could have her to myself.

I glanced over to Broskow, who looked away quickly when I caught him watching us. I saw the pain in his eyes, though. He was likely thinking of Pearl again, and I couldn't really forget her either.

As I closed my eyes, I saw her grabbing at the spider's legs with her bloody hands, the shock on her face as it dropped down on her shoulders. Once again I heard her scream just before it was cut short.

Tossing and turning, I kept trying to get back to the happy place in my memories where I had been with my brothers. I tried to remember my grandmother's smile, Bisa's kiss, but my mind was shrouded in horrors.

CHAPTER 6

A DAY THAT NEVER ENDED

Pearl crouched next to me, shaking my arm. Her face was whole again and a clear spark of anger shone in her eyes.

"Where's my husband?" she cried, and I whimpered, unable to remove her hand from my arm.

"Where is he?" she cried again, leaning in closer like she had when she peered into my dugout.

"I don't know," I whimpered, and jerked away. It burned where she had touched me.

My eyes opened and I frantically looked around. It was Bisa beside me, not Pearl.

"Dahlia, sugar, are you okay?"

I whimpered again as the remnants of the dream dissipated. Shaking, I leaned forward and pulled her into a tight hug.

"I'm so glad it's you!"

She gave a nervous laugh and hugged me back. "I'm glad it is, too. Are you okay?"

I nodded but held her for a moment longer before pulling away. "I thought you were...someone else."

"I came to wake you up because I didn't want you to miss it, but I didn't mean to frighten you. I'm so sorry."

"No, it's okay," I reassured her, collecting myself. "What is it?"

Bisa had lit several lanterns within the shop since the fireplace alone wasn't enough to keep the place illuminated once the sun went down. The shadows made the place unrecognizable, and I shivered at the unease creeping down my spine.

"What will I miss?" I asked groggily and sat up to stretch, but that was a mistake. I winced as a trail of pain made its way from my shoulders down to my lower back. I fell back down on the hay and stared up at the rafters, waiting for the pain to pass.

Bisa leaned in closer and smiled, "It's almost midnight!"

I blinked at her in confusion. "Already?" Sluggishly, I turned my head and looked over to the opposite haystack only to find it empty. "Where's Broskow?"

"He went out earlier but refused to say where." She shook her head. "I know he gave you shelter and everything, sugar, but I don't know if I completely trust the man."

The pain in my back had calmed down to a dull throbbing, and I tried to stretch more gingerly this time before sitting up. This is what I got for sleeping in a damn hollow tree and then on a pile of hay.

"I don't know if I do either, to be honest. He hasn't locked us in has he?"

She shook her head with a smirk. "Do you really think I would have let him get away with that?"

"No, of course not."

I gave Bisa back her cloak and went to the fireplace to warm myself. From the corner of my eye, I saw Bisa fetch me some jerky.

"He didn't exactly say we could have some, but he didn't say we couldn't either," she said with a grin.

It was a meager meal, but after all I'd been through, it felt like a feast. I couldn't remember ever spending a Seeking in a warm building with a roaring fire and even veal to eat.

To pass the time, Bisa told me about how her Seeking wasn't as uneventful as she had hoped either. Apparently, upon not being able to find any Priests at the Exalted House, the mob I had seen yesterday scoured the city, demanding entry to almost every home to search for us.

One person supposedly got beaten with a wooden chair, and Mr. Eddington hadn't fared any better. Not only had his restaurant been one of the first places the mob struck, but they made a mess of his kitchen when he refused to cooperate at first. After they searched the kitchen, they went upstairs and forced their way into Bisa's home. She told me she and Marcus had been asleep when the door got kicked in. The poor boy had started screaming as men with pitchforks and torches went into his room and looked under his bed for me.

"I woke to him screaming, 'Bisa, where are you?' I darted into his room as fast as I could, grabbing my crossbow as I went. You can imagine how shocked they were! 'Where did that seamstress get one of those?' one man had shouted. It's like they all forgot my Pa was a woodworker!"

We laughed, but I couldn't ignore the fear that crept into my veins. There was something so wrong about this Seeking, so unlike any other. It was bad enough to storm the Exalted House when The Seeking hadn't even begun, but to demand entry into homes and stores? To scare children asleep in their beds? It was like Carra was turning into a completely different town.

When the first clock bell chimed, we both grew quiet, barely even breathing. Then the second, and the third.

"Is this it?" I asked.

She nodded, daring to smile. "And I have to say, good riddance!" She hugged me tight and I was already thinking about the celebratory feast we would enjoy together. Maybe if Broskow showed up, we would even invite him.

Four, five, six.

I took her hand in mine and we walked to the front door. I was smiling now; I couldn't help it. I felt like the fear was finally being lifted from my shoulders, and even my footsteps were a little lighter.

Nine, ten, eleven.

Gripping the handle of the front door, I turned it, but

the handle didn't turn. My heart skipped a beat as I looked down at it. Had Broskow fooled us both and locked me in, deciding in the end to toss aside our tentative friendship and reach for the Exalted House regardless?

Suddenly the knob turned in my hand -

Twelve.

I backed away, realizing that my hood wasn't up and in all this candlelight, whoever was in the doorway would be able to easily see that I wasn't Broskow's daughter, but a Priest.

The door pulled away from me, and I stood there holding my breath, not knowing what to do.

Instead of an angry mob with torches, there stood a very gloomy Broskow. He looked between the two of us, shock crossing his features. "What are you two doing answering the door together?" he asked through gritted teeth. "*Get inside!*"

His gaze was locked on me as he spat the words and I felt my heart racing in my chest as I stumbled back a step. My mind was filled with questions, but my old instincts soon kicked in and I hurried over to the shadowy part of the shop. I refrained from asking anything until he had closed the door behind him.

"What's wrong? Why can't we leave?" Bisa wasn't startled like I was, she was angry. "Are you trying to keep us trapped here? Because if that was your plan all along—"

"No, for the last time, that's *not* my plan." He took his hat off and hung it by the door. From where I stood, I could see that he indeed hadn't locked the door. "The clock is wrong."

"What do you mean?" Bisa asked.

He walked over to the fireplace, wet leaves falling off his boots and sticking to the floor. "I mean it's not midnight, not even close."

"You're saying someone bribed the clockman?"

"No, I'm saying I know it's wrong because *I* bribed the clockman."

Bisa gaped.

I thought of my family coming out of their hiding places, little Dameon happily leaving the house he's been safely hidden in all day. My brother Darik would probably leave his friend's house, both congratulating each other on their devious planning. What broke my heart the most, though, was imagining my mother crying in relief at the twelfth chime.

"Why would you do that to them?" I asked, my hands shaking at my sides. "Why would you do that to my family?"

"Because that's how the Priests got their power: cheating and bribery. That's how your family plays the game. They changed the rules in Carra for good. Once someone pointed out that angle, nobody played the honorable Seeking anymore. Since then, everyone has been suspicious of each other, finding ways around each other." He gestured to me with a frown. "Since your family changed the rules on how The Seeking worked, it hasn't been as fun."

"You monster," I hissed. "Bisa was telling me about

the angry mob beating down doors to get to people. What do you think they'll do if they see my little brother? You think they'll ask him to come along nicely? It's not like we have to be brought in alive, and if they've worked that hard to find us, it won't be pretty if they do."

"Was this your plan all along?" Bisa asked. "To keep us here believing you were a good person, then run off to help your buddies capture the prize?"

Broskow glared. "No. And now you two are leaping to conclusions. I promised I would deliver the final payment to make sure the chimes were off. If I didn't make it, the whole thing would look suspicious."

Bisa laughed and rubbed at her eyes. "Oh damn, this just gets better and better. So now you're saying you put Dahlia's family at risk just so you wouldn't blow our cover? How generous of you."

"You could have just forgotten to," I said, my hands balling into fists. "You could have just said you didn't care anymore."

"Oh, come on, kid. Nobody would have believed that. I had to give them a good reason not to think you two were here. I haven't gone home yet; I wasn't sleeping at my own house with my kids. My boy gathered up my dogs for me earlier and is probably worried about me... and Pearl. Instead, here I am jumbled up in this stupid Seeking with you two brats," he growled. "And this is the thanks I get for helping out?"

"You had a good reason," I argued. "Your wife died last night. I think anybody would understand you backing out after that."

A silence fell over the room. Bisa looked at me as though I had just spat in the face of a Gray Person; Broskow, on the other hand, just clenched his jaw and looked like he was trying to prevent the words from flying out of his mouth. I wanted him to say them. I wanted him to let them loose so that I would have more ammunition to throw back at him later.

After a long pause, he said, "I think I'm going to go get some air. It's too stuffy in here. Smells of brat." He slammed the door behind him, causing a few leaves on the floor to swirl.

Neither Bisa nor I spoke. Instead I stood and watched the flames lick at the wood in the hearth.

"Dahlia, sugar, you can't go saying things like that."

"Why not? He deserves it. I can't believe he went out there and bribed the clockman after everything we went through last night! My little brother could be getting beaten up right now, and it's his fault."

She came behind me and rubbed my shoulders. "I guess he felt like he needed to. Maybe he wanted to do something that made things feel normal."

I scoffed. "No amount of money will make this Seeking normal; I already know that."

Bisa sighed and sat down in a chair at my side. "He did say that the Priests were the first to do that, too."

"That was different. The Priests are considered one of the best Exalted Families that have ever been in Carra."

Bisa folded out a pleat in her skirt and leaned back in the chair. Her almond eyes caught the light of the fire and gleamed determinedly. "Maybe to the people who approach you. Maybe even to most of Carra. But do you think my mama thinks the Priests are all so great?"

I turned to look at her fully. "Don't bring her into this. She was living in filth and forced Marcus into it as well. She has nothing to do with this."

"Yeah, she's not the best person, but she's still a member of Carra, isn't she? Doesn't she get to have an opinion, even if it isn't a popular one, or even a good one?"

I forced my hands to relax. "I suppose... I don't know."

"Your family may have found a pretty slick way to get hold of the Exalted House that night, sugar, but like Broskow said, they broke a lot of rules to get there. When you do that, you open the door for others to do it, too. So, if you're willing to break them, you have to be willing to have them broken for you in return. Do you get my meaning?"

I sat down in the chair opposite of her and leaned my head back to stare up at the rafters, searching them for meaning. "You mean I shouldn't get too angry at Broskow for bribing the clockman because that's exactly what my family did."

She nodded. "And what do you think Dameon is going to do when he hears those chimes anyway? Especially after how useless they were at the start of The Seeking."

We locked eyes and I felt the embarrassment settle over my shoulders like a heavy, woolen cloak. "They probably wouldn't trust it at all." My eyes burned; I felt the heat of shame in my cheeks. "Now that you mention it, I don't know why I was so quick to trust it."

"It's not just you, I'm the one who woke you up to tell you. I'd been hearing the chimes go all evening after dark, counting each one. I thought the hours were passing pretty fast, but I thought it was just me."

"It's not your job to keep me safe, Bisa. It's my job, it's my responsibility."

She said nothing to that and instead reached out and took my hand. Her fingers were soft even with the telltale scars from years and years of stitching, where the needle caught her skin instead of fabric. Even blind, I would be able to identify her fingers. I knew that pattern of scars like constellations in the sky.

"In your defense, sugar, you've had a long-ass day."

THE CLOCK DIDN'T STRIKE AGAIN, and it felt like hours passed. I stretched out on the floor in front of the fireplace, focusing on the flames as they lapped at the new log and turned it into charcoal. At some point, Bisa came and curled up behind me, dragging a blanket over us, and folding up her cloak to use as a pillow. I pushed up against her warm body and intertwined our fingers across my stomach.

"I thought you were going to keep watch," I said with a smile.

"I plan to," she said but I could hear the exhaustion in her voice. "You get some sleep, I'll be okay."

I pulled the blanket tighter around us and stared at the fire. Bisa was kind to try, but I knew she wasn't the kind of person who could stay awake all night. Her work as a seamstress was best done in the daylight, and she had a hard time staying awake once it got late.

Sure enough, I soon heard her breathing deepen, felt the slow exhale against the back of my neck. Unlinking our hands, I extracted myself from her and wrapped my portion of the blanket around her.

Pausing as I tucked a corner of the blanket at her side, I couldn't help but notice how beautiful she looked when she was asleep and had to resist the urge to stroke her face. As tired as she was at night, she wasn't that heaviest sleeper and I didn't want to ruin what rest she could get.

Forcing myself to turn away, I went and poured myself a glass of water and looked around for something to entertain myself with. Broskow didn't even have any books here. It was a shop, I reminded myself; all I had to do was wait until dawn and then The Seeking would finally be over.

I had just sat down on the pile of hay I slept on when the doorknob turned. I leapt up and hid in the corner between a shelf and the wall, where the light from the candles didn't quite reach.

The door opened and in stepped Broskow. He lurched inside, leaving the door wide open behind him. For one moment, I thought he had brought someone back from the pub, but then he kicked a foot out and closed the door.

I heard him muttering to himself as he dropped his hat and jacket into a corner, pulled off his belt and dropped it as well, before he made his way back to the piles of hay in the back of the shop.

Bisa shifted in her sleep when he passed her, but didn't wake up at least.

When he was closer, I stepped out from the shadows and whispered, "You're back late."

He jumped; his eyes wide in the limited light. When he realized it was me, he grabbed at his chest and shook his head. "Damn, kid, you just about gave me a heart attack! Don't sneak up on me like that."

"I guess you needed more than just fresh air?"

His shock turned into a sneer as he sat down on the hay pile opposite of me. "I needed to let off some steam."

"You didn't tell anyone—"

"Of course I didn't!" His voice rose above a whisper this time and we both froze as Bisa shifted. "Of course I didn't," he said again, lower this time, and stretched out. "Just because I'm drunk doesn't mean I'm going to rat you two kids out. It's about three in the morning, so we've luckily only got a couple of hours left of this stupidity."

I watched him for a moment, this enormous man with his pink face and the sleeves of his stained, gray shirt rolled up to his elbows. Only yesterday morning I had seen him as a giant, intimidating man, hell-bent on bringing down me and my family in the most embarrassing way possible.

"Why did you help me anyway? I'm the reason

Pearl got killed - she would've been fine if I hadn't chosen to hide out there beyond the Boundary Line." I shifted my weight, turning to face him better. "Why help me?"

He looked at me for a long moment with tired, red-rimmed eyes that were probably irritated by more than just drinking. "You're not the reason Pearl got killed. That was The Seeking that did that. If we weren't out there hunting for you once a year, you wouldn't have had to hide out there.

"When that Gray Person pulled something out of my head, I realized how much of a fool I was. I had trained my dogs and kids for years, been lured into bed with Pearl with the hopes of eventually claiming the Exalted House for myself, and I had spent most of the night chasing a kid through the woods. And right under my nose, these things were waiting. If they hadn't grabbed me, it would've been somebody else, possibly some kid who couldn't take it." He sighed. "Why was I chasing children year after year instead of fighting those spider things in the woods? Why was I making kids hide from my pack of dogs when I ought to be figuring out how to fight the Gray People and protect my family? What the hell was I doing with my life? I have all these skills for catching children when I ought to be out there catching monsters."

I stared at him, trying not to gape. Never, in my years of hiding during The Seeking, did I think that I would ever hear such revelations come out of Broskow's mouth. I looked away, not sure why I felt tears threatening. "I hadn't ever thought of it like that," I said around a shaky breath.

"I hadn't either until last night. It made me reevaluate everything. I thought I understood how the world works, or rather how *our* world works, but I really didn't. I just soaked up the same diatribe everybody had always fed me. I never questioned it, not once." He scoffed. "They said a long time ago they used to choose rulers by counting votes. Can you believe that?" He chuckled. "Sure does sound better than chasing people all day long."

"If we did that," I started, "then the Ritual would fail and all of Carra would lose its supposed protection. I guess we would see more of those spider creatures within the Boundary Line then, wouldn't we?"

His smile faded and his face grew a bit pale. "It's all for those damn Gray People, isn't it? It's all for them." He sat up suddenly and grabbed hay to throw onto himself. "This place is too damn cold!"

I could see the worry in his eyes before he looked away. "Get some sleep, kid. Nobody's going to come to the shop this late at night. The only people still awake are at the pub and trust me, they're no threat."

I nodded and turned away, sensing that I had hit something within Broskow that made him want to shut the conversation down. Had he forgotten about the Ritual that would need to be done to renew the Boundary Line of Carra? It would be happening tomorrow afternoon, assuming both Dameon and Darik evaded capture. Surely, I'd hear the cheers outside if they were caught.

I laid down on the other pile of hay, listening to Broskow's snores and staring up at the rafters, my brain buzzing with thoughts of The Seeking, of Gray People, of Broskow's dogs, and of the Ritual that would hopefully take place tomorrow.

Was The Seeking over yet?

When I awoke, it was to the sound of Bisa's humming. For a moment, I thought I was back in her apartment and I listened for Marcus's voice, asking questions or playing with his toys. Instead I heard Broskow, and suddenly the memories from The Seeking flooded in, causing my heart to sink. I opened my eyes to the beautiful rays of sunlight coming through the windows and let out a long breath.

I made it.

The words rang through my brain as clear as the bell tower's chimes had last night. My eyes were crusted with the tears that had spilled while I slept, but none of that mattered anymore. I had survived another Seeking, which meant another year of investigations, inquiries, and fancy dinners.

You'll have to go through all of it again in a year, and it will be worse next time.

The thought came unbidden, and it took some effort to push it away. That was a problem for next October. Right now it was a beautiful November morning and all the fears I held last night were gone. I had another year to plan for a far better hiding place, another year to find trustworthy allies. Next year I might not even have to worry about Broskow's dogs, which would make everything easier.

I stretched and tried to calm the pit of worry in my stomach that I had grown accustomed to since fall arrived.

"Looks like somebody is finally awake!" Bisa called happily. I groaned and got to my feet, stumbling over toward the counter where she was slicing up more jerky. "I woke up a little after dawn and went back to get a few things." She motioned to a basket of bread and hard-boiled eggs.

"Oh wow, this looks wonderful!"

"It wasn't bad," Broskow said. He sat at the table with an empty plate, sipping on a cup of steaming hot water.

"Were you nervous letting people know you were staying here at Broskow's shop?"

She laughed. "Clearly it's been a while since you weren't the target of a Seeking, sugar. Those streets are near dead the morning after, especially if nobody was caught. There's nothing to be nosy about, so everybody sleeps in." Her eyes narrowed and her hands went to her hips. "Which by the way, I can't believe you let me fall asleep last night! I was supposed to be watching out for you."

I shrugged as I cracked open an egg. "You were

clearly exhausted, and besides, I hid well enough to give Broskow a scare when he came in."

He grunted. "It's true, I guess." There was the shadow of a smile on his lips and that was enough for me.

The air was crisp, and felt cleansing as it drifted through the open door of Broskow's shop.

While I finished eating, Broskow stood outside, rubbing his hands together for warmth as he watched for the best time for me to leave. It was his reputation, after all, that would be harmed if anyone witnessed me leaving his shop of all places the morning after The Seeking.

I gave Bisa a tight hug after I finished my breakfast. "Thank you so much for being here."

"You just be safe going back. I wish I could come with you," she whispered and squeezed me tighter.

"I know, but that would only make things worse for you next year."

I pulled away, and my heart broke at seeing the tears in her eyes. "I always worry about you when I'm not with you."

"I know." I kissed her cheek and turned to head for the door. Broskow glanced at me briefly as I stepped into the doorway; the morning sun feeling warm on my skin.

"Maybe next year," Broskow said without looking at me, "I'll try to make sure there are enough supplies so Bisa doesn't have to bring her own food."

"You mean you're offering?"

He smirked at my surprise. "I don't think I'll ever

want to participate in The Seeking again, but that doesn't mean I'm going to sit back and watch other people chase you down. I'm not the only one with dogs, you know."

"No, but your dogs are the best. That's why you terrified me the most."

He looked down at his feet. "It should be clear now, kid. Get out of here."

"Thank you," I said, giving his arm a squeeze as I stepped out.

I could feel his eyes boring holes into my back as I walked down the hill and towards the Exalted House. The streets were just as bare as Bisa had said they would be. Normally I hid out in the woods and avoided downtown completely, so I really couldn't recall what it was like after a Seeking. I had either been too young to take part in it, or just disinterested until I became the target.

People pulled back curtains as I passed, and one man who was sweeping leaves in front of his shop nearly dropped his broom when he saw me. I smiled and greeted him, but he was frozen with a frustrated frown. I could almost read his thoughts, the town's collective thoughts. Dahlia Priest was not captured, and that meant there was a good chance the Priest family was still the Exalted.

As I drew closer to the Exalted House, more and more people stepped outside to watch me return. Some cheered, while others just glared. I wished they still did votes, like Broskow had said, that way I would know how many people really did support my family. As it was now, it was difficult to say who would gladly hunt me again next October.

Soon the Exalted House came into view, and immediately I knew something was wrong. There was too much activity outside, even for the day after The Seeking.

They didn't look like the group I had seen the night before, with their torches and pitchforks. They were cooks, maids, gardeners, and legal assistants dressed in the cream-colored gowns that I had grown accustomed to seeing ever since my family moved into the Exalted House.

One of the first Exalted Families had put them together, and the roles were passed down from family to family to maintain the appearance and order of the Exalted House. Occasionally, the current Exalted Family had to step in if a position opening appeared and then an influx of applications would flood Father's desk. Being a worker at the Exalted House meant not just that your job was guaranteed for life, but that it was guaranteed to your family if they wanted it.

Two familiar guards stood partway up the dirt path, and one of them had a black eye under his leather helmet.

I frowned. "Kaleb, what happened?"

He grinned, bringing attention to his split lip, but avoided my question. "I'm glad to see that you made it, Dahlia. You weren't hurt, I hope?"

The image of poor Pearl's missing face came unbidden to my mind and I took a deep breath. "No, but it was a rough day."

"The Seeking started earlier than it should have. There was a mob, larger than we had expected, probably twenty or so people." He looked down. "I'm sorry, Dahlia. We weren't able to hold them back."

"We did make them regret trying, though," Marissa added with a smirk. "We're not the only ones nursing bruises today."

I smiled at that. Marissa had always been my favorite. "Thank you both. I'm sorry things were so strange this Seeking."

Marissa reached out and put a gloved hand on my shoulder. "Take care of yourself. Things up at the Exalted House aren't good."

I felt my stomach tighten. "Why? What happened?"

She looked to the ground. "Like Kaleb said, we couldn't hold them back." I looked to Kaleb for clarification, but he also avoided my gaze.

I swallowed. Kaleb and Marissa were the finest of the guards, and knowing that the mob was able to take them out made me concerned for what I would find in the house.

The scent of burning wood hit my nostrils as I approached. I spotted the Exalted Assistant, Rachael, giving orders near the front of the house, her green skirt indicating her important position even from a distance. She was in charge of keeping the Exalted House in order.

The closer I got, the clearer the situation became, and I could see what the excitement was all about. The walls of the Exalted House had been singed in places. At first, I thought it was done randomly, but as I drew closer, I realized the marks formed words. *Death to the Priests* stretched all the way up to the second floor.

I froze, eying the jagged and misshapen letters.

Many of the workers were divided between trying to clean up the mess on the ground and trying to get close enough to handle the vandalism. Shattered pottery and broken timber had been scattered along the base of the house so that it was difficult to even get up there to try to fix it.

I'd evaded capture on several Seekings, but I had never seen so much anger aimed at us. I had never seen people so enraged by our very existence.

At that moment I wished I hadn't evaded capture. I wished I would've given myself in to whoever wanted me, Broskow or anyone else. I wished my family could go back to the simple lives we had before becoming the Exalted Family.

While it was clear that the town didn't want us as leaders, what would they have done if I had given myself over to them? Would capture be enough, or would they have killed me and claimed it was an accident? If I had given myself over, would it have at least saved Pearl's life?

Rachael spotted me and came over. "I am so sorry, ma'am. We're hoping to have it replaced as soon as possible. My deepest apologies to you and your family: I don't think any of us expected to come home to this."

I knew she was trying to be kind. I knew she was trying to make me feel better, but I felt numb. I shook my head, unable to speak, and headed inside.

The rugs that were usually laid out to protect the wood had all been shoved aside. In their place someone had dragged deep grooves throughout the whole house, slicing up wooden floors that had been protected for centuries. More workers were rushing about, trying to figure out what it would take to fix all the damage.

A tear escaped as I climbed the stairs, careful not to step on the deep grooves that had been made on each step. Upstairs was bustling with even more activity and I had to step aside as people ran everywhere carrying singed sheets and blankets. The smell of smoke was stronger up here despite the open windows.

I looked into my room and saw that the floor was littered with feathers from my bed being torn to pieces. Part of the bed must have caught on fire, too, because the floor next to it and the frame were singed.

The tears flowed freely now as I watched one younger worker on her hands and knees sweeping up the feathers, in various charred states, with her hands.

I couldn't go to my room to rest.

I couldn't go downstairs to get away.

There was nowhere to *hide* from this.

"Dahlia?" I turned to see Mother coming out of her room. A whimper escaped my lips as she swept me into her arms. I was afraid I was going to sob, but I was still too numb.

This had to be someone else's home, not mine. Even Mother smelled like smoke.

She whispered something I didn't quite catch before pulling me with her down the hall and into her bedroom, where she closed the door behind us to hide from the prying eyes of the workers. "They took care of our room early this morning before dawn. It took several hours, though, so I'm not sure when your room will be ready for you."

The bed was fresh, and the room had been accented with oils to make it smell better. The floor was covered in overlapping rugs; I could only imagine what it must look like beneath them. If they did all of that to my room, I didn't even want to guess what they must have done in here.

She tugged me down beside her on the bed. "Are you okay?" She peered closer. "Oh, my sweet Dahlia, I'm so sorry. None of this has turned out like it should have."

I nodded, not yet trusting myself to speak, and wiped at my eyes.

"Your father is downstairs working on getting everything fixed. We have the Ritual to do still, and nothing is ready. The food still has to be prepared, but the kitchen is a wreck. I've asked them to make sure the wagon is ready, but there's still so much to do before then. You're welcome to sleep in here with your brother. I want you both to get plenty of sleep before tonight. I can't imagine what it must have been like for you all."

I could hear her voice start to shake and gave her a squeeze. That's when I noticed Dameon was asleep in the bed behind us. He must have been exhausted to sleep so soundly while we were talking beside him and the workers bustled around outside. I wiped at my face again.

"What about Darik? Where is he?"

The panic in my mother's face made my chest clench. "I don't know. I haven't heard from him." She couldn't even look at me as she spoke. "I hope that he's safe, but I honestly don't know. Surely if he wasn't someone would have come forward by now. Surely someone would have claimed responsibility."

I gave her a tight hug and just sat there for a moment, listening to her heartbeat. When I finally let go, I saw she was wiping at her eyes this time. "If you want, I can see what I can find out. We have some time before the Ritual."

"No," she said firmly. "I don't want you going anywhere. I want you to stay here where it's safe. You saw what they wrote out there, I don't want you going anywhere alone."

The excitement I had felt at being able to help dwindled to fear. *Death to the Priests*. For some reason I hadn't even considered that those words would affect my safety, too. The Seeking was over, and it was supposed to be safe to walk around Carra now, to come out of hiding, but Mother was right.

Between the bells chiming long before the stroke of midnight and then ringing ferociously last night, it wasn't just that this was an unusual Seeking. Something had changed.

The entire town ignored the rules.

I thought then of Broskow going off to make the final payment to make sure the bell tower went haywire. Perhaps he didn't do that just to keep suspicion off of me, but perhaps he also did it to prevent himself from being hunted, too.

Looking up, I saw my fear reflected in my mother's eyes.

"It isn't safe," she whispered. "I barely trust the workers at this point."

"Marissa and Kaleb are loyal," I said. "I saw them. Both of them got beaten up last night. I could tell they were upset that they let the mob get past them before midnight."

Mother narrowed her eyes. "And you don't think bruises could be self-inflicted? A mob of that many angry people comes walking up the path to the Exalted House, and they get away with a black eye and a busted lip?" She scoffed. "More than likely they just stepped aside, either knowing the mob was coming, or realizing it could mean their deaths if they didn't."

"Those were only the wounds we could see," I defended, my voice growing more urgent. "They're in full armor out there, Mother. They could have any number of injuries."

She knelt down in front of me and clasped my shoulders. "Listen to me. You are not in a court of law here, Dahlia. You have no defendant to protect. These people don't care about the rules of law any more than they did the rules of The Seeking. If you hadn't interfered with Dameon, the bell tower wouldn't have been their only modification this year. They would have won as soon as midnight came."

I stared at her, shaking.

The world I knew was no longer safe, not even the guards I said hello to every day could be trusted. It wasn't as though I could go anywhere else either. Carra was the only safe place in these woods and I had seen what the woods contained.

The only thing that got me through this Seeking was that it wouldn't last. Once the hunt was over with, I was done, I could relax. Only, now that safety was gone, too.

I felt like The Seeking was just a day that never ended, and the list of my enemies just kept growing and growing.

She rubbed my arms. "I'm sorry, sweetheart. We don't know who's responsible, but if I had to guess it would be Broskow."

I almost laughed. Oddly enough, he and Bisa were the only people I could trust outside of my family now. What kind of bizarre world had I fallen into? I tried to pull away from her, but she was insistent, forcing me to look at her.

"You saw how he and his friends were treating Dameon. You've told me yourself how he harasses you in the street almost every—"

The bedroom door pushed opened and Mother's grip tightened on my shoulders as she jumped to her feet. There were so many people moving in and out of the Exalted House right now she probably didn't want to take any chances that someone would overhear us.

It was only Father, and he stepped inside quickly before closing the door behind him.

"Here you all are," he whispered. He stared for a long

moment into Mother's eyes, his authoritative stance and determined gaze faltering slightly. Then he looked down and gave me a weary smile. "I'm glad you're safe, Dahlia." I rushed forward and hugged him tight. He allowed it for a moment before pulling away. "I've not heard anything of Darik yet, but we're going to have to get ready for the Ritual anyway."

"Oh, Jamel," Mother whispered.

"I know, but we don't have a choice. It's important that we show ourselves as a strong family, impervious to these acts of violence and coercion. We need to show them that we are stronger than they think we are." His hands fisted at his side. "We need to go through the Renewal Ritual with our heads high despite all that they've tried. We *cannot* let them intimidate us."

He glanced down to me, as though trying to impart his strength to me through his eyes alone.

"I'll try," I said. "It isn't going to be easy, though. I'm exhausted and knowing that so many people out there want us dead... I don't know what's going to happen from now on."

"Are they gonna try to hurt us?" We all turned to see Dameon sitting up on the bed, his eyes red and puffy. "What if they try to hurt us at the Ritual?"

Before anyone could reply, Dameon started to cry, and Father went over to him, picked him up, and rubbed his back. "Shh, calm down. The Ritual will go just fine, just like it always does. You don't need to worry."

I listened to his sobs. I was terrified, too.

PART THREE
THE RITUAL

CHAPTER 7
THE ROPE IS CUT

It was strange to take a bath. Not that I didn't want one, but to be worried about cleanliness and my appearance when I didn't know whether my older brother was alive or dead felt wrong to me.

I looked over to the dress they had laid out: a light brown gown with golden embroidery. It was beautiful and meant to represent the renewal of the Boundary Line of Carra. It felt wrong as well, like so much of this Seeking had. The Renewal was a time for finery and celebration to signal another year that our little town was protected from the creatures that lurked in the woods.

But why wear fancy clothes when people down the street from you wanted your entire family dead? Why go through the process of renewing the barrier, when I saw quite clearly how ineffective it was the other night? What was the point?

I hugged my knees against my chest and breathed in the steam from the water. It had taken the workers hours to boil enough water to bring up and fill it: one of the many luxuries of being part of the Exalted Family. I had never had a hot bath in my life before we lived here – at best they were lukewarm like at Bisa's – and that felt like an eternity ago.

My eyes drifted back to the gown. The Ritual itself, the part that I dreaded almost more than the entire Seeking, was when the power of the Gray People was proven to all of Carra, and it tended to carry out like clockwork.

I still had a pit of worry in my stomach.

If Darik didn't come back before the Renewal, what would that mean? Would it mean that we weren't the Exalted Family after all? What if he was lying dead in a ditch somewhere?

Though Darik was known for losing track of time and being late for almost everything, he always showed up after The Seeking: always.

I stepped out of the bath and dried off, appreciating how nice the towels felt against my skin. Each one was embroidered with *Exalted*, a constant reminder of our status and the expectations that came with it.

Shaking my head, I parted my hair down the middle of my head and, using some oils, started detangling it. I tied up half and then began a tight braid against my scalp for the other half, continuing the braid down to rest on my shoulder. Then I did the same with the other half. I had given myself this hairstyle for so long that my fingers knew what to do without any assistance.

My arms ached once I was done, but they always did when I had to braid it. Mother would probably be annoyed that I didn't do anything fancy with my hair, but honestly, I wasn't in the mood to spend a couple of hours working on it.

Toweling off my body, I went over to pull on the ceremonial Ritual dress. I slipped it over my shoulders, sighing at the excess space around my chest that I just didn't fill regardless of the seamstress' insistence that I would grow into it. At least it wasn't too long on me like it had been last year.

Stepping out of the bathing room, the cool breeze of the house felt good on my skin. Normally the place would be warmer this late in the year, but the workers constantly moving in and out made it nearly impossible for the fireplaces to heat the rooms properly.

It was midday and sunlight streamed in through the open shutters. I started towards my room and caught the scent of apple pie in the air. I cringed.

THE GULLY WAS the one part of Carra that was empty most days; nobody liked going there. It flooded in the spring when the rains came, and would occasionally turn into an icy pond if it got cold enough during the fall and winter. But somehow, for each Seeking it was dry and barren, and the elder trees that lined it flourished despite the unpredictable weather.

It was as though their roots went so deep into the earth that the flood waters had no effect on them. It was forbidden to cut them down, so the elders had grown tightly together, their spindly limbs tangled and indistinguishable from one another.

Pathways that were used the year before would be impassable the following year. Getting to the center of the Gully required stepping over limbs, ducking under others, and figuring out what turns to take in order to pass through without going in circles.

As I approached, I noticed the trees' lovely white flowers from summer had fallen away. Now their limbs held plump black berries out for hungry passersby, but everyone in Carra knew better. These berries weren't for consumption. Other elder trees you might pick freely from and even eat the flowers, but these were poison. Some said just plucking one could cause madness.

I walked the edge of the Gully where the thick wall of elders began, Dameon's hand gripping mine. Mother and Father would have already arrived, but all children were to enter separately from the parents. Others were straggling in as well; some stood at the wall, waiting to be led through the maze of trees branches. I had already been told exactly how to enter, so I led.

Dameon was quiet, his feet moving quickly to keep up with my steady pace. We both were terrified something would happen before we were able to get through. There were no guards to protect us here and I couldn't even hide a crossbow in my skirts like Bisa had.

Two people were standing near our entrance, trying to find their way. As I neared, I heard one of them say, "Looks like they're down one."

I felt Dameon grip my hand tighter as I slowed to

stop beside them. I had seen their faces before: a short man with long brown hair and a taller man with short black hair and hard features, both of them maybe ten years older than me. I saw anger in their eyes as they watched us and I searched the trees, looking for the ribbon that had been tied onto one of the branches to signal the safe path.

"What happened to Darik?" The short man with the long hair asked, stepping forward. Dameon moved closer to my side, and his grip was so tight on my hand that it hurt, but I didn't show it. I didn't reply and searched again for the damn ribbon. Where was it? They said I couldn't miss it.

"He's running late," I said eventually.

"Sure he is," the taller man added.

"I heard he disappeared," his friend continued. "Most think something in the woods got him last night." He stepped closer and reached toward me. If I reacted, if I smacked his hand away and yelled at him, then it would draw even more attention to us. If these two were confident enough to harass us, then I didn't know what a larger group would do.

He picked up one of my braids and dragged his thumb down a section of it. I stared at him with absolute disgust.

"So, if they find your brother's body, like we all suspect, what does that mean for the Priests? One child down, two more to go?"

I was shaking. These were the jerks who would have gladly antagonized my little brother to win The Seeking, maybe would have even killed him. These were the kind of people that wanted my family dead.

Before I had thought that Broskow was the only real threat in Carra, but that was simply naïve of me. Broskow didn't act alone, he never did. There was always a crowd, a group of anxious onlookers eager to see what could be done to us. Broskow had been just the loudest of them, the most obvious, but the hatred that bubbled under the surface had been building, perhaps ever since my family took the Exalted House.

I understood how someone could want us unseated; I understood how they thought we had gained power through unethical means. But how dare he talk about Darik being dead in front of Dameon? My little brother had spent the morning crying himself in and out of sleep.

"Maybe getting rid of you might be fun," he said with a grin.

I heard footsteps approaching and wondered if I was even going to make it to the Renewal. I couldn't send Dameon into the maze of trees without knowing how to get through. Would my parents notice us missing and have the guards come for us? Or was this a coordinated attack against all of us?

"Back away from my sister, you ass."

I turned to see Darik striding quickly towards us with a strange, crazed look in his eyes as he approached. I wanted to speak, but I was too shocked at seeing him.

Without losing a step, he shoved the short man backwards, and his arms flew out and pinwheeled as he tried to regain his balance. Too late, he slammed into one of the trunks of the elders. Darik stepped forward as though intending to do worse, but I grabbed hold of his arm.

"What are you doing?"

"Helping," he said without looking at me.

The man with the hard features helped his friend up, and both stumbled away. Dameon released my hand, then rushed forward and wrapped his arms around Darik's waist, crying into his brother's side. That seemed to take the fight out of him, and he rubbed his brother's back absently.

I rounded on him. "Are you crazy? You know everyone out here saw that. They'll take it as our family being aggressive." In my peripheral vision I saw groups of people watching.

"So? Who cares what they think of us?" he snapped, pulling away from Dameon, who only sobbed harder. I reached out and put a hand on Dameon's shoulder to steady him. Darik shrugged. "We won, didn't we? That's all that matters."

"Have you even seen the Exalted House? Do you know what they did?"

"There it is," Darik said, ignoring me, and ducked under some tree branches as he found the ribbon marker for the path to take into the Gully.

"Damn it," I muttered and took Dameon's hand in mine. His palm was wet from his tears.

The sunlight diminished as we stepped into the grove of elder trees. The air grew colder as we walked. I could hear Darik's footsteps up ahead but couldn't quite see him. At least his footprints in the leaves were clear enough to follow. Finally, we reached a clearing where Darik had stopped to ponder the next path.

"You haven't even been back home yet, have you?" I growled as Dameon stepped closer to me. "Where were you this morning, Darik? What happened?"

"I slept in is all," he grumbled. "Damn, I didn't know that was so terrible."

He sounded calm enough, but I could tell something was eating at him. He was drumming his fingers against his legs, ignoring a clearly upset Dameon, and every time he spoke, he couldn't look me in the eye. I wanted to slap him.

But before I could retort, Dameon spoke in a stuffy, shrill voice, "They tore apart my bed, Darik. They wrote nasty things on the walls." Darik stared down at him with hollow eyes, and Dameon continued. "Everybody is scared. I thought you were dead!" He looked like he wanted to hug his brother again, but decided against it this time.

For a moment the woods were silent, and then I heard very light footsteps - not from behind us or even in front, but from the side. They weren't the same heavy, noisy footsteps we made through the under-brush. No, they were so delicate that it could have been the sound of falling leaves. I pushed Dameon behind me and heard him gasp, but he knew better than to speak.

We had lived in Carra our whole lives, so we knew exactly what walked like that. Darik's eyes were wide as we each stepped back to the entrance of the clearing, ready to bolt.

That was when the Gray Person came into view.

Sticks and brambles that would have scraped my skin dragged against her legs, but she didn't seem to care. The Gray People were made of hardier things than flesh and blood.

Even in the diminished sunlight her skin gleamed like ashy wood. The black pits where her eyes ought to be were fixed in our direction, and she pushed a sapling out of the way with a taloned hand.

Did I mention that the Gray People were always nude? She was no exception, but I had never seen their bodies so distinctively before. It was like she had been carved out of wood, and the slight indentions of the blade could still be seen on the surface of her skin, sometimes in spirals and sometimes extending all the way down a limb. I might have considered her beautiful if she wasn't so terrifying.

She gave us a cruel smile, and Dameon gasped again. Her gaze darted to him like a cat watching an injured bird, and Darik and I closed in the gap between us to keep her from seeing our brother.

A hoarse laugh escaped her crude mouth. "Don't worry little ones, he's not the one I'm after today."

I remembered Broskow talking about its eyes, that they were how it fed from him. With a little bubble of panic in my chest I looked away from its gaze, though it was surprisingly difficult to do so. Was that what Broskow had felt when he was wailing over Pearl's body?

If it was hard for me to look away from it when I was already on guard, it must have been terribly difficult for Broskow that night.

Finally, the Gray Person turned away from us and moved through the underbrush toward the Gully. I noticed that where she walked, the elder trees parted for her. A shiver went through me.

"Are you two okay?" Darik asked in a wavering voice.

Dameon squeaked his affirmation.

"Dahlia?"

I honestly wasn't sure if I was ever going to be okay again, but I had to say something. He was being the protective older brother, just like he had been when that jerk tried to threaten us earlier. All the hair on my arms was standing on end, though, and I couldn't shake the image of its hollow eyes from my mind.

"What do you think it meant?" I asked finally.

"I don't know," Darik said. I could see now that his hands were trembling, though he was trying to hide them. "But at least it's not after us."

He led the way again as we followed the path the Gray Person had made toward the Gully. Up ahead, I could smell the sickeningly sweet aroma of freshly baked apple pie.

Darik might feel better knowing the Gray Person wasn't after us, but I didn't.

Who was it after?

~

Stepping into the Gully was like stepping out of the night. Never before had I so appreciated the warmth from the sun, even though there was still a cool breeze. We must have been one of the last to arrive because the edges of the Gully were almost full of people. Most of them were sitting down, but a few were standing, looking for the first chance to leave. Almost every person in Carra would be here, though. It was expected.

The guards, Marissa and Kaleb, would be walking through town making sure that even newly born babes were here. The more people present, the more powerful the Ritual supposedly was, and the more likely that the people of Carra wouldn't be attacked by the creatures of the woods.

Higher attendance bought better protection from the Gray People, too. However, there were always a few who didn't make it. Some had reasonable excuses such as illness, or others, like Bisa's mother, just didn't want to attend anymore. This year I was surprised at the turnout, considering so many had vandalized the Exalted House. I had assumed they wouldn't want to see us step into another year of power, but here they were.

Of course, Broskow had probably explained what happened to his wife by now, and many would have blamed it on a poor attendance last year. I thought of Pearl's face, her missing eyes so similar to the black pits that I saw on the Gray Person earlier. Perhaps that was the real reason for attendance. Everyone was scared.

As we approached the pedestal where the Exalted Family was to sit, Mother was already running down the steps, her arms outstretched. Darik barely had the chance to smile before he was pulled into a tight embrace.

"Don't you frighten me like that again," she pleaded.

Dameon stayed at my side, clutching my hand, still shaken from our encounter with the Gray Person. He wasn't rushing to see Mother, which surprised me.

"I'm sorry, okay?" Darik said, trying his best to disentangle himself from her grip.

"I don't care if you're sorry, just promise me you won't do it again!"

There was a fleeting look of fear in Darik's eyes and I noticed his hands trembling again at his sides. It was disconcerting.

"I promise," he said in a meek voice.

"Good," she said, finally letting go of him and allowing him to breathe. "Don't forget it either!"

"We saw a Gray Person on the way here," Dameon said so casually it alarmed me. "I've never seen one during the day before. They're really creepy."

Mother looked up and across the Gully, her eyes following movement along the tree line. "Yes, I know, honey. There are many of them here today. It's...unusual."

I turned to follow her gaze. At first, I saw just a bunch of people sitting on the rim, chatting, eating handfuls of apple pie from clay pots. Then I saw something pale flash behind them and looked harder.

I saw them. There had to be at least twenty. They

weren't standing on the ground like us but perched in the trees. They reminded me of vultures.

Mother put her arms around me and hugged me, breaking through my terror. I took in a deep breath, my lungs aching. "I'm glad you made sure your brothers made it," she said with a little laugh.

"I didn't do anything." I forced myself to smile, trying to focus on my family, and hugged her back. "Dameon wouldn't have left my side even if I asked him to, and Darik found a way to track us down. I don't know how—"

She cut me off to ask in a whisper, "What's wrong with him?"

"Who, Darik?"

She nodded, her chin digging into my shoulder. "He seems so scared. Was it the Gray Person?"

I had never been very good at lying to my mother since she had an uncanny way of seeing through me, just like she did with my brothers. "No, he was like that before we saw her. I don't know what's wrong with him."

She squeezed me again before letting go. "Keep an eye on them, will you? Your father and I will have to head down soon, and I want them to be okay." She sighed deeply. "The sooner we're done with this the better."

I nodded, trying to show that I was calm to ease her nerves. "At least The Seeking is done. Now it's just the Renewal. That's not so bad, just standing still."

She shook her head in disbelief. She and I both knew it was far more than just standing still, but neither of us liked to talk about it before the Ritual. Even talking about it afterwards was difficult.

Mother took my hand and together we headed up the stairs, Dameon following behind and still oddly quiet.

"It's a good thing I had a daughter," she commented. "I don't think my heart would have been able to deal with only boys." We laughed and it helped ease the tension.

Soon we settled into our chairs. Father sat on one end and Mother on the other. I sat in the dead center between my two brothers, staring out at the far end of the Gully.

After a moment of silence, Father stood and addressed the people. His robes billowed around him as a gust of cold wind blew, carrying the scent of apples and spice. The words he spoke were the same ones that were said every year, but I didn't miss the strain in his voice. He was a nervous wreck just like the rest of us.

"The Seeking has officially ended, and once again the children of the Priest family have been able to remain hidden for the full day before All Hallows' Day. The Priest family will therefore inherit the title of Exalted Family and live together in the Exalted House on the hill.

"With this fulfillment, we ask that the Gray People of the woods please grace us with their protection in our dark times. We promise that we shall mind the barrier that you have provided to us. We seek your promise to defend that barrier and to protect us. We have lived in the sanctuary of Carra for centuries, and our pact of trust and respect shall not be broken this day."

I smelled something else on the breeze, too: the bitter scent of elder trees, which you could usually only smell when they were covered with flowers. It mixed with the earthy aroma of dried leaves.

There was a palpable anxiety in the air, a restlessness that couldn't be named. Several people on the rim were on their feet instead of sitting on the ground, as was custom.

Father moved in front of me, but around his cloak I had a clear view across the Gully and into the patch of elder trees on the opposite side. I could see more and more of the Gray People arriving.

I watched their pale bodies climb into the branches, perched and waiting. It wasn't just on the opposite side of the Gully; it was all around us. Their pale bodies registered in my peripheral vision around the rim. They were amassing, and again I thought of vultures.

"Darik," I whispered. "Do you see them all? What are they doing?"

"Falling asleep, I guess," he said with a snort. He was talking about the audience, not the Gray People.

"No, look." I nodded to the side, not too far from us where the pale bodies sat motionless in the trees. His laughter fell away, and he shifted closer to me in his chair.

"What are they doing? Have they ever done this before?"

I shook my head. I had forgotten that I had the best eyesight of my siblings, and that Darik easily had the worst eyes of the three of us. "I've never seen them do this before."

Mother stood up next to Father and they held hands. Her voice had no hint of the fear it had earlier as she spoke. "Together we stand, and together we offer ourselves up to the Gray People for protection."

They walked down the steps of the pedestal and into the center of the Gully, where the yellow dandelions grew thick. Unlike the ones that marked the Boundary Line of Carra, these dandelions glowed day and night and lit Mother and Father's legs as they walked through them and up the opposite ridge, until they stood midway between the edge of the Gully and the bottom.

"Our children hid from their pursuers," Mother continued, "so please protect us from our enemies, just as you have before."

I gripped the arms of my chair as I saw from the corner of my eye a Gray Person climb into a tree only a few feet behind me and my brothers. On the opposite end of the Gully, the string that held the wagon in place shook. The Ritual was about to be performed, but I couldn't figure out why the Gray People would be so keen to see it now as opposed to in years past.

In fact, the Ritual was never exciting, and so many people slept through it each year after finding a grassy spot to lay. Only children were really interested in seeing the Ritual pass.

Behind us, I saw the Gray Person give a crooked, open-mouthed smile as she dug her black claws deeper into the elder tree. She looked like a cat ready to pounce.

There was nothing different this year as far as the rules went, I told myself. We had all succeeded, we had all done precisely what we needed to. So why was I breaking out in goose flesh?

As my mind whirled with possibilities, the rope snapped and the wagon went barreling down the edge of the Gully, straight toward my parents.

CHAPTER 8
THE MOTHER OF THE GRAYS

A hush came over the Gully, so that all I could hear was the rattling of the wooden wheels as they hit every possible rock on the way down the incline. The wagon itself buckled and leapt, almost turning diagonally before straightening again.

Mother and Father stood with their hands clasped together and their backs facing the wagon as it careened toward them.

Any moment, a Gray Person would dart over and shove the wagon out of the way, just like they had been done every Ritual. They would destroy it without any trouble. However, as the wagon got closer and closer, I realized it wouldn't be stopped. It was too late to stop it.

I jumped to my feet and screamed, "Mother, no!"

Darik held me back, wrapping his strong arms around me. I screamed again, hoping she would hear my voice and move out of the way, hoping she would push Father aside, too, but I knew that wasn't their way; both had promised to stand together in the direct path of danger without flinching. As the heads of the Exalted Family, they had made vows that if this day came, they would accept whatever fate awaited them. In that instant I hated them both for their pride and dedication.

When the wagon hit them, Mother was flung forward, and Father went straight under the wheels. His screams echoed up from the Gully, amplified by the steep, bare walls.

The wagon wheels continued forward, now red. Father's cries had stopped. Mother was on her knees, one leg turned at a terrible angle from how she'd landed. Where I stood, I could see she was dazed and there was blood on her temple.

She crossed her legs in front of her, in a feeble attempt to stop the wagon somehow, but it had been turned sideways after hitting Father, and she never had a chance. Her upper body was flung backwards, but unlike Father, she didn't scream. Maybe she just didn't get the chance.

The wagon rolled once more before landing solidly in the patch of dandelions. It was then that I noticed their glow was gone - for the first time ever, they looked like regular plants.

I couldn't bring myself to look at the bodies of my parents, even as cries and screams rose up from the audience. I just stared at the patch of yellow flowers that only grew to fill the bottom of the Gully. Someone was wailing in my ear. I turned to see Dameon clutching my arm, fat tears rolling down his cheeks.

Numbly, I turned to Darik on my left and instantly recognized his guilt. He had let go of me at some point and had a look on his face like he was either going to pass out or puke, and even that wasn't really why I knew. No, it was something in my gut that told me.

Five years of working in courts and hearing people try to lie their way out of fines or housing issues had fine-tuned that instinct, and Darik was guilty of something. But I couldn't think on that now, and I hated the fact that my instincts kicked in when I could barely remember how to function.

My parents were dead.

They had died right before our eyes, right in front of all of Carra.

I made myself look towards Mother's body, crumpled into a shape that didn't even resemble her anymore.

No, the dandelions, I told myself. *Look at the dandelions.* The tiny yellow petals exploded on each stem like a miniature sun. *What if they're not dead?*

The thought crept into my mind and I felt a hot tear roll down my cheek. No, I couldn't be stupid. I saw what happened to them; the wagon killed them both, and if they weren't dead yet, they would be soon.

It was when Darik was lifted from the chair beside me that I was knocked back into reality.

A black-clawed hand covered his face, tearing long scratches across his cheeks and temples as he was picked up, a long, gnarled arm around his waist like he was a child's toy.

I was on my feet before I knew it and must have

grabbed Dameon, too, because his hand was clenched in mine.

The Gray Person who had picked up Darik was not like the others. She was even taller and wore a pair of silver antlers on her head, which had been carved with spirals and swirls. Her torso was painted the same shade of silver, though it was faded and dirty in patches.

She smiled at me as she climbed across our stairs, an arm still wrapped securely around Darik.

The people on the rim of the Gully grew mostly quiet. I could hear sobbing coming from various places in the crowd, but all eyes were focused on this Gray Person holding Darik.

"The Ritual has failed," she hissed out. "This child was captured." She dropped him to the ground, and he groaned, blood seeping from the woman's claw marks across his face.

"As Mother of the Grays, I declare our protection is at an end." She smiled at all of us before glancing over her shoulder. "Feed well, my children."

From the trees came the Gray People with long, loping strides. The first victim was a tall man at the far end of the Gully. He hadn't even heard the creature drop from the tree and approach behind him. The Gray Person turned him around and stared into his eyes. Something clearly died within the poor man as he started twitching and collapsed into a frothing, convulsing heap on the ground.

I shuddered.

Then the Gray Person moved onto the next human.

The Ritual had turned into a feast.

~

I DIDN'T STAY to see what happened to the others. Instead I pulled my knife out of my shoe, bit the blade between my teeth, and picked up Dameon, despite how heavy he was, and ran. I needed to get out of the Gully as fast as I could.

One Gray Person saw us trying to escape and rushed to cut us off.

"Dahlia, watch out!" Dameon's cry came too late.

The Gray Person swiped out with his claws and missed me, but grabbed one of my braids instead. My head jerked back as a burst of pain covered half my skull and I screeched.

It was trying to turn me around, but Dameon pulled the knife out from between my teeth. It took a few seconds, but the blade finally cut through my thick hair. The Gray Person laughed, letting go to grab another woman trying to escape.

I stumbled forward and saw movement from the side of the Gully, near the Boundary Line. A spider creature emerged, similar to the one I had tried to fight the other night. And while I was already eager to escape the chaos, seeing that thing again brought on a fresh burst of adrenaline.

The Boundary Line. I thought of how the dandelions no longer glowed in the Gully. The Mother of the Gray People had said it, hadn't she? Their protection was lost.

Darik: I thought of Darik with his slashed face lost somewhere amid this bloodbath and recalled the way the creature had chosen Pearl simply due to a single cut. He wouldn't last long, not with those wounds.

I only had the briefest moment to consider, and turned for the woods, holding Dameon close to my chest. I could save my little brother, but I couldn't save Darik any more than I could have Mother or Father.

I wouldn't have been able to bring Darik, too, I thought trying to allay the guilt already spreading within me. *I couldn't rescue him if he was being attacked.*

As I stepped into the shelter of the elder trees, I pushed back the panic that threatened to slow me down. The Gray People were our protectors. They were supposed to help us and defend us, but all it took was one mistake for them to turn on us.

I stopped thinking and ran.

The path through the elder trees was more difficult with Dameon in my arms, but I didn't dare put him down, even though my arms were burning. I nearly fell once while stepping over a pile of branches, but he tried to help where he could, reaching out to pull limbs aside for me.

When we finally made it through the trees, I saw others fleeing as well; all of them were heading toward town.

My feet moved without my conscious thought, following the others, but I didn't know where would be safe to hide. I knew what both the Gray People and the creatures of the woods were capable of, and if they wanted to slaughter every person in Carra, there was very little we could do.

The helplessness of it all enraged me. Even on Seeking nights, I always felt as though I had some control of the situation, no matter how small. I knew places around Carra that were easier to hide in than others, I knew people who could be trusted.

Now there were no safe places.

I realized Dameon was struggling in my arms and stumbled to a stop. "What's wrong?"

"I can walk, Dahlia. It's okay."

It was at that point that I realized my arms were shaking so badly that I was close to accidentally dropping him. I imagined him falling to the ground and scraping a knee. Would that be enough blood to attract those monsters? I wasn't sure.

As I carefully lowered him down, the pain broke through the cloud of adrenaline surrounding me. My arms didn't want to straighten at first, but once I let them relax, they hung limply at my sides.

Dameon put his hand in mine and started leading me toward the Exalted House.

I shook my head, and it took a moment for the words to swim back to the surface of the barren pool of my mind. "We can't go back home."

He looked up at me in confusion. "We can't stay out here, though. They'll find us!"

"The Exalted House has been torn apart. We'll be easy to reach there," I rambled as we approached downtown. "I can't go to Bisa's either. Mr. Eddington's restaurant on the ground level might attract them."

A surge of emotion threatened to overtake me at the thought of Bisa and Marcus, but I pushed it down. I couldn't think about her right now, not unless I wanted to curl up and start bawling here in the open field.

"Maybe Broskow's place..." I shook my head even as I spoke the suggestion. Broskow was a butcher, and slabs of meat didn't seem very safe either. However, his smokehouse wasn't at his shop and I didn't recall seeing any food items there other than the jerky and what Bisa had brought.

Another wave of emotion came at the thought of Bisa, one strong enough to make my eyes tear up, but I bit my tongue until it went away. I just couldn't give in, not yet — eventually, yes, but not now.

"Broskow's place? Really?" Dameon looked up at me with incredulous eyes. He assumed I was joking. He had no idea how things had changed from the night before, but maybe it would seem more plausible now. Maybe the world had changed enough that even that gamble would make sense.

We had only gotten a few blocks into town when a scream rang out amid the buildings. I turned in a circle, but couldn't see where it had come from. We froze and Dameon clutched at my dress, going silent and watchful, too. The scream came again, but this time it was abruptly cut off.

I picked him up again, and he allowed it even though we both knew my arms couldn't hold him for very long.

Broskow's shop was only a few blocks away. As we passed through the second intersection, I heard Dameon gasp and felt him pull on my dress, urging me backwards. I did as he asked, but I didn't know what had spooked him until I looked down the road to our left.

There stood the woman who had screamed earlier; I recognized her. It was the old woman with the watery eyes, who just two days ago was laughing at me in Broskow's doorway. Something was wrapped around her and at first, I thought it was something hairy, but then I realized that those fibers were legs. It was a giant millipede, with feet as long as my arms. A few of its legs were still on the ground; the rest of its body was wrapped around the woman. It had a stinger on its rear that it had shoved into her abdomen. That must have been what halted her scream.

I traced the body up to its head, which looked like it was giving her an enormous kiss on the cheek. It bobbed backward like a bird as saliva and bits of the woman's flesh came off in its mouth. It swallowed down its morsel, then went to bite again, its eyes rolling up into its skull and its mouth opening larger than it looked capable of.

And she just stared at me, her eyes wide and glassy, her cheeks wet with tears. She didn't try to struggle or even move; it looked like the poison had paralyzed her.

My throat was dry, my breaths came up as short, shallow rattles. I was so close to Broskow's shop, so close to relative safety. So, I took a careful step forward. I felt Dameon's fists grip my shirt, but neither of us spoke. We knew better than that.

Dameon might have always stayed at a friend's house during The Seeking, but he knew how to hide, how to be quiet. In a way, we were more prepared for this than anyone else in Carra, and I hated that.

A few more steps and I was midway through the intersection when I saw the millipede arch his head back again. The old woman was missing a good chunk of her skull, yet still her glassy eyes just stared ahead. I hoped she couldn't feel what was happening to her. I hoped she was oblivious to what it was doing. I couldn't imagine the torture it would be otherwise. I didn't want to even consider it.

Finally we were through the intersection and moving down the next block. I stepped nearly soundlessly on the dirt road, preferring that over the noisy wooden platforms of the storefronts. At this point, Dameon and I breathed so silently that we could've been ghosts moving through a deserted town. We tried to look everywhere at once, searching for any kind of threat, no matter what form it might take.

Our terror kept us alert.

When I turned onto the final block to Broskow's place, I stopped in my tracks. The door to his shop was closed and there were lights on inside, but just outside the door on the beaten dirt path grew a single glowing dandelion that I knew hadn't been there this morning. The ground was cracked around its roots as though it had suddenly forced itself out of the ground somehow. The piles of leaves which had gathered near the steps of his shop were gone, too.

I braced myself as I approached the front door, not sure what I would find within. If I needed to flee, I would flee. Dameon kept a lookout over my shoulder as I reached for the handle, which turned without complaint.

THE GLOW of the fireplace and the burning candles within made me pause in the doorway. The flames threw shadows throughout the room, hiding potential dangers, and I didn't want to be caught off guard. Not now, not when we were so close. I pushed the door open further and suddenly a torch hovered near my face - I winced at the heat it gave off.

"Oh!" a familiar voice cried out and I tried to see past the light to the face behind it. "It's Dahlia! And thank goodness: Dameon, too!"

Bisa. She stood just behind the door, and the look of surprise on her face had to have matched mine. I gaped at her, my mind trying to make sense of her presence there. How had she gotten here? How had she survived the Ritual and made it back?

Then I felt gruff hands take hold of my arm and I nearly sped out the door on the spot.

"Don't be stupid," Broskow growled, pulling me and Dameon into the house. "Don't you know what's out there?"

My instincts were screaming at me to run, to be on

alert, to be ready to fight again if we had to. Dameon slid down from my arms and went to give Bisa a huge hug. He wasn't crying, but he was shaking from head to toe.

Broskow was talking to me, but I didn't hear him. I was checking the room for any dangers, anything that could be hidden from view. The windows were all boarded up. Sleeping areas had been created near the fireplace, and bundles of blankets were rolled out as well. The smell of cooked vegetables was in the air and everything seemed safe. So why couldn't I calm down?

I felt Bisa's arms wrap around me, warm and soft and comforting, gripping me around my waist. "It's okay," she said into my ear. "It's okay, calm down now. You're safe here. I've got you."

I felt my adrenaline start to ebb away at her words, but it was replaced by a wall of sadness and despair. "I can't," I said, rubbing a hand on her arm as I stepped away. "I'm afraid." the words caught in my throat as I said them, realizing how fully entrenched I was in my paranoia.

She gripped me tighter and pulled me back into her arms. I felt her lips on the side of my neck and a shiver went down my spine. "It'll be okay, Dahlia. Calm down, sugar. You need to calm down. You survived, you made it, you're safe now. Please."

Her words were like a balm to my soul. I felt my muscles relax, felt my breathing deepen again, felt the pain in my arms from carrying Dameon halfway across Carra. Then the tears came, hard and sudden, as the weight of the day came crashing down on me.

Bisa pulled me to the wooden floor and cradled me against her, rocking me as though I was a child. Normally I might have been appalled, but not today.

I needed her now.

I needed her more than I ever had in my entire life.

CHAPTER 9
THE SEPARATE SHEEP

I don't know how long I cried, but once my tears were all spent, I sat cross-legged on the floor, staring into the fire. Bisa sat curled up with me, an arm draped around my shoulders. Broskow brought me a blanket and a cup of water; oddly, the well water tasted cleaner than ever before but I drank it down without commenting on it and he brought me another one just as silently.

Dameon moved to sit with Marcus - Bisa's little brother had been spared, too - near the makeshift beds. They looked so alike there, even though Dameon was three years his senior. I could only imagine what all Marcus had seen with his sister out in the Gully today, and I hated how both of them were forced to grow up so fast.

"How did you all make it?" I asked, my voice hoarse from crying.

"Remember how the Gray Person back in the woods

killed that spider creature?" Broskow asked, pulling up a chair beside us.

I furrowed my brow. It felt like a lifetime ago. "It used a torch. It caught fire like a kindling log."

He nodded. "That's right. It turns out that's the one thing these things are afraid of. Bisa nearly got attacked by one, but I put my makeshift torch in its face, and it lit up like a candle." He motioned to the torch sitting near the door. It was a large piece of elder wood wrapped in the remains of a shirt.

I thought back to the craziness of the Ritual. "How did you light it there? Nobody stopped you?"

He smirked. "Unlike you, I wasn't sitting up on a precipice for everybody to see, so nobody gave a shit about what I did. When all those Gray People started gathering around, Bisa and I thought we needed a little bit of protection."

Bisa smiled. "Let's just say it's a good thing I had my mirror."

I gripped her hand so hard that her skin blanched. Was that really all that stood between her and a gruesome death: a grimy sliver of mirror that had barely survived for centuries?

"I didn't think any of you had lived. I thought Dameon and I were alone." Broskow and Bisa exchanged a look and I tensed, realizing that they were hiding something from me. "What is it?"

"There's someone else you should see." Broskow gestured to the rolled-up lump beside the fireplace. I hadn't even noticed it before, even though it was only feet away from me. I glanced between them suspiciously. Why had they not mentioned this person sooner, and why were they so tense about telling me?

I approached the bundle of blankets cautiously and had to step up to the fireplace to see the person's face since they were so completely covered. The firelight threw odd shadows, so it took me a moment to realize that I was looking at bandages instead of an actual face.

"Darik," I said through a gasp. He was fast asleep, but I could see that he had bled partway through the bandages.

A flood of emotions spilled over me at once: shock, gratefulness, and disgust. But my hatred was the worst. I loved my brother, but in that moment, I wished he had died at the hands of that Gray Person. She had said he was responsible for all of this, that he had lied about not being captured on the day of The Seeking. I needed to know if her accusations were true or not.

I shook his shoulder, slowly at first then more vigorously when it took him time to stir.

"Dahlia, he needs to recover," Bisa chided, stepping forward, her voice filled with concern. I ignored her. She was right of course, but I needed answers. We all did. People were being slaughtered outside, and we probably wouldn't last more than a day because of his stupidity.

I thought of Mother's worry for him before The Seeking, back before our home was vandalized and before all of Carra was turned into a bloodbath. Back before she *died* beside my father.

"Wake up, Darik!" I couldn't keep the anger from my

voice. His left eye blinked open. His right one was hidden beneath a bandage.

"Dahlia? You survived!"

"Was she right? Was the Mother of the Grays right about what happened during The Seeking?"

He sat up slowly, some of the bandages loosening or falling off completely. The scratches were dark ruby and deep. What I had assumed were bandages were only bits of cloth that Bisa had found lying around. He would be lucky if they didn't get infected, but at that moment, I pushed away any concern. I was back in court, demanding an explanation in order to hand down judgment for all the wrongs that surrounded us.

"Look, it's not what you think, okay?" There was real fear in his gaze, a fear I recognized.

I thought of his superfluous attitude before the Ritual, how he didn't show up until the last minute, forcing Mother and Father to worry for him all the way up until the last minute. He was a selfish distraction, only concerned with himself instead of thinking about others.

Of course, if he had caused something this terrible, then his avoidance and nonchalance made sense. If he acted like nothing was wrong and none of it mattered, then maybe it wouldn't. Sometimes I hated how well I could see through people.

"That was why you were acting so strange before the Ritual. You actually were captured, and you were trying to play it off like it was nothing."

"No, look, it was an accident. I was hiding in my

friend Jo's closet, like I normally do during The Seeking, and he thought it would be funny to lock the closet door on me. When I woke up the next morning, I realized I was trapped, and he unlocked it and let me out. He thought it was funny and I just thought he was being an ass. I didn't know it would cause the whole Ritual to fall apart!"

I didn't care if he was four years my elder. I slapped him as hard as I could. A few more of the makeshift bandages fell off, fresh blood spouting in places where my hand made contact.

He stared at me with wide, terrified eyes.

"Dahlia, that hurt! Shit..." His hand hovered over his cheek, wanting to touch it but afraid to cause more pain.

"Good!" I screamed. "I'm glad it hurt. You deserve at least a hundred more for what you did."

"I didn't do it," he said, his voice hard with anger now. "Jo did. He's the asshole who—"

"Yes, but you could have said something! You could have told them. Jo should've been up there doing the Ritual with his parents - they should've been the new Exalted Family."

He stared at me with his mouth open. "But it was just a joke! It didn't really matter."

"Well it did! As soon as he locked that door, he captured you. You were his prize, and it didn't matter how hidden you were for the rest of The Seeking, at that point, the game was over. Our family lost, and Jo's family should have stepped up to take over. It should have been them down in the Gully with the wagon barreling down on them!"

He stared at me with wide eyes. "I didn't know. Nobody ever told me."

I rolled my eyes. "I was never told either, you idiot. I read the damn rules! I did that years ago, when I first had to take part in it. I wanted to know the ins and outs of it. Are you telling me you never thought to read them?"

He looked down at his blankets, his eyes glassy.

Of course it would be some stupid move that brought the Exalted Family down. I just wished it hadn't been one of our family to make it. I wished it hadn't been our parents who had to stand there and allow those wheels to crush their bones and shove their bodies into the dirt. They didn't deserve that. They were good people.

Now nothing could change where we were, holed up in Broskow's butcher shop once again, hiding from things that wanted to suck off our faces and pump us full of poison. This was where we were, and no amount of slapping my brother would solve the problem at hand.

I turned away and saw Bisa and Broskow staring at us, shocked, while Dameon and Marcus watched me with wide, fearful eyes. I looked away, filled with resentment and terror. I didn't know what was going to happen to us, or how we could possibly survive.

Then I heard a shudder get ripped off outside.

Bisa jumped and moved to stand in front of me. Dameon and Marcus came running over to stand with us near the fireplace.

"What was that?" Broskow whispered.

The buzzing of large wings reverberated against the far window, almost as if in reply. It sounded like a bumblebee, but so much louder. I spotted enormous yellow eyes through the slots of wood nailed across the space. Long spindly legs reached through, feeling with their hairs. If it could rip off the shutter, it wouldn't be that difficult to pull a board away.

A mandible came through a large triangle of space and a long tongue coiled out, as tall as me.

"Go away," Marcus pleaded.

I thought of the spider from the other night scenting Pearl's blood in the air. It could probably smell Darik's blood.

"Dameon, you still have that knife?"

He nodded, pulling it out of his waistband and handing it to me. It might not work for their limbs, but it might work on a tongue. I moved to the wall near it.

"Dahlia, get back here," Broskow hissed. "What by the Grays are you doing?"

As angry as I was at Darik, I didn't want to see this thing get inside and tear his flesh off. I couldn't deal with that, and I wouldn't.

The loud buzzing came again as the bee readjusted itself, then more hairy legs reached through and the tongue stretched out. This time I was ready for it and slammed the blade of the knife down on it. It emitted a high-pitched squeal; the noise made my head vibrate. Part of its tongue fell to the floor and flopped around like a fish. Gray blood oozed out of it.

The creature left, and for a moment I thought we were free of it.

Then the buzzing grew louder, and *slam!* I jumped. Somehow, by trying to get it to leave us alone, I had only made it angrier.

I moved away from the window, my hands shaking so badly I had to consciously keep myself from dropping the knife.

Slam! Bits of debris fell from the wooden boards.

Slam! I saw a hairline crack form in the center.

That's when my stomach dropped. It was only a matter of time.

I looked to the door, then to Broskow and Bisa. Would we be any safer outside than we were here? Did we have a choice? Bisa picked up Marcus and I grabbed Dameon. Broskow put an arm around Darik's waist to help lead him.

Slam! One of the boards fell away, and Marcus screamed.

Bisa had a hand on the doorknob when we heard a scuffle outside. Broskow put a hand on her shoulder. Something was struggling outside with the bee. He left Darik's side as he crept to the window.

"Be careful!" I hissed.

He waved a hand at me as he peeked out through the gap made from the fallen board. His eyes grew big and he waved for us to come. Reluctantly we followed, but we kept our distance from the window.

I blinked. A Gray Person held the bee creature by the stinger and was slamming it against the ground. It took several smacks before its outer shell cracked. The noise it made was horrendous. Its long, hairy legs groped at the sky until the final smack. Then the Gray Person dropped its body to the ground, its forearm covered in blood.

Darik stepped back, whimpering as the Gray Person looked into the window at us. I gripped the blade in my hand tighter. If it wanted to come at Darik, it would have to take me, too. Except the Gray Person merely smiled, its empty eye sockets staring at each one of us in turn. Then it held a finger to its lips before reaching down to pick up the corpse of the bee and hoisted it over its shoulder. He nodded at us, then walked away.

Broskow let out a slow, shaky breath. "What was that all about?"

"I don't know," Bisa said and put Marcus down. She picked up the board and looked for a way to somehow patch the gap again with it. "But I don't want another of those things getting in here." Broskow went to help her, then froze.

"Wait a moment," he muttered. "There's one of those glowing dandelions out there now!"

"I know, I saw one at your door when I came in. I don't know where—"

"No, there's one outside this window now. There wasn't one there just a moment ago. That Gray Person must have planted it."

I crept closer and looked. Growing between the wooden slots of the deck that surrounded Broskow's shop was the single plant. It looked like it had been growing there for weeks, slowly making its way up between the boards, but I knew better. That was definitely not there when I left for the Exalted House yesterday. And unlike the weeds that grew in the Gully, this plant was glowing brightly despite the late afternoon sunlight streaming in.

"You said there's another one at my front door? What do they want with my place? I haven't done shit to them!"

"No," Darik said, peering out beside me. "But I have. The Mother didn't kill me when she could have, she just marked me." He shivered. "I don't know what they want with me, but it's not to kill me. I know that much, at least." His voice dropped to a whisper as he said, "Somehow that makes it worse."

I grabbed hold of his hand and squeezed. It was like we were kids again and I had to give him the courage to go on his first Seeking night.

I thought then of the way the Gray People had fed on Broskow and on the others in the Gully. We were food to them, clearly, but somehow our little group was something more. They wanted something from us, but I wasn't sure what. Why would some sheep be put aside while all the others were slaughtered? A special meal, perhaps?

Darik pulled his hand from my grip and rubbed it. Apparently I had been squeezing it too hard. "Are you okay?" he asked.

"I don't know," I said with a sigh. It was the truth; I didn't know what I felt anymore.

Bisa and Broskow finished securing a fresh board in

place and the afternoon sunlight made long streaks across the floor where it peered in through the gaps. I looked around at the four walls of the shop, realizing for the first time how small the place was, especially for six people.

But it was different from the underground hiding place I had made for myself. That was a bunker of my choosing that I could leave if I needed to. Here, we were trapped at the will of the Gray People, waiting for whatever plans they had to play out, and I hated it.

It was different when I saw this place as a safe house. Now it was merely a cage.

BROSKOW MADE a beef and vegetable soup for us as daylight began to fade. It was incredibly salty because everything here was preserved with salt, but none of us complained. At least there was plenty to eat.

I would occasionally go by the window and peek through the slots at the glowing dandelion outside. It was multiplying. Now there were two of them growing through the cracks in the deck as though they had always been there. I pointed it out to the others, but they didn't seem as bothered by it as I was.

"Well, at least the monsters out there won't be able to get us as easily," Broskow said as he chewed on a piece of jerky. "Apparently some of the Gray People are still protecting us." He must have seen my disbelief because he continued, "You saw what they did to that bee, kid.

The stinger on that thing was big enough to skewer you and your little brother at once. If that Gray Person hadn't come along, we would all be dead."

"But you know they're not keeping us here for a good reason, right? They're doing it because they have other plans for us. They aren't doing it because they like us." I scoffed. "Why do they want us alive when they want everyone else dead? What makes us so special?"

Broskow shrugged, not meeting my eyes, and I could tell it bothered him more than he let on. So why was he acting like it was no big deal? We weren't safe; we were corralled here. Why was he digging into his soup instead of taking this seriously?

I looked around the room. Darik had been quiet ever since the attack, and I knew it was because of our argument. It was as though my words took the life out of him.

Meanwhile, Dameon had taken on the role of keeping an eye on Marcus. The boy had been utterly distraught ever since the bee attack and hadn't wanted to leave the far end of the room where the hay was laid out for our beds. Bisa tried to calm him, but nothing really worked until Dameon came over and talked to him for a bit. Once Broskow made soup, Dameon fetched bowls for each of them, and the two boys sat next to each other eating and speaking in low voices.

I was proud of my brother for being strong, even though I knew he was terrified like the rest of us. I just worried that I was the only one that seemed to be taking this seriously.

"Slowly those dandelions are going to circle this

whole building, and that will be our Boundary Line." I faced Bisa. "Then we'll be stuck here for however long they want."

She nodded. "I mean you're right, sugar, but I don't know what to do about it. We don't exactly have much power here."

I turned to Broskow next. "You had one of the Gray People feed on you. You know what it was like. I don't want that to happen to our little brothers."

"Do you have to remind me?" He dropped his spoon into his bowl with a look of disgust. "I'm beginning to wish I'd never told you about any of that!"

"If my parents were alive, they wouldn't want to cower in a building like this. They would be trying to escape."

"No, they would want their kids to be doing the cowering for them."

I gaped. "This is not the same thing. The Seeking had rules. Sure, there were risks, but we knew that going in."

Darik pushed away from the table and turned his back to us, retreating to his now familiar spot by the fireplace. I glanced his way, not sure if I ought to follow him or not. More and more I felt like I was the outcast here, and I couldn't comprehend how so many people were perfectly fine with carrying out the rest of their lives stuck, caged.

"Yeah, you're right," Broskow said sarcastically. "The Seeking had rules, and this doesn't. This is what happens when it fails; everything falls apart. You're upset 'cause you don't want your brother to have his brain sucked out by a Gray Person? Well my kids are out there somewhere, and I don't know what happened to them. I couldn't find them at the Ritual, and I sure haven't found them now. For all I know, their minds are all gone, or they're pumped full of poison somewhere."

"I'm sorry, I—"

His eyes glistened with tears, but he wouldn't let them fall. "I don't know where they are, let alone if they're safe. If they are alive, and I do find them, I'm going to have to tell them that I watched Pearl die. I'll have to explain that I sat there screaming and didn't do a damn thing to stop it."

He stared at me with all the ferocity that he had that night, like I wasn't even a person anymore.

"I'm sorry to hear that," Bisa said in her calm, steady voice to break the silence. "This has been a difficult time for all of us. One simple mistake has led to almost the entire town being killed. It was a mistake that could have happened at any time, but it happened now." From the fireplace, I saw Darik turn back toward us, but he remained silent. Bisa sighed. "If they are keeping us for food, then I guess that means they're keeping us for breeding, too."

Broskow nearly choked on his soup. "What are you even talking about?"

"You heard me. You keep dogs. How do you keep them generation after generation?" He blanched, but Bisa went on. "My point is that I'm not trying to embarrass anyone in this room, but I'm not interested in a damn single one of the men here. Dahlia and I like women, and I think I speak for both of us when I say that neither one will be a breeder to repopulate this devastated spit of a town. We never liked it that much to begin with."

I took her hand and squeezed it hard, feeling her fingers shake: perhaps the only signal of how difficult all of that was to say. Bisa and I had made no secret of our relationship, but we certainly hadn't gone around advertising it. I never thought she would be spelling it out for Broskow of all people either. It was hard to see Darik's expression with the fireplace behind him, but I thought I saw the shadow of a smile on his lips.

"We're not dogs, we're not sheep, and we're not about to be treated like them," Bisa continued. "If they're trying to protect us, that means they need us."

I finally understood what she was saying. "Which means we have leverage over them!" I pulled her close and kissed her for a good long moment. "Bisa, you're brilliant!"

When I pulled away again, she was grinning. "Oh, sugar, I thought that's what *you* were getting at."

I laughed and she put an arm around me.

"But what are we going to do? I got the impression the Gray Mother isn't exactly interested in negotiating terms," Darik said, stepping towards us.

"She kept you alive, didn't she?" Bisa added, "If she wanted you dead, she would have killed you on the spot."

Darik pursed his lips. I was hoping that would reassure him, but apparently not, based on his glower.

I stepped forward, still holding Bisa's hand. "I know this isn't going to be a popular idea, but I think we need to show that we're more than just livestock to be protected and bred. We need to go find the Mother and demand that she listen to us."

Broskow laughed so loudly and so suddenly that I felt Bisa jump. "You've clearly lost your mind, kid. Maybe you missed what happened at the Gully, but I sure didn't. You want to go find their Mother? That's suicide. You may not like being locked up here, but at least it's safe."

"Safety comes at a cost," Bisa retorted. "None of us are truly safe here. They may want us to think that, but if they come in here and demand that we pop out babies to restock the stables and we refuse, suddenly that promise of safety is gone."

"What if they decide not to protect you?" Darik asked. "What if you head off into the woods, and no Gray Person gives a damn if some bug attacks you?"

I thought for a moment and turned again to Broskow, "You figured that part out. The bugs are afraid of fire. At least, the spiders are."

"No, the millipede things are, too," Darik said distractedly. "When I was trying to escape the Grove, one of the guards had a torch. It was Marissa, I think. She was wielding it like a blade along with her sword. She's the one that helped me up after the Mother attacked me. I got separated from her when everyone scattered, but I saw how the millipede kept its distance from her, scuttling away when she aimed the fire in its direction." His gaze was distant. "I was too panicked at the time to think. I should have noticed more. I shouldn't have been so distracted."

I went over and took his hand, noticing Dameon and Marcus had come closer to the fire to listen to our conversation. "You weren't distracted, you were bleeding, hurt. You're lucky you didn't get targeted in all that mess."

Darik couldn't meet my eyes, but he squeezed my hand tighter. "I should have done more." A tear slid from his exposed eye and down his cheek.

"You're the only one that saw her up close, Darik," I said. "Do you think we have a chance of doing any kind of negotiating with her? Do you think she gives a shit about us at all?"

He looked at me finally, and there was hatred in his eyes. "She looked at me as though I was worth less than dirt. She could have torn me apart in a moment, but she didn't. I thought I was dead, but instead she just scratched me up and then dropped me."

Broskow snorted from where he sat.

Lost in thought, Darik reached up to touch the ragged piece of cloth used as a bandage on his cheek. Bisa had redressed it while Broskow cooked. "I think she left me alive to send a message. She wants us to remember the mistake, and that's why we're alive. We're supposed to learn from this and obey without question." He smiled and it was first glimmer of the light-hearted boy he used to be that I'd seen in months. "But you know me, I've never been good at obeying orders. If I'm going to grow old and have children of my own, I don't want them to live under some ridiculous rules. I don't want them to have to risk getting their friends slaughtered like we did."

"I don't think anyone should have to watch that, kids or not," Dameon spoke up, his voice barely above a whisper.

"What if you all are wrong?" Broskow said, gaze stern. "What if you walk out there and you're dead before you even reach the forest line?"

"Then we're wrong," Darik said. "But at least we tried. At least we didn't cower in our cages and accept our fates. I'm only here to serve as a lesson to others."

"What if it makes them angry? What if they turn their rage on us and punish us for your stupidity? They did it before. They killed most of Carra because of your inability to follow instructions."

Darik's eye went wide and he spun on his heel to face Broskow. "I told you, *that was a mistake*."

Broskow walked around the butcher's table. "Damn right it was. Now I'm trying to prevent another one from being made. I'm not going to let you be the cause of our deaths."

Bisa stepped between them, putting her hands out to separate them, the firelight reflecting off their pinched and angry faces.

It was Darik that swung first, trying to box Broskow in the ear, but scuffing Bisa along the jaw in the process. She was knocked backward, and I ran forward to grab her and pull her out of the way. The two men started fighting and never before had I wanted so badly to be out of this building.

If someone had told me a week ago that Bisa would try to break up a fight between those two in Broskow's butcher shop, I would have never believed them. If I had been told that the entire city I had grown up in would be mostly gone, I would have probably thought they were crazy.

We had fallen to this point and I wasn't sure if there was a way to climb back up. The Gray People wanted us to stay here, they wanted us to be subservient, to be so busy fighting among ourselves that we wouldn't fight them. But they needed us.

"Are you okay?" I asked, eyeing the men warily.

Bisa nodded and rubbed her chin, which would probably be bruised tomorrow. "Your brother is stronger than he looks." She turned back to me but looked over my shoulder. I felt a tug at my back and looked to see Dameon and Marcus standing there, each holding a sack with supplies.

"We're ready, come on." He pulled harder at my dress when I just stood there in surprise.

"You two want to come with us?" I asked and he nodded.

Marcus was hiding behind Dameon, his eyes watching the two men still fighting in front of the fireplace. Broskow was punching Darik in the side while Darik kicked at his knee.

I shook my head. "We're not ready, we need food and plenty of torches."

"We've got all of it." The seriousness in Dameon's eyes terrified me. I had never seen him look so solemn in my life. He looked at least five years older than he did just the other day. "Darik said we need to hurry. If Broskow notices, he could try to stop us." He looked toward Broskow and I realized what he meant. Darik had never intended to come with us. He planned to stay behind. I looked at Darik again, and when our eyes met there was desperation in his.

Bisa and I took the satchels the boys were carrying. Dameon's had soaked torches, at least forty. Marcus's had food and waterskins: mostly jerky with some dried fruits, but enough to last at least a week.

I bit my lip and we inched toward the door. When I looked back, Darik was on the ground, having lasted as long as he could, and Broskow seemed to have run out of energy, too.

When we opened the door, Broskow turned to us with the same look I'd expect to see on a wild dog. "What are you doing?"

Bisa slipped out first with the two boys right behind her, and I followed after them. Broskow came to the door and reached out to grab me. He might have been able to reach one of my braids if Dameon hadn't already sliced it off earlier.

We hurried out into the street and I turned to see that Broskow only made it a few steps before stopping in the doorway. He couldn't pass the line of glowing dandelions that now bisected the boards in front of the door, he was too terrified. He stood there bewildered and confused, his face a mixture of terror and anger.

Tears were in my eyes for Darik's role as a distraction, but I was glad to be away from Broskow. I wasn't sure what he would have done to make us stay. At least the monsters of the woods didn't attack their own kind.

PART FOUR
CONFRONTATION

CHAPTER 10
BEYOND THE BOUNDARY LINE

I knew once we got out of the building, it was going to be difficult for Bisa and me, not to mention the fact that we had two little boys with us as well. Danger is hard enough to face on your own, or with your loved one, but is ten times worse when you have to protect children, too.

While Bisa and I were willing to sacrifice ourselves for this chance at freedom, we weren't willing to sacrifice them. The stakes were suddenly so much higher than either of us had expected, and we shared a grim glance.

About a block away from Broskow's shop, I stopped and pulled out a torch. Darik had made sure we had everything we needed, even a tiny metal lighter at the bottom of the bag. I didn't know he even owned one of those. It was a relic from some long-ago world that he had somehow found a way to refill.

It took me a minute to figure out how to strike a light. After only burning my fingers once, the torch lit and we stood there in the chilly late afternoon air, staring at the fire like it was some goddess. I just hoped it would protect us.

I took Dameon's hand as Bisa took Marcus's and we headed further down the street. The place was barren. Except for maybe the day of the Ritual, Carra was never so empty. There was usually someone hanging up laundry to dry, or the scents of foods, or a whiff of horse manure. Now I didn't even hear birds chirping. It was like everything had been slaughtered.

As we walked, we'd occasionally pass evidence of a struggle. One road had a huge bloody spot that extended from one end of the dirt path to the other. I wasn't sure if a person could even produce so much blood: maybe a horse? Either way, we picked up the pace.

Some buildings were fully intact, others weren't. Many looked like creatures had either broken through the shutters or through the front doors. The road was mostly strewn with pieces of wood. We didn't explore inside any buildings, even though I was sure there would be supplies we could find. I couldn't handle seeing the bodies of people I knew, and I didn't want to expose the boys to that either.

Nobody spoke. We walked quickly, panting into the cold air. We were almost out of Carra when I heard Marcus gasp. I turned, expecting to see a creature near him, but there was nothing. He had stopped in the street, still holding Bisa's hand. Bisa had walked a few steps forward before she had noticed.

Marcus lifted a hand and pointed. The poor boy was

staring off down a road making small squeaking sounds with each breath. I followed his gaze to see the house he had grown up in: his mother's house.

The building, I had seen for myself during the investigation, was an absolute wreck inside. Unlike the other buildings, though, all of the shutters were open, and the door was swinging wide. What had frozen Marcus in his tracks were the two long black legs sticking out. They bent up to the top of the doorway and out into the street, long black limbs that were covered in tiny black hairs - I knew what those legs belonged to. I had seen them up close the night of The Seeking.

Through the windows I spotted things wrapped in white gossamer, large masses that seemed to swing gently from the ceiling. The legs of the spider shifted on the outside as it sorted through its stores of food within.

Bisa didn't wait, she picked up Marcus and the three of us hurried on. She fell in step beside me and I could hear her voice barely above a whisper as she spoke to her brother.

"It's okay, honey, it's okay."

Marcus buried his sobs into his sister's shoulder.

I kept looking back to make sure it wasn't following us. Seeing one of those spiders again, seeing the size of it compared to a house I knew quite well, made me break out into a sweat. When I had been holed up in the tree that night, it was hard to discern just how big the creature was. Had it been that big, or had I only encountered a baby?

As the sunlight dwindled, I would occasionally catch

the distant sound of buzzing going past, and maybe spot a large round shadow dart across the road in front of us.

When we reached the edge of town, we came to a stop. The ring of dandelions that surrounded Carra and protected it for so long was barren. The plants looked like shriveled black vines, looking as lost as the rest of the town.

"No need in hesitating anymore I guess," I whispered to the others. My voice seemed loud in the silence, but somehow I wasn't as scared to speak here as I had been downtown. Here I could hear crickets and the chirping of birds bundling down for the night; the darkness would be coming soon.

"You think we should camp here?" Bisa asked.

I looked back toward the buildings. "No, I don't trust it. There are too many of them still out there. We'll move farther in and camp there."

Bisa reached into my satchel and pulled out her own torch. At my questioning look she said, "I'd rather be extra safe."

I nodded and looked down to the boys. "You two ready?"

Dameon stepped over the Boundary Line without a word and we huddled together as we entered the forest.

I was grateful for Bisa's torch. The darkness was thick and we could barely see the light that was still along the horizon.

Not for the first time that day, I hoped we had made the right choice.

WHEN WE DECIDED to make camp, I was once again grateful to have the boys present. They started picking up sticks and logs for the campfire as we went. Once we found a clearing, I made sure we had enough wood to make a large fire for the four of us. When we lit it with one of our torches, the flames were taller than Marcus.

We ate the jerky that Darik had packed for us and rolled out our thin blankets in silence. We were passing around the waterskin when Bisa curled up beside me, slinking her arm around my waist. Without even thinking, I leaned into her and put a hand on her knee.

I used to be reluctant to show such affection in front of my family members, but now I just didn't care. It wasn't that they disapproved of us exactly, but Mother especially hadn't liked us being so openly involved together. As a member of the Exalted Family, she thought it made us as a whole look bad. Now she was dead, along with most of Carra, and it didn't matter anymore what anyone thought of us.

We sat there in silence, enjoying each other's warmth and scent, and simply *being* for a few minutes. As we stared into the flames, I thought back to Darik and Broskow. I wondered how my brother was doing and if he was even still alive. Had Broskow regretted his actions and set about nursing him back to health? Or did he roll him out to be eaten by the spider that was in Bisa's old house? The memory of that creature's legs poking out of the front door sent a shiver down my spine, and Bisa held me tighter.

"Are you cold?"

"No, just remembering too much." I closed my eyes and listened to her heartbeat.

"I keep second-guessing what we did," she said. "Then I think of what it was like staying in that damn shop and listening to Broskow. He wasn't that bad at first, but it was as though the longer he stayed there, the worse he got. He was entirely different on The Seeking than he was when we left. It was like he just couldn't get his anger under control."

A log cracked and sank deeper into the flames sending a shock of embers up into the dark sky. I felt Bisa's chest rise and fall as she spoke again. "I think Pearl's death made him rethink everything. I think he was afraid then, and that's what made him kinder. That's what made him actually stop and listen. When he's alone with his own thoughts, that's when he gets worse."

"I couldn't believe he attacked Darik like that," I said. "I feel bad about leaving them alone. Do you think we should have stayed behind to help? Do you think he even got out?"

Bisa gave a deep sigh, the kind she gave when she was trying to explain bad news to Marcus. I had heard that sigh when she told Marcus he would be moving, after she had just gained custody of him and he wanted to know if he would ever live with their mother again.

"Darik knew what he was doing," Dameon said from

across the fire, his eyes glowing in the light of the flames. He had his arms wrapped around his knees, unlike Marcus, who was sleepily eating jerky beside him. "He said Broskow was itching for someone to punch and didn't want it to end up being either of you."

Bisa rubbed at the large bruise that had formed on her chin, giving her skin a painful reddish-purple hue.

I looked into the flames. "I still wish he could have come with us. I feel like I let him down. He could've at least told me his plan. As it was, he put us in a terrible position. How was I supposed to know their fight was all a ploy?"

"If I had known, I wouldn't have gotten between them," Bisa added with a small laugh.

Dameon looked down. "He wasn't sure if he could trust you. You were so mad at him when you found out what happened, so he was afraid you wouldn't believe him. He wanted me to tell you that he was really sorry for everything." He wiped his nose on the back of his sleeve. "I wanted him to come, too, but he refused. He said he had messed up enough already."

I didn't remember much about what I had said that night, but I remember slapping him so hard that his wounds reopened. The memory made me cringe. Oddly enough it made me think of Broskow beating up my brother, too. But I was upset at the time; surely that was excusable considering I had watched our parents die right in front of us.

Only Darik had seen that, too, hadn't he? He had been there right beside me. He even kept me from running down there, and possibly getting myself killed in the process. Yes, he had been missing for most of The Seeking, but that was just his way. He had always preferred to be on his own and not to team up like other siblings sometimes did in the past.

However, whenever he was with us, he was always trying to protect us: from those guys who tried to intimidate me and Dameon before we entered the Grove, to preventing me from getting myself killed during the Ritual, to helping us escape a man who I believed had become my friend and ally. Somehow, Darik saw right through that and knew we needed to get out of there before it was too late.

My stomach clenched and I felt a wave of guilt sweep over me. I pulled away from Bisa and got to my feet.

"Sugar, are you okay?"

I gave a weak nod but couldn't bring myself to speak. My heart hurt and I felt tears threatening to overwhelm me. We had enough to deal with right now without me crying everywhere and getting Marcus upset again or worrying Bisa or Dameon. So I turned away from the fire and wiped the tears that had spilled down my cheeks. I took deep breaths and tried to calm myself as best I could.

Everything hurt. I had been so wrapped up in my annoyance with Darik that I had completely overlooked how he was helping. I had let my anger at him blind me to the good that he was doing. In that regard, Broskow and I had a lot in common.

I was disgusted with myself. I wished I could walk

farther into the woods to get more privacy, but I knew better than to stray from the firelight.

I watched a shadow move closer and my body went rigid. It moved again and I moved back toward the fire. Bisa was right behind me, and we were so close to one another that she must have noticed me tense.

"What is it?" she whispered.

There was more movement, close enough this time that I could spot the segmented body wiggle by. It was one of those long millipedes, one of the ones that I watched wrap itself around the old woman with the watery eyes. It was just close enough to make me wary. I gestured to the others to stand and heard Dameon pull Marcus to his feet.

Bisa saw it, too, and she pulled out the unfinished torches from earlier and relit them.

The millipede was circling us slowly, curiously, probably trying to decide how safe it was to approach. I turned and urged the boys to come around to our side of the fire. They obeyed without a word. Soon, Bisa and I were standing on the outside with the kids behind us and the fire behind them.

The millipede was circling closer and closer.

"It's too hot," Marcus whispered. I turned to see his poor face covered in sweat, but I didn't know what to do. If he wasn't careful and broke from the group, it might target him, and I wasn't sure if I could pull it off of him if it wrapped around him like it had that old woman.

"Dahlia, watch it!" Bisa cried and instinctively I dove to the side. I heard a horrible ripping sound and looked down to see that the stinger of the creature, which I suspected was filled with poison and measured about the size of my forearm, had caught the skirt of my dress and pinned it to the ground. I pulled on the fabric, but it wouldn't budge.

When I turned back around, the thing's face was only a foot away from mine. Its mouth was open with multiple rows of teeth lining the inside, and its eyes had rolled up into its skull; it probably thought it had poisoned me and that I was ripe for the taking.

I only had a second to react, but I remembered the Gray Person the night of The Seeking and how it had handled that spider. I switched the torch to my other hand with the flames aimed downward, then threw it into the creature's gaping mouth.

Suddenly all I could hear was its horrific wail.

The sound hurt my ears and I crouched down to the ground, trying to make myself as small as I could. I felt its legs crawling frantically down my back. Then something hot and wet dripped down my back, sticking the fabric of my dress to my skin.

Someone grabbed my leg and yanked so hard I thought it might get pulled from its socket. I thought I heard a ripping sound again, but the wailing of the creature was still so loud it was hard to hear anything above it.

Then I felt Bisa's arms around me, pulling me backward. I couldn't open my eyes; my head was ringing terribly. I was covered in some disgusting muck, and the warmth of the fire burned against my back.

Finally, the wail subsided into a ringing noise and I felt Bisa shaking me.

I opened my eyes and saw her lips moving, but I couldn't hear a word. I shook my head and said, "I can't hear you", as the words echoed in my skull. Bisa's eyes went wide, but she nodded as she forced me to turn around so she could check out my back.

Beside our fire was a gray trail of slime from where the creature had tried to escape into the woods. It must have pinned its stinger into the ground too well, though, because it couldn't go far.

The body had collapsed against the wide trunk of a tree, and I could see the smoke rising from within its body and into the sky. I wondered if it would attract other things. Did anything eat the giant insects out here?

I felt a hand wrap around mine and looked down to see Dameon as he mouthed dramatically, "ARE YOU OKAY?"

I nodded. The ringing in my ears was pulsing now with my heartbeat, and even though Bisa was trying to peel the back of my dress off, I pulled my knees to my chest as the adrenaline high slowly wore off.

Marcus rushed to his sister's side, clinging to her leg while Dameon wrapped one of his arms around mine with a look of concern that seemed far too old for his young face. I untangled my arm, and reached out and put an arm around him, hugging him close. He was a good kid, he always had been, and in that moment I was especially glad he was alive and with me. Dameon was always the sensitive one, the one who worried for everyone else, the one people tended to protect more than the others, but still he was wise for his years. It really was no wonder Darik had trusted him over me earlier.

I ruffled his hair and he grinned with what appeared to be a laugh. I thought it looked forced, the sort of teasing that came at the absolute wrong time that only siblings can provide.

By now, the pulsing and ringing in my ears had dwindled down to a low drone and sound slowly started coming back to me. The crackle of the fire was a constant, but I also heard Bisa speaking with Marcus.

"...only had my thread, maybe I could make something more for her. We don't even have any water to wash it with."

"What about this?" Marcus asked reaching for something I couldn't quite make out.

"No, that's our waterskin, sweetie. That's for drinking, not cleaning."

I smiled. It was odd, and I wouldn't have expected to want to smile again after that ordeal, but I had survived an attack; we all had. Sure, it was probably ninety percent dumb luck, but I was still pleased.

The woods also seemed fairly peaceful now. The drone of crickets had returned, something I realized I hadn't heard since we started the fire almost an hour ago. Perhaps they were our true warning sign, the normal insects. And perhaps the wail of the millipede would chase off anything else that might want us for a late supper.

"The fabric is going to dry hard, I imagine," Bisa said with annoyance, her eyes meeting mine. "But it will dry. I'd say we should hang it up by the fire, but I don't think you're wearing anything under this, sugar."

"Just my underpants," I flirted with a smile.

"Then sit with your back to the fire and it should dry faster. I'm sorry."

I turned around, noting how sensitive my back was to the heat. "I think I got burned a little."

"You were right under it when it caught on fire," Dameon said. "I thought for a minute you had caught on fire, too." He squeezed my hand; my fingers throbbed with the force he used, but I didn't let go.

It dawned on me that I was Dameon's only family now. Mother and Father were both dead. Neither of us would probably see Darik again; either he would die somewhere out here or Broskow would kill him.

I laid down on my side and Dameon laid down with me, refusing to leave me. I smiled, keeping my back to the fire despite the pain from the heat. "Bisa, can you—"

"Take first watch?" she finished with a smile. "Sure, sugar. Get some rest. Dameon and I can watch tonight, can't we?"

I felt Dameon nod in my arms.

"But he's only a kid," I said, staring at her. She gave a resigned shrug.

Dameon craned his neck around to look at me over his shoulder. "Just because I'm a kid doesn't mean I can't help. You two need to sleep, too."

I let the tears fall and laid my head down on my arm.

A day full of adrenaline and emotions, of terror and relief, of loss and pain, was finally done with. Tomorrow it would begin again.

~

I AWOKE to the feel of a cold hand on my cheek. I jerked awake, barely holding back a cry from my lips as my instincts kicked in. But it was only Dameon looking down at me, his face shadowy in the early morning light. I had to unstick my eyelids when I opened them again - the corners were crusty and painful.

I looked around and saw the fire was far lower than it had been last night, but it was still lit. As I shifted to look around further, the skin of my back felt like rawhide, and every pull and tug of my muscles made the dull ache hurt worse.

"Everything okay?" I whispered. He nodded and offered a hand to help me up. My right arm was asleep from using it as a pillow all night, and my joints all complained about my sleeping on the ground, but I got to my feet all the same.

The first thing I noticed was the smell. When it was trying to attack me last night, the giant millipede didn't have a smell that I could recall, but now that it was dead and its foul gray innards were seeping into the forest floor, the tang of it made me cough. I held the back of my hand to my nose and looked at Dameon. He was busy waking the others.

The woods were filled with the sound of birds. They

sang all around us and I was amazed that they hadn't woken me from my sleep. Then again, I was dead tired and Bisa looked about as exhausted as I felt. She yawned as she got to her feet.

"Do we have everyone?" she asked, her eyes red and swollen. I thought of her keeping the first watch. Had she volunteered just so she could have a good quiet cry for a few hours while we all slept? I reached out and took her hand and she gave me a warm smile despite everything. Dameon tried to wake up Marcus, but the boy just rolled over with an angry huff.

Bisa picked him up and held him in her arms. "You'll have to lead us for a bit," she whispered to me. "This boy loves his sleep."

I smiled and then felt something get pushed into my hand. I looked to see Dameon was passing out slices of jerky to each of us. He went back to fetch the waterskin as well. "Keeping us all well fed, Dameon?"

He gave me a serious nod and passed the water around. "We have enough to last us at least a week, but water is more limited. It would be good if we could find a stream somewhere."

I nodded, realizing that I hadn't the slightest clue where any body of water was out here. There was a river that went along the south side of Carra, but we had surely ventured far from that by this point. If I was smarter, I would have directed us there instead of straight into the woods, with no knowledge of how to get to the Mother of the Grays or whether she would kill us on the spot or not.

Despite our lucky first night in the woods, it had been far too close for comfort. If every night was that risky, I wasn't sure we would last another day, let alone a full week.

Pushing those doubts aside, I reached into a nearby sack and pulled out a torch to light it on the dwindling fire. "Did you all have any trouble last night?"

"I saw a lot of movement," Dameon said. The ease with which he said it made me almost drop my torch into the fire. "I think there were two spiders, but mostly there were Gray People."

"Here? Why didn't you wake us?" I asked, unable to keep the fear from my voice.

He shrugged. "None of them approached, but they watched us. Some were in the trees; most of them were on the ground. They didn't come near, though, and neither did the bugs," he shuffled his feet. "So I didn't see a reason to wake anyone."

I glanced toward Bisa, but she was struggling with Marcus, who was awake enough to want jerky but not awake enough to stand on his own. Had she seen anything? Why did the Gray People just watch us? What were they waiting for?

Despite the lit torch in my hand, my arms were covered in goose flesh. I kicked out the fire and felt a touch of fear grip my heart as the gray haze of morning descended upon us.

I turned to Bisa, feeling agitated with myself and frustrated with Marcus for wanting to be babied. "Are you two ready?"

There was a clip in my voice and both Marcus and Bisa turned to look at me, all the humor draining from their features. She put Marcus on the ground and gave him a piece of jerky. At least the boy didn't fight her then.

They took hands and Bisa said, "We're ready, sugar. Are you okay?"

I nodded and turned to pick up my pack, but Dameon had already shouldered it. We locked eyes. "If you end up getting into a fight again, I don't want our food supplies to catch on fire."

With a trembling hand, I patted his shoulder. He stayed in the front with me as we passed the hulking body of the dead millipede.

We walked deeper into the woods, away from our brief place of safety.

CHAPTER II
MAMA

After about an hour, the trees seemed to grow closer together and the brambles that we had been dealing with disappeared. The bedding of dead leaves under our feet gave with every step, as though we were walking on cushions. It was a testament to the age of this part of the forest.

The canopy overhead blocked out most of the sky and our daylight, so that the only light we had, besides the torch, was gray and dim.

If there was any forest that could go on forever, it had to be this one. It felt like we could walk for hours and see the same trees growing in the same patterns. The birds that we heard back at the clearing were silent.

I was gripping the torch so tightly my fingertips were white. I tried to look everywhere at once, not wanting to risk the chance of missing something, of not seeing some kind of danger approach.

Then, I heard Marcus' squeaky voice behind me say, "Mama?" It was so quiet and his voice so high-pitched that it made me jump. I spun around to him with wide eyes and glanced toward Bisa.

Both of them were looking off to the side and I followed their gaze. Walking towards us was a woman dressed in worn rags of cream and brown. She had a limp and was barefoot. I tried to see her face, but it was wrapped in a scarf that had almost fallen to pieces.

Bisa was gaping at the woman, her face a mask of horror. "What is she doing here?" she asked in a high-pitched whisper that could have been a muffled scream.

Marcus was pulling away from her, eager to go see his mother, and grinning from ear to ear. I put myself in front of them both, pushing them and Dameon behind me as the woman picked up her pace. She looked like some dead banshee lumbering toward us.

If this was their mother, then she had diminished even more than when Bisa and I rescued Marcus from her house. From where I stood, I could see the dirt and blood caked to her toes. Then there was the question of how she even got this far out. Her home had been turned into a spider's nest. This wasn't right at all.

She came to a stop only a couple of feet away from us. "Oh," her voice stopped then cracked as though she hadn't spoke in days. "My babies, I'm so happy to see you!"

She clutched the scarf to her face, and I could see her eyes darting back and forth between them. Her fingers were bloody and her hands dirty in the gray light. Why would she suddenly be interested in seeing her children? She could have gone to see them every day before, but she preferred to stay holed up in her home and shroud herself in darkness.

She dropped to her knees with such force that I was afraid she had broken something and beckoned with one claw-like hand. Marcus broke free of Bisa's grip and ran past me.

"Marcus, don't!" Dameon cried and the emotion in his voice broke my heart.

The woman wrapped him in her arms, which were more bone than anything else. Now that I looked at her, she looked like she had been starving for some time. I thought about the supplies in our bags, about what hunger could do to a person.

Bisa whimpered.

"Marcus, come here," I demanded, mimicking my father as best as I could.

The boy turned and looked at us, but the woman was busy removing the scarf from around her face. "Hold on, baby, hold on. Let Mama see you."

He stood still and waited patiently beside her. He hadn't changed that much from the well-trained boy he had been when he still lived with her. When she pulled the scarf back, though, everyone gasped and even Marcus took a few steps back. Her eyes were clear, and her face was probably the cleanest part of her body, except for the wounds. Down her cheeks were long, dark trails of blood. They were caked on top of each other, as though they had been left to dry before being reopened again and again.

"Mama, what happened to you?" Marcus asked, reaching out to touch one of the wounds.

"Marcus, don't touch her!" Bisa nearly shrieked and ran forward to grab him.

"What happened to you, Mrs. Figg?" I asked.

Zola Figg had once been a normal woman. Upon marrying her husband, she had joined him in tending the orchards like his family had done for generations before. But when he died, everything changed.

The woman became a hoarder and would only come out of her house at night. She was eccentric to the point of giving Marcus an unhealthy lifestyle; but even at her worst, she was nowhere near as disturbing as the almost inhuman being crouched before us.

I remembered giving her papers explaining how her son would be re-homed with her daughter, and the woman didn't shed a single tear – she'd understood the reason. She was unsociable and most certainly a hermit, but never like this.

"What happened to you, Mrs. Figg?" I repeated when she didn't respond.

She ran her bony fingers through her hair anxiously as she climbed to her feet. "Oh, I met a wonderful man. He saved my life."

"What?"

"I was asleep when I heard the screams outside, and I

peeked out to investigate. Monsters roamed everywhere. I knew something terrible had happened, but I wasn't about to leave my home. I locked up my doors and curled up in a corner to wait it out. I must have fallen back to sleep because when I woke, there was an enormous spider trying to make its way inside. I screamed and begged the old gods, the Grays, anything that would listen to help me. That's when he showed up." She hugged herself tightly and a smile spread over her lips. "He showed me what it was like to truly live."

Who was she even talking about? Who would be able to save her from one of those giant spiders on his own? The small one I had seen took Pearl out in a matter of minutes.

That's when the Gray Person jumped down from a nearby tree, landing with barely a sound on the cushioned ground. I jumped back, holding the torch up to protect us. His black, empty sockets looked through all of us. He easily towered over me and his grayish-white skin seemed to gleam even here in the dim light.

He put a hand on Zola's shoulder and forcefully pulled her back to stand beside him. She nearly stumbled.

"Darling," she said, "These are my children." She draped her bony fingers along his shoulder and chest.

A cracked smile spread across his face and I gripped the torch tighter. "You're her offspring?"

"We are, yes," Bisa said, then indicated myself and Dameon. "These are my friends."

"We're on a mission to find your Mother," I mentioned. "We need to speak with her."

His empty eyes went wide at that. "*You* want to speak with Mother? What business have you with her?"

I swallowed down the dry patch in my throat. "As a member of the Priest family, I want to negotiate on the future of Carra."

This seemed to greatly amuse him, and he stepped forward to study us. He smelled of dried leaves and damp, decaying logs. "You don't know where you're going, do you, little humans?"

I felt goose flesh on my arms again. "We need a guide."

He smirked.

Behind him, Zola had wrapped her arms around his arm, pushing her body up against his. She adored him, and I couldn't fathom why. Was it because he had saved her life? Did he have her under some sort of spell?

"I will take you to her, but I require food in return. My supply is almost gone."

I glanced to Zola, understanding what he was obviously getting out of their relationship. I didn't know if it went farther than that, and I honestly didn't want to know. She kissed his arm.

"You don't need more than me," Zola said, playfully hitting his arm after placing one last kiss. "I'm all you need."

The Gray Person sighed. "Excuse me, but I've all but lost my patience with this one."

He turned to Zola and she grinned so widely she looked like a skeleton. Then the air seemed to shift. He looked deep into her eyes and I could feel the energy spark between them. Zola was laughing at first, but then the wounds near the creases around her eyes opened up again, and blood flowed down the worn trails along her cheeks.

Her laughter turned to sobs and her entire body started to shrivel in on itself - even more blood flowed.

"No," Bisa whispered next to me.

Zola's eyes rolled up and she screamed, a ragged sound that seemed to echo among the trees. The air was electric, and the Gray Person seemed to become even more luminescent. Finally, Zola fell to her knees, still unable to look away from him. Blood trailed from the corner of her mouth and dripped from her ears onto the remains of her scarf.

"Why...?" she whimpered.

"You bore me," he said simply. "And your energy is quite mad. Goodbye." He reached down and wrapped one of his huge hands around her skull and gave it a quick twist, like turning a knob. There was a sharp snap, and as he released her she fell to the ground in a heap.

"Now," he said, turning back to us, "you need an audience with Mother?"

I DIDN'T RESPOND. My eyes were transfixed on Zola Figg. Her legs were still twitching despite the fact that he had twisted her neck as easily as tearing a twig off a tree. My body felt icy cold and I couldn't move. All I could do was stare as the twitching slowed.

Bisa took a tentative step toward her, covering her mouth with both hands. "Mama?" Her voice sounded like a child's.

I heard the high-pitched squeaks from Marcus again; each breath sounded like tiny screams. Dameon's fingers dug into my arm so hard that it hurt.

Suddenly Bisa fell to her knees beside her mother. Zola's body finally stopped twitching, and Bisa reached out to her, stroking her cheek as though not entirely convinced it was real, or that this was the woman who raised her.

Soon her wails echoed throughout the ancient forest. The trees towered over us in silent indifference.

I knew what she felt. I knew the pain that made her cry out, but I couldn't feel it. I was numb.

It was like my head was attached to a string and floated above me. It was another body, another victim, another person that the Gray People had killed without care and without remorse.

I looked into its empty black sockets with as much hatred as I could muster. I thought of Mother and Father, the old woman with the watery eyes, and now Bisa's mother. I thought of my brother and Broskow, and even Broskow's son. An idea sprung up so dark and so disturbing that I almost wondered if it was truly mine.

"I'll be your supply," I said, walking towards it and

ignoring Dameon's pull on my arm. "You can feed on me."

To my surprise, the Gray Person took a few steps back. His smile, which had been so confident before, faltered into a frown that cast shadows on its face like wet timber. "No," it hissed. "Not you."

"Why not?" I demanded, my voice rising. "Suddenly you're picky now? Why the sudden change?"

He was backing off quickly, no longer trying to hide his unease, but I kept my furious gaze steady. I reached out, grabbed him by his arm, and pushed him as hard as I could against a tree trunk that was as wide around as my arms would reach. I thought he would be difficult to move, but he was incredibly light.

He slammed into the tree and bits of gray matter snapped and shattered off behind his skull. He slumped down, now at eye level with me. He looked dazed, and I was about to do it again when I felt Dameon beside me.

"Don't do it," he whispered, pulling at the pieces of my gown. "Please don't."

A part of me was angry with him. I could maybe kill one of the Grays, so why was he stopping me? Why shouldn't I try while it was helpless and scared? But another part of me, the big sister in me, understood. Dameon still had his wits about him. Dameon kept a cool head in the face of adversity and understood that killing it might bring about consequences. I might be able to take down one, his words implied, but not a whole swarm of them.

"Yes," the Gray Person hissed. "There would be consequences."

I slapped it across the face and his head flung to the side. I could see the cracking on the back of its head more clearly now. They were far frailer than we had always been taught.

It turned back around to look at me, and I felt the shift in my brain. I could feel it frantically reading my thoughts, like a shadow falling over my shoulder. It was trying to figure out what I was thinking, to predict what I would do next. If I concentrated, I could feel its fear; it tasted coppery, like blood in the back of my mouth.

It's the anger, I realized as I felt its frightened thoughts jumping around like the fluttering of a trapped moth. The anger makes them weaker. I felt the truth in my realization through his mind. I looked away from his gaze, and put my torch near him, close enough that it was mere inches away from his chest. His gray skin singed like a piece of kindling.

"Dahlia, don't," Dameon said behind me, but I ignored him.

"Don't," the Gray Person whispered in that same terrified voice and I realized he was staring at my little brother. He was trying to feed off Dameon's fear while he stood right in front of me.

I slapped him again and held its jaw in place, putting the torch close to his nose this time. He tried to push my arm away and clawed at me with his taloned fingers, but I didn't let go. I had felt brambles that were worse.

"How dare you. I ought to kill you right now." I

watched his face start to darken like wood about to catch fire.

"Stop!" he cried. There was pure emotion in his voice this time, not some false feeling that he was stealing. I pulled the torch back just an inch.

"You will lead us to your Mother, and you will feed off of no one, do you understand?"

He nodded.

"If we don't make it, then you don't either. I'll light you up like this torch."

He stared into the flames, his black eye sockets empty and cavernous. "Alright," he said. "I will take you. Just please - *don't*."

I pushed his head harder against the tree. "Don't anger me again, and I won't have to." With a snarl that I have never made in my life, I finally let go and he fell to the ground, gasping and trembling. I stepped back and felt Bisa wrap her hand around my arm, pulling me toward her. "What?" I asked, not turning toward her.

"Just...be still," she whispered as she wrapped her arms around me. She squeezed me tightly and that's when I noticed that the torch in my hand was shaking. My entire body was shaking, and I suddenly felt cold despite the heat from the torch.

Would I have really killed him? I wanted to, but wanting and doing are entirely different. I tried to calm down, to let the hatred pour out of me. I looked to Dameon and Marcus, who both looked terrified - not of the Gray Person, but of me.

I had turned into Broskow, I realized. I was no better

than him. But this wasn't someone I knew; this was a creature, not a person. It had killed Zola right in front of them. Surely that counted for something.

"You saw what it did to your mother," I said, weakly trying to defend my actions.

"I've never seen you so angry before," Dameon whispered.

Bisa released me and rubbed my arm. "I think I've seen enough death, sugar."

I nodded, taking a deep breath to calm myself.

The Gray Person stood, its face a mask of disgust that had been darkened by the torch's flame. It turned in the direction Zola had come from. "Mother's woods are this way, humans."

I nodded and took Bisa's hand in mine. She looked as though she had aged five years in the span of a few minutes when she turned to her mother's distorted body behind us and stared.

"Should we bury her first?" I asked.

"No, there's no point." She bent down and kissed her mother's forehead. "Goodbye, Mama. I'm sorry."

I could hear Marcus' squeaking breaths again and went over to him and Dameon. I gave my brother the torch and pulled both of them close on either side of me. "Walk close to me, okay? I don't want either one of you out of my sight." I rubbed Marcus's back with my fingertips, feeling his shoulder blades buckle with every breath he took. "You're going to be okay, Marcus."

He wiped a tear from his cheek and nodded. "I'm trying."

I squeezed his shoulder and followed the Gray Person's lead. Bisa stepped up to walk beside her brother so that each of us had a hand on him.

We were all trying to be okay, but I wasn't sure if any of us would be again.

CHAPTER 12
SCORCH A NEW PATH

I had never seen woods like these before. They looked nothing like the ancient trees we had seen earlier, or the brambles that we cut through at the beginning of our journey.

The trees bulged out of the ground like bulbs that lived on the surface of the earth and shot numerous thin trunks into the sky. The leaves exploded at the tips in a mixture of greens and browns, making it look like an enormous aboveground onion. The ground here was also very dry. Some places were so cracked that it looked like broken pottery.

"What is this place?" Dameon asked, his voice a whisper at my side.

"I don't know," I said, not sure what else I could add. I knew my brother was looking for reassurance, but at this point I was just as confused as he was.

Bisa came to a stop beside one of the trees and just

stared at its bulb. "Dahlia," she gasped suddenly. "What is this?"

From our side the tree looked normal, so Dameon and I shared a glance before walking around to her side to check out the enormous cyst that grew on it. It was oval-shaped and about twice the size of a person, made of completely different wood than that of the tree.

Marcus picked up a stick and poked at it. I should have stopped him, but instead I stood there in rapt fascination as he pressed it against the thin wood that had a foul smell. It left a deep impression, but then bounced back into place when he pulled the stick away.

Then a hand pushed back from the inside in that same spot.

Dameon gasped and ran to my side; Bisa grabbed my arm and pulled me backwards.

"Is there someone inside?" Marcus asked, his eyes widening as Dameon reached out and pulled him further away, too.

The thing inside the cyst shifted around, and I could see its form better. It was far larger than a human, and where its face ought to have been it looked like a bare skull.

I turned to the Gray Person and asked, "What is that?"

He was leaning against one of the trees, watching us with a disturbing smile on his lips. "You are jumpy creatures, aren't you?"

He had barely spoken a word the entire way here

except when there was precarious footing, and suddenly he was back to being arrogant again.

I held the torch up with a glare, but he held his palms out to me. "I was merely making an observation. There's no need for violence."

"I asked you a question," I said.

Smiling again, he knelt down beside the cyst and put his arms around it, leaning the side of his face against the soft wooden exterior. "This is what you would call a baby. He'll be born very soon, I imagine."

All around us were these trees with pustules attached, some moving, others not. There were a few that looked like they had burst, and the hard edges remained, exposing the blackened wood where the *baby* had been. There had to be dozens of them.

"So many," I whispered.

The Gray Person laughed. "Of course. That's really not a surprise after the Great Feast."

I stared at him for a moment and considered the number of Gray People I saw at the Ritual. So many of them had eaten their fill there, and yet he had chosen to go save Zola Figg and steal into the woods, far away from the others of his kind. Why did he choose to leave them when they all worked together?

"You're not like the others, are you?"

His smile faded for a brief moment before returning. "No, I'm not. I'm far more intelligent."

"So why don't you live here with the babies and your Mother?"

"My kind does what it will. We are not tethered to a society like you; we move where we want."

I considered the Gray Person from my dreams, the woman who crawled into my room as a child. Had she fed on me? Was that why I could never remember what happened after that? Was she not supposed to, or did they even care?

But then I remembered how the Gray People patrolled Carra on a regular basis, making sure nothing slipped past the Boundary Line.

"That's a lie though, isn't it? You all had to protect Carra. You had patrols. You also planted the dandelions around the edge and planted more at Broskow's shop after the Ritual failed. You have roles the same as we do."

He glared at me. "It's not the same at all. Your kind are disgusting and dirty, with bodies made of little more than flesh and flimsy bones. You couldn't survive anywhere on your own."

"What's your name?" Dameon asked suddenly.

The Gray Person looked at him as though the question was an insult.

"What do you call yourself?"

He glanced at me, and more specifically at my torch, before answering. "I am He Who Wanders." He looked away. "Come, the daylight is fading, and we should be closer before nightfall if you fragile creatures are to survive the night."

So, he's an outcast, I thought to myself. *Or in exile.* That had to be why he was out there by himself, not with others of his kind. Perhaps his desire to steal humans from their homes was the reason for that.

Eventually we left the birthing trees behind, but the foul smell of them lingered far longer. When the air finally cleared, the woods were so dark that we had to light a second torch, leaving us halfway through our supply at this point, and I was nervous. If we lost our access to fire, the Gray Person would surely kill all of us.

"We ought to camp," Bisa said after Marcus tripped over a root and nearly fell.

I turned to the Gray Person. "Is this a good place?"

He shrugged. "No place is a good place, but I suppose this will do."

We put our bags down and decided that we would go in pairs to fetch wood for the fire, always leaving one adult behind to make sure the Gray Person didn't try anything.

Meanwhile, he climbed into a tree and sat on a long branch to watch us work. He seemed curious about how we stacked the wood, how we laid out the stones, and when we finally got it to light and encouraged the flames higher and higher, he nearly fell from his tree in surprise.

"You're so fragile you must master dangerous arts in order to exist," he observed. "How long must your kind sleep anyway?"

I glanced up to his gray face, shifting with the flicking flames. "A number of hours. I suppose you don't have to?"

He smiled. "We are of the earth and sky, we are the leaf and grass. We are beyond the reach of sleep."

"I'll take that as a no." Whatever the Gray People were, they certainly were not conversationalists.

Dameon handed out double helpings of jerky and dried fruit since we hadn't had the chance to stop for lunch all day. It was strange, eating and trying to relax with our watcher in the tree, tracking our every move like a starving cat. He must have lived with Zola for days, so I had thought he would at least have a basic understanding of how we ate food. Though, I supposed they did eat with their minds instead of their mouths.

I pushed away the memory of him trying to feed off of Dameon when I had him pinned earlier. There was no telling if he would stay put while we slept. He had no real reason to, and part of me kind of wished he would leave even though it meant we would be lost here.

He looked like a ghostly specter when the firelight hit his gray skin just right.

"Will it be safe for us to sleep with you here?" I asked. "Or are you going to kill us as soon as we nod off?"

"I could, of course," he said with a smile. "But I won't. What was it you said? You would light me up like a torch if you didn't make it to Mother? So I suppose my course is clear."

I cringed. I don't know what I had been thinking threatening him like that. The anger had been so easy to tap into earlier, but now it felt like a coal that had lost its spark. I turned to Bisa, "I'll take first watch tonight."

"If you say so," she said. Normally she might insist otherwise, but I could see the exhaustion in her face, her still puffy eyes.

"I am curious," the Gray Person continued as though I was still talking to him. "I want to see what Mother does with you lot. I want to see what she says when I bring her four little lost strays from the forest."

Ignoring him would hopefully make him be quiet, so I didn't acknowledge him. I wasn't curious what Mother would say. All I wanted for us was freedom, but that seemed incredibly unlikely now. The most I could hope for was that she would order the Gray People not to hunt us, but I had little to barter.

My conviction at the beginning of this journey that Mother didn't want to lose us was quickly waning, and the more time we spent in the woods, the more I questioned the intelligence of my decision.

I cuddled up beside Bisa and started to wrap my arm around her only to have her push it away and lay down in my lap to stare into the firelight. Her sadness was palpable, and I could feel her tears hitting my leg. I dragged my fingers through her hair, massaging her shoulder and scalp, trying my best to help, but knowing nothing I did would fix it.

Nothing would bridge the gap that had existed for so long between her and her mother, and nothing would bring Zola back. She had lost her mind long ago, but that certainly wasn't the fate she deserved. With enough time and proper care, she might have eventually come around to be a decent mother to her children again. Now they would never know either way.

Eventually, Bisa's breathing slowed and her chest

rose and fell rhythmically. I gently shifted her over to her bedroll and covered her up.

"So you don't sleep then?" The Gray Person at least had the decency to talk in a whisper, but it was clear he was intent on having a conversation regardless of how little I wanted to.

"No, I don't think so, not tonight. Not with you here."

He smiled. "Am I a distraction?"

I lit a torch from the bonfire and his smile disappeared. The smoke filled my nostrils and almost got rid of the horrible smell of the birthing trees that lingered long after we'd actually seen them. "I wouldn't say a distraction as much as a liability. You're dangerous and untrustworthy, and I won't let you harm us tonight."

He cocked his head to one side, and the angles of his face were thrown into sharper relief by the firelight. "So you're protecting them from me? Or from others of my kind?"

"Both."

Unlike the trees we camped in earlier, this area had tree trunks that spread out to where the firelight made a ring around us, but beyond it I had no idea what watched us. At least in the dense foliage our enemies had to move around obstacles to reach us. Here they would have almost a clear path. We were like an island of light surrounded by dark ocean waters.

The Gray Person stared at me with an intensity that made my skin crawl. He reminded me of the praying mantis and how it sat in wait for its prey to be foolish enough to approach it.

"A praying mantis, such an odd name."

I turned away, frustrated that he had been reading my thoughts. "It's just a bug."

He smiled, and it was the only part of his face that moved. "A mantis is just a bug. A *praying* mantis, however, is very different. Tell me, are you a daughter of the Priest family?"

It was strange to hear the way he pronounced the syllables out of my last name as though through a grimace. I wasn't sure if I ought to answer truthfully or not, but part of me was so tired and exhausted that I just didn't care anymore. "Yes."

He cocked his head to the side again. "Do you know where that name came from?"

"It's just a name. It's been passed down within my family for generations, like any other."

"No, it's not just a name. Any more than a bug is just a bug - as you should well know by now."

I stepped toward him, gripping the torch.

"Are you threatening me?"

"Not at all, simply attempting to educate in whatever small way I can. Your kind forget things so quickly it's almost incredible that you are able to build and harvest and hide at all. Information gets lost and forgotten, like a fallen tree that has been hollowed out and eaten from within. It may look healthy on the outside, but with one step, it can be crushed."

I was tired of listening to his insults. He was gloating now, trying to find a way under my skin. I stepped forward with the intent of smoldering his skin like I had his face before, but he held up his hands, black-tipped fingernails gleaming against the light.

"Priest. Does that name have no meaning? Your people kept faith, they worshipped gods, they performed rituals for sanctity and purity. Over time that faith was lost. Over time it spoiled like fruit."

I stared at him. The flame of my torch wasn't quite close enough to scorch his palms, but I was too mentally exhausted to threaten him more than that. "My...people?"

"Yes, you were born from a family of believers. At first, Carra was leaderless and chaotic. It was your family's faith that led them to create the arrangement with us. They believed strongly enough to convince the others in Carra to join them. They were healers and helpers, leaders even. Some of them were charlatans and deceivers, especially towards the end of your religion, but for as long as it existed, your family was there to lead it. Now you plan to begin a new faith, scorch a new path."

I was shaking; there was no way I could hide it with the way the torch wavered. All I could do was stare at this creature and try to process its words. Was it speaking the truth or feeding me lies to save itself?

"I want to see it," he admitted with a hiss. "I want to see you overthrow Mother and her children. I want to forge a new arrangement with your kind. I'm tired of being He Who Wanders. I want to be more."

I shook my head. "No, we don't want any more to do

with your kind. We don't want any more slaughter or ridiculous rules."

"I would not require something so base. My rules would be fair and straightforward. My kind can live in conjunction with yours like we used to do, if we wish."

"Is that why you killed Bisa and Marcus's mother?" The determination in my voice surprised me. I felt the same anger from that morning building up inside, and I wasn't sure if I could hold it back this time.

He waved a clawed hand absently. "That woman was broken long before I reached her. I merely hurried her to her end." The Gray Person looked away from my scowl. "Consider my offer, daughter of the Priests. You show more determination than any other human I've encountered, yet you will not survive in this forest for a week. Why do you think you could live forever on your own without protection from the creatures that live alongside you? The world has changed, and your kind needs help if you wish to truly live."

I didn't know what to say, but I lowered the torch at his words. He was right that we depended on him. At the very least, we needed his help to reach Mother, to demand our freedom, but what then?

We wouldn't survive on our own. That was made clear to me the first night that we slept beyond the Boundary Line of Carra. In fact, I was lucky to have convinced this Gray Person to work with us, but the more he spoke, the more I began to doubt that partnership.

"I will ensure the safety of you and your friends, but I

request an answer come morning. Sleep, or you will be useless against Mother."

I gave a slow nod, and with a flash he leaped into an adjacent tree and out of sight. I watched the leaves on the branch tremble briefly before going still. The Gray People were always quiet and quick, but I hadn't realized they knew so much about us. They knew more about us than we did, and He Who Wanders was far more talkative than any other I had met.

In the darkness, outside of our rim of light, I heard a screech cut off as quickly as it started, and a familiar pungent scent hit my nostrils. The Gray Person saved us from a bug, possibly a millipede like the one we faced the other night. Had it been waiting for me to fall asleep, or perhaps for the fire to die down?

I shuddered but felt an odd sense of relief at knowing that he was out there hunting on our behalf. The weariness of the day descended upon me, and like a child following a parent's orders, I curled up behind Bisa and wrapped an arm around her waist. In her sleep, I felt her grab my arm before she resumed her light snores.

I thought about my ancestors, the Priests with their gods and religion to keep them safe. I thought of them putting together the Gully and agreeing to the rules of The Seeking. Were they drawn to the significance of that day? Did they congratulate themselves for keeping their children safe, even if it meant dooming their relatives centuries later?

I thought of the Gray Person's offer and turned it around in my mind. If I was to make a true pact with him, I needed to make sure I'd considered everyone it would eventually affect. I didn't have to worry about just the four of us, but for generations down the road, assuming we all lived that long.

I WOKE JUST in time to catch myself from falling face-first into the dirt. I vaguely heard Bisa's yelp of surprise, but I did hear the urgency in her voice as she shook my shoulder.

"Dahlia, wake up! You fell asleep! The boys look okay, but I don't see any sign of the Gray Person."

I pushed myself up, willing the adrenaline rush away. "It's fine," I muttered. "The Gray Person is guarding us."

That was when she grabbed my arm and pulled me into a seated position. Her voice was somewhere between a hiss and a snarl, and it jolted me fully awake. "Since when do we rely on him to protect us? I thought that was the whole reason why we didn't want to leave him alone with the kids last night? You saw what he did to Mama yesterday, and now you're just going to sleep with full faith that he won't kill us in the night? What is going on?"

I pushed her hand away and rubbed at my still blanched arm. "He made me an offer."

Her glare softened to pure confusion.

"He gave me the night to think about it."

"I counted at least three dead bugs last night," Dameon said, his voice calm and focused as he walked around the dying fire. He sipped gingerly from the waterskin.

"How is Marcus?" I asked.

"He's asleep still. I woke up when I realized it was daytime and got Bisa up."

I took a deep breath and then gave a shortened account of our discussion last night. These two were the closest I had to advisers. When I had been a prosecutor for Carra, I had a whole team who had decades of experience to advise me on how to proceed on different cases. My father had handpicked them to work with me and to consult with me on the best options.

Now I had my girlfriend, who didn't trust my judgment, and my little brother, who seemed like he might never smile again. As much as I hated putting this on their shoulders, I knew I alone couldn't take on this task. Sure enough, they peppered me with dozens of questions.

"Are there other Gray People he's working with?"

"Why does he want to overthrow their Mother?"

"What does he want in return?"

"Why us?"

I certainly didn't have answers for everything, but perhaps the most important question came from Dameon. "What happens if we refuse?"

That stumped all of us. The options didn't look good, and it certainly didn't seem like we would make it to Mother without his help.

"This was all a terrible idea," I said. "I shouldn't have dragged you all with me on this."

Bisa rubbed my back. "Don't get discouraged. You didn't know how bad it was out here. None of us did, sugar. That was the whole point of the Boundary Line, wasn't it? If we never left Carra, how would we ever build the courage to leave?"

Between the three of us, a plan started to form. It wasn't surrounded in superstition or death-defying rituals, but it did permit an open alliance between us and the Gray People. If we wanted to roam the woods, they would accompany us. If they wanted food, we would willingly open our minds to them, on the condition that no one was to be killed or their minds damaged. Slowly, we hashed out something that actually seemed doable and humane for both sides.

By the time we were done, the sun had climbed partway up the trees, the bonfire had all but died out, and Marcus was munching on some dried fruit in Bisa's lap. I got to my feet and stretched.

I looked up to the familiar branch, expecting the Gray Person to be crouched there, watching and waiting, but there was nothing. "He Who Wanders?" I called out, but all I heard was the chirping of birds and the few remaining crackles of the bonfire.

"Did the bugs get him?" Dameon asked.

"More like his own kind," Bisa said.

I heard Bisa gasp and spun around just in time to see him fall effortlessly from the trees up above. Judging by how hard he hit the ground, he had to have been a long way up, but he got to his feet with a smile.

"I assure you, it was neither," he said.

It was difficult to keep my anger in check. "Did you hear everything?"

He cocked his head to the side. "I heard what I needed. Your conditions sound acceptable for the most part, but I didn't want to interrupt the intensity of your planning to tell you otherwise."

"So there's something you disagree with?" I asked, standing as tall as I could, even though I barely reached his shoulder. This close to him, he smelled like burned wood, but with a powerful tang like that of a sprig of spruce tree on fire. I could still see the discoloration on his face from where I'd threatened him with the flame.

"Your kind breeds like rabbits when left to your own devices. I'm but one and given time, I'll be unable to keep my end of the promise without aid."

Bisa laughed for the first time since her mother died. "I don't think you'll have to worry about that with us." She pointed to herself and to me. "Two women together aren't going to breed anything but trouble."

He looked annoyed. "I need sustained nourishment. You four alone won't sate my hunger."

"That's going to be a problem then," Bisa said, folding her arms. "Cause you and you friends have killed off anyone else we might have brought with us."

He seemed to consider this for a moment before agreeing. "I suppose that is true. Then we will simply have to steal from the other flocks." He turned and headed deeper into the forest. "Come, we must make a path to Mother before nightfall. She will not approve of humans sleeping so close to her den."

Dameon kicked the bonfire out, then took my hand. "What does he mean by other flocks?"

I gave a heavy sigh. "I honestly don't know."

"He can't mean flocks of birds, can he?"

"No, but he can mean flocks of people," Bisa said, falling in beside us.

"Other towns?" I turned to her. "You mean they're keeping other towns?"

"Remember what we talked about in Broskow's shop? That's how livestock are kept. Different groups are divided up according to what purpose they serve."

I watched He Who Wanders walk in front of us, his footsteps barely making an impression on the earth. "We're not like sheep though, Bisa. We're dangerous," I said. "We think too much, we're too suspicious. Of course they would split us up. If they hadn't, we would have resisted ages ago."

PART FIVE
MOTHER

CHAPTER 13
THE PIT OF DEAD STONE

The sun was beginning to set when we approached a rocky cliffside. It overlooked an enormous drop, where the tops of ancient trees looked like ants beneath us. Beyond, we could see other cliffs like this one: rocky and foreboding. The wind was powerful here and made my ears hum. My dress, which was hardly anything anymore, whipped around me and goose flesh had broken out all over my exposed skin.

With one arm, I hugged Dameon at my side, a little ball of warmth against me. Bisa had to carry Marcus, who started crying as we got near the cliff. The distance between us and the ground below terrified him, and he refused to let her get too close to it.

"This way," He Who Wanders called, following a crooked path down along the edge of the cliffside. The walkway was narrow and steep, and more than once, Dameon fell. Bisa took her time, even though Marcus was crying in her ear. The wind was so strong that it sounded like he was wailing as his voice came and went.

We finally reached an enclosure, and I rubbed my arms, trying to bring warmth back into my limbs.

"It's so cold," I said through chattering teeth.

Bisa nodded and put Marcus down. His cheeks were slick with tears and his face was puffy, but he had stopped crying. He stood beside his sister, gripping her skirt with one hand.

"Do you want me to carry you for a bit?"

"No!" he said as he tried to hide behind her skirts to stay away from me. I couldn't help but smile.

"The stone," Dameon said suddenly. "It's warm." He had moved behind me and I turned to see him dragging his fingertips across the smooth grain that went along-side the walkway. As he tried to grip one of the knobby stones that stuck out of it, two small crevices opened near his hand.

"Ahh!" he cried and backed into me. I stared in horror as the two crevices closed then opened again - then the stone turned. That was when I noticed that it wasn't stone at all, but one of the Gray People camouflaged perfectly with it.

It sat up, and gray dust shifted and puffed around it. The knob Dameon had been messing with was its nose, I realized. It stood and stretched, "Humans...out here?" It looked like a woman. She squatted to the ground and reached out to grab Dameon by the jaw.

Before I realized what was going on, she pulled Dameon towards her, her eyes hungry. "Begging to be my food, child?" Dameon at least knew to avert his eyes, but that wouldn't save him for long.

I cursed myself for not lighting a torch as soon as we found cover. The wind prevented us from carrying one, but that shouldn't have stopped me. I had no weapons that were useful, only my words. Then I remembered when I attacked He Who Wanders after he killed Zola. I remembered what made his claws feel like dull thorns and his strength weaken to that of a child.

I had my words and Dameon had his emotions, and that was all we needed.

"You always were the weakest of us," I told him even though it hurt to say the words. I was terrified for him. It only hurt worse when he looked at me with those big, terrified eyes. "I guess you'll always be the victim, won't you, Dameon? You got beaten up by Broskow just the other day, and you remember what happened to Bisa's mother."

Dameon looked like he wanted to cry as the Gray Person dug her claws into his arm, drawing blood. I was frantic, trying not to let my fear take hold of me as I resisted the urge to run up and attack her myself. If I did that, she could kill him before I'd even reached them.

"You remember Zola, don't you? And what happened afterward?"

Recognition registered in his eyes and the terror narrowed into something hard and cold.

"How dare you!" he shouted at the Gray Person, but his voice cracked and betrayed the fear he still felt.

"Don't be the weak one, Dameon," I said, balling my

fists tight to keep from running forward, my nails digging into my palms. "Prove all of them wrong about you. Just because you're the smallest doesn't mean you're the weakest!"

This time he pushed her back with so much force that she slammed against the stone wall, her head knocking backwards.

"You don't have the right to touch me," Dameon sneered. "Don't you know who I am? I'm the son of Jamel and Ivory Priest." He pushed her again and this time I heard the cracking of her head against the stone. "I'm the youngest of the Exalted Family of Carra!" He shoved her again and this time she crumpled to the ground with a wail.

She held up a hand to stop him from attacking again, but my brother wouldn't stop. All the pent-up frustration and anger had finally let loose. When he kicked at her head, he knocked her chin back and I heard it snap like a broken tree branch. The Gray Person took two deep gasps before collapsing to the ground, as still as the stone she had hidden in.

"Dameon," Marcus whispered, his voice small and frightened. He stepped forward, but Bisa shook her head and held him back.

I waited a few moments before approaching Dameon. I waited for his hands to stop shaking, and for the hatred in his eyes to fade. I waited for my brother to come out of his rage and return to being the boy my mother always worried about the most, the boy who she always made sure had a safe place to stay during each

Seeking.

I wrapped my arms around him and held him tightly, like Bisa had done for me so many times before. He didn't resist me, but his breathing was heavy, if not ragged, and it took a moment for him to hug me back. We stood there in silence for what felt like several minutes before I heard his soft sigh.

"I'm sorry, I didn't mean to do that."

"I know, I know. It's okay. You were scared."

"I was at first, but then once you reminded me, I got so angry. I didn't think I was capable of doing that, even to one of them."

I dragged my fingers through his short, coarse hair, wishing I was the one who was attacked instead of him. He didn't deserve such a weight on his shoulders. He didn't deserve to always be the one targeted. I wanted to be able to shield him from the anger in himself, but I knew that was impossible.

"It's okay. She was going to kill you."

After a few more minutes he finally pulled away and wiped at his eyes.

"Are you ready to move on?" I asked him and he gave me a short nod. He looked younger than he had in days with his puffy, red eyes and trembling lip.

Bisa came to my side like a bird swooping in. She took my hand while still holding Marcus on her opposite hip. "Is he okay? We ought to look at his arm."

"It doesn't look deep; I think we should wait a bit. I feel terrible, though."

She squeezed my hand and leaned closer to whisper

in my ear. "I think you both handled it perfectly. It's encouraging, knowing we have some kind of weapon against them."

"Don't assume it will always work," He Who Wanders commented dryly. He leapt from the outside lip of the cave, moving with surreal ease and landing soundlessly on the stone ground beside us. "Anger will only work for so long. When injured, your kind can't help but be fearful, and that benefits my kind."

Bisa advanced on him, letting go of my hand. "Where were you when Dameon got attacked? Up there hiding?"

"Of course," he said with a grin. "She was looking for something to report back to Mother. The longer before she knows, the better. I could probably escape if she sent her guards to kill us, but you wouldn't be so fortunate." He turned to look at Dameon beside me, who sidled up closer to my side.

"I don't appreciate your threats," I stated and He Who Wanders merely stared at me, his empty eye sockets hinting at no emotion. I felt him sift through my thoughts, probably tasting a bit of my mind, but I didn't push him away. "Don't forget," I said, breaking off the connection and turning toward the path ahead. He shifted slightly and I hoped that it threw him off. "We're your reliable and willing food supply. If you fail to protect us again, I will kill you. Your Mother will know we're coming regardless." I took Dameon's hand. "If you cower again, you won't live to see her. I'm sure I can find another Gray Person eager and willing to work with us for a steady meal."

I started walking down the steep slope and Dameon had to walk at a faster pace to keep up with me, but he didn't try to pull away. He knew I was gambling, and I hoped it was a smart move.

Eventually He Who Wanders fell in step beside me. "Very well, Dahlia of the Priests. I will protect you and your clan as best as I am able. You do entertain me, that is certain. I just hope Mother is in a good mood this eve, or else this will be a short arrangement indeed."

"Better to die trying to escape than go back to living like animals," Dameon said beside me. I squeezed his hand and kept my gaze forward as Bisa moved closer behind me with Marcus in her arms.

We started down the path again as the sun began to dip past the edges of the hills that towered over us.

It felt as though we walked for hours. I could tell that the sun was still up because the sky above us was streaked with orange and red clouds. But down here, in the pit, it may as well have been night. We had already gone through one torch.

The wind that had been so terrible higher up was now little more than an occasional breeze. Down here it was oddly warm, as though the stone had soaked up the heat throughout the day and emanated it back into the air.

There were no trees, no grass: nothing except the smooth gray stone on all sides and the spiraling dirt path always descending. Not even a bramble attempted to crawl out in between the cracks. It was as though nothing was permitted to exist down here. Yet here we were.

When the path finally flattened out, I nearly tripped over my own feet. I stomped as I regained my balance, and the noise echoed around us. I held out the torch and looked around, waiting for something to emerge from the darkness and come toward us, but once the echoes died down, everything fell silent. That was when I realized just how quiet it was.

When we were walking, I had heard our footsteps shuffling along the stone, but now that we all stood still, I realized I couldn't even hear crickets, let alone the owls I always heard at dusk.

"Are you okay?" Bisa asked in a whisper. Only there was no way to talk quietly here.

I had intended to say "fine" in my normal volume, but it came out weaker. It was easier to be angry up there in the daylight, surrounded by living things, than down here in the pit of stone, where the fear was almost palpable.

I turned to He Who Wanders and asked, "Why is it so quiet?"

He looked at me, his face expressionless. "We are accustomed to silence, and we keep it so here."

"How?" Dameon asked, his voice stronger than my own. "How do you keep things from living down here with you?"

He gave an eerie laugh. "Simple, child. We merely

exist. The living avoid us: most do, at least." He gestured with his black-clawed fingers. "Come, we shall reach Mother soon."

"I haven't seen any others since the one that Dameon killed. Where are they?"

"We all felt her death, and I can assume that Mother wishes to see you since she didn't attempt to have you killed again."

"But how does she know we're here?" I asked.

He Who Wanders replied without turning back. "She has eyes everywhere. You grew up in Carra; you should be used to it."

Slowly the little light we still had dwindled, and as rock formations emerged above our heads, I couldn't tell if we were merely entering a narrow section or if we had entered a large cave. Soon the light from the torch only reached so far, and there was no telling what was above us any longer.

I had no idea where we were going or what would be waiting for us, especially since the Mother of the Grays seemed to know we were coming.

It had to have been a good ten minutes before I realized we were being followed. I heard more than our own feet shuffling whenever we walked. I froze and put out a hand, and just for a brief second, I heard something else's footsteps before they came to a stop behind us.

Only they were clearly not shoes hitting the ground, but something softer.

I turned around with my torch and examined the emptiness. I took one step forward, then another.

"You've noticed our guest then," He Who Wanders said with amusement. "Had I not been here, you would be dead."

"Who-what is it?" Bisa asked. She had pushed the two boys behind her and was standing a few paces behind me. "More of your family?"

"Of course not. We are not nearly so noisy." He strode past us and into the darkness. Sweat broke out on my forehead as he disappeared beyond the reaches of the light. More subtle footsteps sounded that I knew were not his. But they were familiar somehow; I just couldn't place them.

Then a leg stepped forward, followed by several more. He Who Wanders returned, this time followed by one of the horrible spider creatures, like the one that had killed Pearl Broskow and the other that had hung bodies up in Zola Figg's home. It was larger than either of them, though, with a body that was at least twice the width of both and hairs that reached as long as my arm. Its long, prehensile neck stretched forward like a snake, bobbing from right to left.

I backed to one side to let it pass by us. Bisa pulled the boys to the opposite direction, and there was such a gap between us that they were almost out of the safety of my torch's firelight.

"Fear not, little Priest clan. She won't harm you as

long as you do not harm her. You are safe in my presence." He grinned. "She is tame, unlike those that were unleashed upon your little town."

The flippancy with which he spoke about our home sparked anger within me, but I pushed it down, knowing this was not the time to lose my temper. I waited until He Who Wanders and the bulbous body of the giant spider had moved past, then ran to the other side of the passage to be with Bisa and the boys.

"She's so big," Marcus whispered.

"She should be bearing her young soon," He Who Wanders said and reached his arms around the snake-like neck to drag his fingers along it; she twitched under his touch. "A large nest, certainly. She is a mother much like my own, keeping our lands safe from intruders." The spider seemed to nuzzle his hand and he smiled.

"From intruders or from escapees?" I asked, trying to hide the fact that every inch of my body was shaking.

He gave me a displeased glance before releasing the spider creature. "Go on then. These are mine, not yours."

She made a noise that was something between a hiss and a series of clicks before she skittered away into the darkness with a speed that made the hairs on the back of my neck stand up. Even after she left the ring of firelight, I could still hear her footsteps and I couldn't move until they faded into silence.

"You tame them," I said, finally able to breathe again.

"We tame many creatures, yes."

I nodded, beginning to understand our place in the

complex, ugly web we were stuck in. I locked eyes with Bisa and saw the fear I felt reflected there.

I think we both knew this wasn't going to end as well as we had hoped.

I KNEW we were reaching the end of our journey when we finally spotted light. As we drew closer, I saw that it was a short distance away from the mouth of the cave we were exiting. The light was actually a small campfire, put together hastily by someone who obviously didn't know what they were doing, but it put off far more light than my pathetic little torch could.

"Ah, she has welcomed you all," He Who Wanders stated as though we all were supposed to be grateful.

"Is that what this is supposed to be?" I asked.

He gave another disturbing laugh. "No, the fire is only part of the welcome." He pointed and I spotted a man with disheveled hair and glazed eyes standing beyond the firelight. His mouth was ajar as he stared up at the roof of the cave. His expression was eerily similar to Zola Figg's before she was killed.

"Broskow," Bisa whispered and I glanced at her, confused.

"What?"

"That's him," she said again, her eyes wide.

"That's not—" I looked again: past the scruffy, unkempt beard and the torn pant leg, past the bruised body and the way he swayed side to side as if drunk. I stared into his listless, blue eyes.

For so many years I had only seen hatred there, a keen disgust that got worse with each Seeking my family won. It had softened for a day after Pearl was killed, but that anger had come back with a vengeance after Carra fell.

Broskow had always been a passionate man: dangerous yes, but always with a strong opinion and a zeal to be right. Now I saw nothing. His eyes were empty, as though everything that made him...him had been taken away. I saw no excitement or rage, no affection or loss. He was just a man who happened to look like Broskow, but wasn't.

I ran over to him, not even thinking of the possible dangers. "What happened to you?"

He looked at me and blinked several times, his eyes clearing for a brief moment. "Dahlia," he whispered, his words coming across like his tongue was too big for his mouth. "There you are. I was wondering where you went."

"They took you, didn't they?"

"They brought me here. They took things from me. I don't remember what, but they probably weren't that important anyway."

My head hurt from the intensity with which I stared at him. Broskow, who insisted on staying put instead of risking the dangers of the forest. Broskow, the man who could be so quick to anger. Broskow, the man who had wept for his lost family.

"Do you remember Pearl?" I asked him. "Do you remember what happened to her?"

"Pearl?" He tried the name on his lips like tasting a new food.

"Pearl. She was your wife. You went with her on horseback searching for me during The Seeking, remember? You loved her."

His eyes went clear again, and he scrunched up his face trying to remember. "She died?"

"Yes, she did." I wanted to reach out to touch his shoulder, to shake him, anything that would rattle some sense back into him. Yet I felt that wouldn't be permitted. He likely wasn't alone out here, not like this. Something had fed on him, and recently.

"That spider took her head off." He had a grin on his face, not from the memory surely but from the ability to remember it at all. "They...took me..."

"After we left, yes, they brought you here."

He stared straight into my eyes, easily looking twenty years older than when I had last seen him. "They took Darik first." Tears filled his eyes. "Then they took me from me."

He looked away and the tears streaked lines down his dirty cheeks. "My wife, my children...you. They took all of it from me." He fell to his knees. "I can't remember their faces! I can't remember what they even looked like!"

I felt a tap on my shoulder and saw Bisa there. She was staring down at Broskow with little sympathy. "Dahlia, our Gray guide has found a friend."

I looked and saw He Who Wanders staring intently

into the eyes of a Gray Woman. Her eager smile made me uncomfortable. "What are they doing?"

"I think they're talking, but I'm not sure. Neither one of them is moving their mouths."

I felt a tug on my hand and looked down to see Broskow on his knees before me. "Please," he said, his eyes wide with terror. "You have to tell me everything. You have to give back what they took from me."

I stared down at him. Did he really want me to recount all the horrible things that happened to him? Or the horrible things that he did? I wasn't sure if I could even recount all of it; those days seemed like another lifetime ago.

"Please!" He pulled so hard this time that I nearly fell forward and Bisa had to grab my arm to keep me from tumbling.

The Gray Woman appeared at his side, and placed a hand on his shoulder. His body stilled and his eyes went glassy. His grip on my wrist loosened and I pulled away.

"He'll need some work," she said to He Who Wanders. "I wasn't expecting him to be needed for anything useful."

"That's fine," He Who Wanders replied. "That's perfectly fine."

"What's fine? What were you two talking about?" I asked.

"The Priest Clan has no breeders, as you said," he stated simply. "I'm pulling from other sources."

Bisa leaned in next to my ear and whispered, "I don't know if this is a good idea. You remember what happened last time we tried to work with him. That's how we lost Darik."

Broskow was on his knees before me, trembling from head to toe with glassy eyes, tears still streaming down his cheeks. Could he still hear everything going on? Could he still think and feel inside that hollow shell of his?

I thought of him beating up Darik in front of the fireplace, and the way my brother had pleaded with us to leave with just his eyes. If Broskow was right, the Grays took him, too.

I crouched down in front of him and grabbed his chin to turn his face toward me. "Where did they take my brother? Is Darik still alive?"

His face went even paler as a terror overcame him. He turned his gaze away from mine, unable to look at me.

"Tell me!" I demanded.

He made a sound between a whimper and a sob, but he refused to look at me, and words seemed lost to him. I let go of his chin and got to my feet.

I slapped him. Not as hard as I had slapped Darik, though I wanted to punch him in the nose, too. Broskow wasn't worth it then, and he certainly wasn't worth it now. He toppled to the ground from the blow and had to reach out an arm to grab at the dirt.

"You've always been a coward," I said. "It didn't matter if you were hunting down children on horseback with dogs, or beating the crap out of my big brother, you've always been a coward. It's just more obvious now, isn't it?"

He was sobbing, covering his face with his hands. I brought back a foot to kick him but was pulled backwards and off balance. "Bisa, not now!"

"Don't do it." Dameon's voice was small and pleading, his gaze intense. I looked down at him in shock.

"You know what he did to Darik. You saw what he did."

"I know, but—"

"He told me not to tell anyone," Broskow whispered. I was on him again like an unleashed dog. I grabbed him by the remnants of his shirt and shook him. The broken man didn't fight me or even resist. "I promised him."

"Damn your promise!" I shouted, fully aware that even the Gray People were watching me now. "Tell me what happened."

"He went with them. The tall one, she came and demanded to talk, so he did. They made some sort of arrangement and healed him. I don't know how they did it, but they did - with their minds, I think. Then he left with them and left me with...her." He looked up to the woman who had clearly been feeding on him. She smiled as she approached.

"And now he's part of your clan, Little Priest." She stroked his hair as if he was a pet dog. "His mind is a mess at the moment, but it will clear over time. Then I'm sure he will have all sorts of stories to share."

There was a smile on her lips that seemed to imply she knew more than she was letting on, but I was too weary to demand more information. She looked to He Who Wanders, asking, "A farewell sip perhaps?"

"I see no harm in it," he said.

She grabbed Broskow around the back of the neck and his whimpering intensified.

"Please...no more..."

She pulled him to his feet, and he seemed barely able to stand as she held his jaw between her hands and forced him to look at her. In his defense, he tried to look away, but once he looked into those empty eye sockets, he was lost. A shudder went through him and a tear rolled down his cheek.

"I suppose that's all I can have for now, but perhaps I'll visit on occasion, Mr. Broskow." She let go and he collapsed to his hands and knees, trembling.

"Is he okay?" Marcus' voice broke the tense silence that had descended upon us.

"No, he's not," He Who Wanders said in annoyance. "That was more than a sip."

She smiled. "I couldn't help it. Some minds taste better than others. His is full of fear and wrapped in a shell of hatred, folded in on arrogance. If you drink long enough, you'll taste that bitter seed of love in there somewhere."

She glided past him with a smirk, her footsteps not making a sound. Then she laughed, a horrible sound like the rattling of dried leaves in a wind, before disappearing into the darkness.

"That was certainly uncalled for," He Who Wanders said as though he were talking about a spilled drink instead of the mental abuse she had inflicted on

Broskow. The poor man was still on his knees, his entire body shaking.

Broskow had described what it was like to be fed on by these creatures, and I had seen the effects on Zola, but I had never seen it done to this extent. He Who Wanders had tried to feed on Dameon when I threatened his life with the fire, but it was never so gut-wrenchingly strong. She had said he would recover his memories and I assumed his mind over time, but was that still the case after her last assault?

I ought to help him, I thought to myself, but I couldn't bring myself to.

I should have tried to attack her with the torch or focus my rage, but I hadn't. It wasn't because I was afraid of her. Dameon had shown what anger could do to them, and I was certain He Who Wanders would've let me kill her. It wasn't because I was exhausted either, because I knew I could have fended her off.

It was because it was Broskow.

Broskow, with his dogs who had chased me into the woods. Broskow, who had made me hide in a tree and nearly get devoured by a spider creature. Broskow, who was my friend during The Seeking but turned on me the moment he grew afraid. Broskow, who had attacked my brother without any provocation, only because he was afraid of angering or insulting the Gray People.

I realized in that moment that I hated him more than I hated the Gray People, and that terrified me.

It was Dameon who broke loose from our group and

ran over, knelt down on the ground, and wrapped his small arms around Broskow's shaking shoulder to try to help him stand. My little brother, who had been bullied for years by Broskow and who had known Darik's plan from the start. Somehow, he had more sympathy than I did for a man who had brought so much fear into our lives. If he could find a way to forgive him and help him, then surely I could.

Was forgiveness even something I understood anymore? Did I even remember what it felt like?

Fear and anger seemed to rule my life these last few days, but Dameon had suffered just as much, if not more. Even though Broskow and his friends bullied him, shoved him to the ground and made him cry, he hadn't forgotten how to forgive or how to sympathize. I clearly had. Anger was a useful tool, but it could consume. I couldn't let it, though. I had to remember how to care... even if it was Broskow.

Dameon had gotten Broskow to his feet, although the man still appeared lethargic and weak. He looked at me with red-rimmed, but otherwise clear eyes and I knew that if we hadn't come across him this night, he would have been dead come morning.

He dropped his gaze to the ground as I approached.

"If you come with us," I started, "will you promise not to harm any of us again? I can't have you joining us if you can't manage at least that."

He gave a slow nod.

"I need to hear it."

"Yes," he managed to reply, his voice a hoarse whisper.

I felt Bisa's hand on my arm, warm and comforting. It gave me the strength to continue. I knew what I needed to say, but I was still fighting with myself to even let him come along. Part of me wished he had died when the Gray Woman fed from him that last time.

"Will you promise not to get in our way?"

At this, he looked at me again, his eyes narrowing. "What?"

My face burned from his question. There was that fight I knew he still possessed, even as broken as he was. There was the hard rock that I knew made his core, the part that resisted regardless of all attempts to smother it.

A part of me was happy to see it was still intact, but another part of me was glad I was making the conditions of his joining us clear. That resistance might not have cropped up right away, but it would have eventually. I needed to weed it out now while I still could.

"Promise that you will not get in our way or try to prevent us from making decisions. I'm not saying you can't give input, but you are not leading us. I will not put our safety in your hands. Any move that you plan to make needs to be approved by me or Bisa first."

He grunted in frustration. "What happens if I don't?"

He Who Wanders stepped forward. "Then I'm sure she or one of my kind will be happy to take you on. Judging by the way that She Who Feasts spoke of you, that wouldn't be difficult."

"You would just pass me off to another one?" He looked between both of us now. "Why can't I just go back home? I didn't ask for any of this."

I kept my voice firm as I explained. "Carra is having a new beginning, one that you won't be part of unless you agree to our conditions."

Broskow gaped at me.

"Your decision then?" As cruel as it would be, I wasn't above letting the other Gray People have him if it prevented our group from being poisoned from the inside again.

He blinked, trying to focus, before waving a hand at me. "Fine."

"So, you promise then?"

"Yes, I promise, damn it."

I held out a hand and he took it. As I clasped his hand in both of mine, I tried not to smile.

CHAPTER 14
MOTHER'S DEN

I was wary of leaving the safety of the campfire and the light that it provided, but we weren't exactly in the safest location.

Our pace was slower than before thanks to Broskow, but it meant that Marcus was able to walk on his own more. At one point, Dameon broke off a tree branch to give to the man to keep him from nearly toppling over every few minutes, and I half expected something to attack us, but nothing did.

We were surrounded by trees, but they were all dead. The trunks and branches looked like skeletal hands reaching for the sky. Their bark was almost the same shade of gray as the stone nearby. Still, I preferred it to walking through the cavern with those spider creatures able to sneak up on us.

As the light of the campfire disappeared behind us, we were plunged back into the darkness we had grown accustomed to, with only the light of our single torch to lead the way.

After what felt like an hour of walking, Bisa put the intimidating feeling to words. "This darkness goes on forever."

"Nonsense," He Who Wanders said. "We will reach Mother soon, she merely has her ways." He paused, then added, "You may want to renew your fire moving ahead. That one is nearly out."

I blinked at him for a moment before realizing what he meant. The torch in my hand had grown dim and none of us had even noticed. Dameon was way ahead of me and started getting one of our last torches ready. I didn't want to think about what would happen if we ran out here.

As I held the new torch up, Bisa gasped.

On either side of our path stood dozens of Gray People. Their bodies gleamed in the light as they stared at us. A few walked around the others, but their footsteps never made a sound.

Marcus started squeaking when he breathed, and we all moved closer together. Broskow reached a hand out to pull Dameon in, and the boy dropped the fading torch onto the ground, forgetting completely about stomping it out.

"So many," I whispered.

He Who Wanders smiled. "They, too, are curious to see what Mother does with you. There has never been a group of humans who dared to approach her." His empty gaze turned to me. "You asked me to guide you to her, but you said nothing of my protection after that."

My mouth went dry at his words, but I gave a brief nod. "Y-yes, I understand," I stuttered.

He came closer and I tensed. This had to be what he was waiting for. He had brought us as far as he was willing, and now was his chance to devour us – something he likely had been pining to do for over a day.

I turned the torch toward him, and he paused. Behind him, in my peripheral vision, I saw the other Gray People go disturbingly still.

"However, I must say that I've grown rather curious about your clan, little Priest. I would like to see what becomes of you. May I accompany you to her throne and provide my services should the need arise?"

"What kind of services?" Dameon asked beside me. He was standing close, apparently ready to lunge in an instant. "Are you going to eat us?"

"No, that would be rather wasteful. Should she not wish to permit you to live, would you like me to provide an alternative solution? The Priest clan as a whole spoke of it not long ago." He met my eyes again.

"What's he talking about?" Broskow asked behind me, but I ignored him.

He was talking about the arrangement, about the conditions we set up before. Why had I forgotten about them? Probably because of all the danger we had faced since then. This was the moment we determined whether we died here, or if we went on to create something greater than the snare that was Carra.

"Yes," I said with a deep sigh that felt like it came from my bones. "Please provide an alternative solution should the need arise."

When He Who Wanders smiled again, it was like a crack along the grain in a slab of wood. The disturbing delight in it made a shiver go down my spine that had nothing to do with us being surrounded.

"Come," he said. "Mother is there." He gestured into the darkness, and it took us about ten steps forward with the torch in hand to illuminate the cave entrance.

"Of course, it would be another cave," Bisa muttered. She was standing so close to me that I could feel her breath on my neck.

We climbed the short steep hill inside and left behind the swarms of Gray People that had been so eager to see us. They didn't take a single step up the incline to follow, and I wondered if it was fear or their allegiance to Mother that kept them back.

ONLY A FEW STEPS past the entrance to the cave, we heard the low whistle of a wind whipping its way through. Only it wasn't coming from behind us; it came from in front. At first, I thought the cave itself had strange acoustics, but then the creaky wind shifted into words.

"...guessed it would be you, He Who Wanders. But I must ask. Why have so many hideous children made their way into my home?" I recognized the voice. It was the tall Gray Person who had lifted Darik and slashed his face at the Ritual.

It was Mother.

Her voice echoed off the walls and seemed to come from all around us. I heard Marcus start squeaking again and turned, looking to see if she had approached us from behind, but there was only the empty cave entrance. Then I noticed He Who Wanders remained facing forward, stoic and still.

"They are the members of the Priest clan," he said with a hint of disgust in his voice. "I believe they can tell you themselves why they have come to seek your audience, Mother."

That rattling wind came through again, then shifted. "Send them forward I suppose."

He Who Wanders looked to me and nodded. As I stepped farther into the cave, he fell in step beside me. Bisa picked up Marcus and moved to my other side while I felt Dameon huddle in close behind me. Broskow was farther back, though I could hear his makeshift walking stick scrape against the stone with every step he took.

The torch's light illuminated what looked like a small cave in. Dozens of stones were piled up in the corner, each about as large as my skull.

Then I saw her.

She was lounging on the seek pile, surrounded by what looked like dead branches, similar to those on the trees that we saw outside.

There were other Gray People there, scurrying about

behind her. One brought her a headdress with the silver antlers we saw at the Ritual, which gleamed in the torch light like white fire. She took it and placed it on her head. Her body was still covered in that dull silver shade from days before, but now I could see dried blood splatters on top of it. That was the blood of the people of Carra, my people, my family's people.

I gripped the torch tighter and stiffened as I approached her. "Madam, I would like to plead our case."

She smiled and rested her chin on her long, black-clawed fingers. "Oh? How quaint. Go on then, child." She held out her other hand, and a Gray Person hurried out of the shadows to file her outstretched claws. They, too, were stained with dried blood and I couldn't help but think of Darik. Was that his blood, or was it all that remained of the bloodbath from the Ritual?

"We understand that Carra failed to uphold its contract with the Gray People. We have come to-to—"

"No," she said, lifting her chin.

I stammered to a stop. Were this a normal case back in Carra, I would have ignored the interruption and kept going. But here? Here I had no power. I had no title and no name. I barely had functional clothing.

"It was not the citizens of Carra who failed to uphold the contract."

Mother got to her feet, looming over the other Gray People as she stepped down the pile of rubble, her foot-steps not making a sound on the treacherous rocks beneath her feet. Her gaze was fixed on me, and although

I knew I ought to look away, I found it difficult to do so. The silver antlers drew my eyes in the darkness, and since it framed her face, it was impossible to avoid her intense gaze.

She held out a hand and I thought for certain that she would claw me across the face just like she had Darik. Afterwards she would feast on Dameon, Bisa and Marcus and there wouldn't be a damn thing I could do to stop it. Startled back into focus, I felt her fingers glide beneath my chin, her gray skin surprisingly smooth if just as cold as the walls of the cave.

"Carra kept its contract with me for centuries. It was the Priest family that brought it to ruin."

At the mention of my family's name, the other Gray People in the room hissed. Mother drew her fingertips away, her claws dragging across the tender skin under my chin. The shock and pain threw me off guard. I put a hand to the wound, feeling blood drip through my fingers. It wasn't much, but it would be enough to draw the attention of her bugs if she wanted.

Blinking, I mulled over her words. She was the Gray Person who created the original contract? Were these creatures immortal? I thought of all the trees with the large boils on their trunks that we saw before. Would all of those be immortal, too?

She held her arms out to her sides. Servants, who up until this point were constantly moving in the corner of my eyes, ducked and backed away.

"Of all the people of Carra, of all the Exalted Families

who have come and gone, it was the Priests that brought them down." She turned and pointed at me, her black, jagged nail still wet with my blood. "The Priest family founded Carra and the Priest family destroyed it. In one day, your family destroyed every person who lived there. Do not blame Carra for its ruin; it was your family's doing."

"It was an accident!" I snapped. "Darik didn't know he was even captured. The rules are ridiculous, how are we to know—"

"*Silence!*" Her voice hissed like sandpaper on stone and I felt a sharp pain in my ears. I went to cover them, but the discomfort passed by the time I tried.

I heard the clatter of wood and turned to see Broskow had dropped his walking stick and fallen to the ground. Marcus and Dameon were trying to help him back up. Bisa remained close behind me, not wanting to leave my side. They must have been in pain, too, but neither made a sound, neither cried out. We had all gotten so much stronger since we fled into the woods.

"Your brother was the cause of all this. He was the weakling in your tribe, the one who faltered where others did not. His failure was the downfall of your entire pathetic town."

"No, he was not weak!" My fists clenched at my sides. "The whole Seeking is a ridiculous requirement that doesn't make any sense at all! Why do you even want children to hide? Why put the entire weight of whether a town is destroyed or not on the shoulders of children? We don't deserve that!"

She smiled, a crooked, dead thing that sent a tremor through me. "My people could treat you like cattle. We could cage you, breed you, tag you, make you live inside sheds your entire lives, but we don't. It makes the mind less palatable.

"So, we compromised. We let you rule your little cut of land. We let you determine who led and who followed. The only requirement was that we were offered a bit of entertainment ourselves."

"That's disgusting," Bisa whispered, which made Mother break into peals of laughter that bounced back toward us from everywhere. In the distance, I heard the snickering of her followers, unseen beyond the torch's light.

"We live a long time, children. We live a very long time, and it can get quite dull." She gave a wide smile. "Watching you scramble each year is quite entertaining. This year, we begin anew, though. We will begin a new breeding."

I thought of Pearl with the spider attached to her face, and how the Gray Person didn't appear until after she was dead. Had it been in the woods, watching and enjoying the spectacle? The very thought made my insides twist.

Dameon stepped forward, his voice trembling as he asked, "What about my brother? What did you do with him?"

I could already guess the answer, and I was horrified that Dameon was the one to ask the question. Surely he had guessed that his brother was already dead, given what they did to Broskow.

"I approached him on a treaty and he graciously agreed."

"What kind of treaty?" Bisa asked.

She nodded to one of her followers and he crept off. "He was in a vulnerable state, and probably would have died had we not approached him. Your friend in the back made sure of that."

Before I could turn to Broskow, I heard her followers snickering again. Something was being pulled into view, and it took me a moment to make out what it was.

Bisa gasped and pulled Marcus close, trying to obscure his view with her skirts. Broskow cursed.

My brother, his eyes vacant and bleary, was underneath the bloodied cloth that wrapped his wounds - I could see the scars that they had made on his once clear skin.

He was limping badly, and I realized it was because his feet were so bloodied from being barefoot on the stone ground. When he met my gaze, his eyes lit up with recognition and he tried to rush forward to me and Dameon, but his escorts held him back. He looked at them with pure terror before resigning himself to standing still, slightly swaying side to side.

Dameon cried out and started to walk toward him, but I leapt forward and pulled him back. I didn't want my little brother to be held prisoner, too.

Darik looked at me but didn't speak - couldn't speak

for the strange black thing that had been stuffed into his mouth. I thought it was black cloth at first, but the long, furry tendrils waving slightly in the breeze implied otherwise. Was it alive, or was it just some strange kind of plant life?

"What did you do to him?" Dameon sounded like he was about to cry.

"He volunteered his life for Carra. A noble decision, but ultimately useless. We were going to spare his little town regardless, but his continued torture keeps my people entertained. They've been trying all sorts of things out on him."

Mother walked over to look Darik up and down, and my big brother just kept his eyes downcast, as though he had grown completely accustomed to being treated like an animal. It was hard to believe this was my older brother, the one who always tried to look cool when things got bad, who always looked out for us, who always ran late to everything in the world.

Now he had been twisted into something else.

"We have been protecting humans for a long time, but we rarely get the chance to have one up close for prolonged periods. We get hungry and usually devour any who are foolish enough to wander through our woods. We've been examining the muscle tissue and the frailty of human skin. We learn more every day."

I felt Dameon's shoulders shake. I knew it had to tear him apart to see what had become of Darik, the man he had looked up to.

I was upset, too, but instead of crying, I was redirecting it into anger. My parents were murdered and almost everyone I knew had been killed. Despite their torture, my big brother not only knew me, but he wanted to come to us. That meant his mind wasn't lost yet. That meant he could be saved, and I refused to lose another family member.

A plan began to form in my mind. It was a crazy plan, but as I stared at Darik, who was riddled with scars and not even permitted to speak to us, I knew I needed to get us out of here.

"We were fools to make an agreement with you," I said aloud, turning to Mother. "We should never have done it."

"Dahlia," Bisa whispered, but I ignored her.

I stared into Mother's empty gaze with as much fury and hatred as I could muster. I thought of all the people who I knew that were dead. I thought of their faces, of every good thing they had ever done for me, of my father holding my hands, of my mother hugging me tightly.

I let the rage overflow in me and a surprising thing happened; Mother grew uneasy. Her sweeping movements, once open and confident, suddenly became more controlled. Then she looked away and I knew I could do this. I just had to hope it worked.

"My family should never have trusted you, or agreed to take part in your Seekings. There was no other way for it to end except in slaughter. You knew that, though, didn't you?"

My lips curled in disgust. "Yes, it was the Priest

family that was the Exalted at the end, but it could have been anyone, could have been any kid who didn't know better. We were just the unlucky ones. We should never have agreed to it, but I doubt you gave them much of a choice, did you?"

She was advancing on me, her gaze averted from my eyes but her anger was still evident.

She lifted up a hand as though to strike, when He Who Wanders spoke. "Perhaps I can offer an alternative solution?"

Her head whipped toward him so fast I thought that her antlers might fly off. "An alternative? From you?" She stalked toward him and yet He Who Wanders didn't back away. Instead, he stood perfectly still.

"Yes, Mother."

"The outcast? The recluse? The one they call *He Who Cowers*?"

There was more snickering from the shadows, and He Who Wanders sighed. "Some do call me that, yes."

"What is your proposed alternative?"

He explained his desire to create another town for us to live in. There were a lot of details he left out, though, including the arrangements we had made and the required concessions for both us and the Gray People. In fact, his description was very similar to Mother's current setup. Perhaps that was why she started laughing.

This time, it was an open laugh and the roar from her followers was so loud that it sounded like the wail of cicadas. He Who Wanders remained resolute, though, and while Mother laughed, he made pointed eye contact with me.

I certainly hope you have a plan, Dahlia, his voice in my mind made my stomach clench for a moment, but I pushed it away.

I showed him what I was planning, every minute detail of it. That was when he faltered, when he looked like if he could bolt for the exit he would've. But that wasn't an option right now, not with Mother so close to him.

"Perhaps I should rename you," Mother said at last, petting his head with her claws and causing him obvious pain by the way he flinched. "He Who Wanders isn't suitable for someone so foolish. He Who Dreams is far more appropriate. For that is what you do, foolish little one: *dream*." Her tone of voice at the end turned shrill and biting, and I winced at the renewed pain in my ears. "Now, my children," she called out, "who wants to watch me feast on these humans?"

The hissing grew excitable and slowly they began advancing on us. He Who Wanders was watching me, not Mother, for he knew what I planned to do.

I drew Bisa and everyone to me and backed away from Mother toward the pile of stones.

"Look at this, my children! Even until their end, the Priest clan remain cowards!"

I motioned for Darik to join us, and he pulled away from his distracted captors to hobble over. The crowd was closing in around us; He Who Wanders was trying to push his way to the front.

"You're foolish, Mother!" I cried out at the top of my lungs as the hisses grew louder. "You should never have tried to destroy the Priest clan!"

I threw the torch onto the branches near her throne, into the dry twigs that had probably been there for ages. Mother lunged forward, but He Who Wanders shoved her back. Suddenly the entire floor was alight; old leaves, twigs, and whatever else carpeted the ground caught on fire. It spread across the cave floor like water.

In the light of the blaze, I could see the blood that was soaked into the pine straw and leaves. The fire would destroy all of it.

The branches on either side of us were already burning out, even as the fire on the ground spread further. I urged everyone to start climbing the stones of Mother's throne. Once we got past the heat from the branches nearest the throne, we found the other stones were still cool. It at least gave us some time.

The kids went first, then Darik, Broskow, and Bisa. As I climbed, I could hear the screams of Mother's children all around us as they tried to escape - the fire had spread too quickly, too far. I thought it might even consume most of the cliffs, and I was perfectly fine with that.

He Who Wanders stepped around us, moving so quickly I could barely see his limbs. He began removing the top boulders, one at a time, and dropped them over the edge.

"What are you doing?" Broskow demanded.

"Getting us out of here," he stated, oddly calm. What

I could see of him, though, was already getting singed with the heat.

He made an opening at the top, revealing the sky above that had turned a purple-blue with the early onset of dawn. Bisa and I climbed further up to help. We couldn't lift the heavy rocks, but we could take care of the lighter ones.

The smoke was getting thicker, and it was hard to see through our watery eyes. We were all coughing, and as soon as the hole was big enough, I lifted Dameon out while Bisa grabbed Marcus. Slowly, we started assisting everyone else out. He Who Wanders climbed out on his own, no longer interested in helping us that much.

Finally, Bisa and I were the only ones left. I had just helped her up when I heard a god-awful shriek coming from behind me.

The sound felt like two ice picks being shoved in on either side of my brain and I screamed as well. The pain was so acute that I only vaguely realized I had fallen to my knees.

Hot blood dripped down the sides of my face as the heat built around me. It was when I felt Bisa's soft hand on my arm that I finally opened my eyes and saw she had climbed back down.

I couldn't hear anything except that scream, rever-berating over and over again in my ears, but she didn't seem bothered by it and helped pull me out.

Once I was out in the open night air, I noticed how dark the plume of smoke was coming out of the hole we had climbed through. My back felt hot and sore, the skin tender with every move I made. The previous burn there hadn't healed and the heat from the flames only made it worse. I worried I would have scars, but I couldn't focus on that now. We had to survive first.

Turning, I found Dameon sitting on the ground coughing and Marcus lying on his side gasping for air like a fish on land. I rushed over and started pressing on his back, trying to relax the muscles. Broskow was doubled over in a coughing fit. I spotted Darik, bent over in the woods puking. Whatever they had put into his mouth must have been terrible to pull out. He Who Wanders was some distance away, examining his own singed skin. Bisa moved to stand beside me, talking to Marcus, trying to help him breathe again.

"We need to get him to cleaner air," I said, and my voice sounded incredibly loud in my head. I glanced around, relieved to see that others could at least hear me.

He Who Wanders said something, but I shook my head. The scream that had pierced my mind had dulled down to a ringing noise, but lingered and blocked out the outside world.

When he realized I couldn't hear him, he looked into my eyes and his voice was suddenly clear, pushing at my anxiety. *Follow me. If we take the opposite side to the top, we may yet survive. You do realize that was an incredibly foolish move, don't you?*

There was clear reprimanding in his voice, though he smirked at the same time. He turned away before I could think of how to respond and I understood that we didn't have much time to discuss my lack of planning skills.

Of all the Priest children, it was a shame that I was the only one capable of taking action in that cave. Darik should have found a way to fight off Mother himself, single-handedly defeating her and making all her children bow to him instead. Dameon could have safely negotiated with them, but he was too young to even attempt such a thing.

My mother would be proud of me, though. She was right; I was a survivor after all.

I scooped Marcus up into my arms and followed He Who Wanders and the others. For some reason, the thought of my mother's praise made me smile. It was the first happy thought I'd had about them since their deaths.

Tears started to stream down my cheeks, and I couldn't tell if it was from the smoke or from remembering them.

～

HE WHO WANDERS LED us to a steep, rocky cliffside that must have formed the backend of Mother's cave. Even out here, the smoky air scratched at my throat, making me cough constantly.

Dameon was trying to light our last torch. In the silence left by my inability to hear, it felt like a holy act. With each failed flick of the lighter, I wondered if their heartbeats sped up like mine did as it pounded away in my ears.

Broskow took a single look behind us, as though a

flood of Gray People were going to clamor out of the same hole we escaped from, but nothing came.

Darik reached out as though he wanted to help Dameon, but he could barely stand and was leaning heavily on Bisa. Finally, the torch lit, and relief spread over all of our faces. And goodness, what a mess we were.

Dameon's face was streaked with tears and dirt. Bisa was grinning, and Darik had a grim smile, as though he was in a lot more pain than he was letting on. Broskow's relief was clouded by his fear and the obvious desire to keep moving. Marcus had fallen asleep in my arms. I might not have been able to hear his breathing, but I knew what his chest would look like if he was having an attack again.

I set my jaw and eyed the rocky path as Dameon started to work his way down.

"Wait, be careful," I said in what felt like an overly loud voice. He said something back, but I couldn't hear him and then realized He Who Wanders was the only one who knew I couldn't hear.

Dameon descended easily at first, but it wasn't long before he took his first misstep. A rock that he'd thought was secure slipped out from beneath his foot, and he had to hold himself up with his hands. I think he cried out. I wanted to go down after him, but I still held Marcus.

My little brother pulled himself up, with muscles I didn't even know he possessed, then started his slow descent again, this time checking his footholds before putting weight on them. I had always thought of

Dameon as a young boy, but in that moment I had to accept he was quickly becoming an adult.

When Dameon reached the bottom, I let out the breath I was holding.

Bisa offered to help Darik down next, but my big brother refused. I was happy that he hadn't changed that much at least. He followed Dameon's path, and though he was slower and had to stop to catch his breath regularly, he made it. Broskow went after, followed by Bisa.

Before she descended, I leaned over and pecked a kiss on her cheek, which was visibly flushed despite the soot that mostly covered us, as I passed Marcus to her. She looked absolutely shocked by this, though I had kissed her numerous times before. For some reason, here in this place it must have felt blasphemous.

It was only when she reached the ground that I realized He Who Wanders had already dropped down to the bottom. I had to descend on my own. So, taking the same steps all the others had, I began my climb down. I felt some of the rocks give under my feet, their stability uncertain. Knowing that so many others had gone before me and made it emboldened me to plow ahead, until one of these weak rocks fell apart completely on me, and I didn't have Dameon's upper arm strength.

I hung there for a moment, then uttered a terrified cry before I tried to grab another stone. It, too, fell apart. Below, I saw the others saying things to me, their lips clearly moving, but I couldn't hear any of them.

"I can't hear!" I cried as my arm began to shake and I

reached out with my other hand. "I can't hear any of you!"

I finally found another, sturdier rock and clung there like a squirrel trying to avoid a hawk, gripping those rocks as tightly as I could.

I panted, and the smell of the earth calmed me for some reason, made me think of the hiding place that I had carved out for The Seeking. It made me think of home.

A tiny earthworm dragged its body over my pinky finger, and I watched him crawl back into the dirt between the stones. I was halfway there; I had to finish what I started.

Taking a deep breath, I continued on, even though my hands were scraped and my arms shook. When I reached the ground, it was Broskow who grabbed me by the waist to make sure I didn't fall. I turned around to gape at him, shocked, but he merely smiled and rubbed my back for a few moments. The absurdity of it just baffled me. Even on The Seeking, when Broskow showed me that first shred of kindness, I never thought he would be willing to catch me like that.

I was still shaking. I hadn't really felt afraid when I was standing in front of the Mother of the Grays in the cave. Perhaps my anger gave me an extra boost, or perhaps I was too headstrong to notice it. Either way, I felt that fear keenly now.

Bisa grabbed my arm and pulled me closer. She looked me in the eye and exaggeratedly mouthed, "Are you okay?"

I laughed and nodded. Bisa had little Marcus in her arms, still fast asleep, though his breathing looked normal now.

Bisa nudged me and I looked up to see He Who Wanders pointing up ahead. He said something aloud to the others before looking me in the eye. *We will head up this path. I think we should be safer here than if we back-tracked.*

"Whatever you think is best," I said aloud. I must have said it too loudly because Broskow jumped at my side.

I flushed and looked away, noticing Bisa's arms were shaking as well. She had carried Marcus a lot over the past few days, and her arms were starting to show the strain.

I took Marcus when we started the long climb to the top. After a few minutes, I was already regretting it. My arms were tired, and it was only going to get worse.

WE WERE ABOUT HALFWAY up the slope when my hearing started coming back. We were high enough that I could hear the distant singing of birds above us and see that the sun had just crested over the edge of the cliffside.

We hadn't seen any Gray People, and I was grateful that He Who Wanders had suggested this path. If we'd tried to escape on our own, I didn't think we would have made it out alive.

The fire we left behind only grew worse. The steady

stream of black smoke streamed up into the blue, cloudy morning sky. At first it was just a trickle, but the higher we climbed, the more visible the smoke became, turning into a dark cloud that seemed to spread and darken the further it traveled.

I had been forced to pass Marcus off to Bisa again, and I could see the worry in her face as she took her sleeping brother. He still hadn't woken, and although his breathing had gotten better, he didn't even stir when we passed him back and forth. He was as limp as a doll.

It was hours later when we finally made it to the top, and the sun had climbed up with us until it was almost directly above us. The wind up here was warmer than it had been the other day, but it was just as strong.

"Can we rest here?" Bisa asked, her voice nearly blown away by the wind.

"We must keep moving," He Who Wanders insisted. His eyes were on the path at our backs, the one we had used before.

And so we followed him into the woods. Once we were under the cover of trees and the wind had died down, I decided to probe for answers. "You're afraid of their wrath?"

He glanced back to me. "I'm afraid you have turned Mother into a martyr. Of course we will feel their wrath."

I shook my head. "We don't even know if Mother died."

"You heard her shriek. Her gift was her voice. Before she became Mother, she was known as Speaker of Pain." He shrugged. "An appropriate name, don't you think?" I shuddered, recalling how her shriek had made my skull feel like it wanted to shatter. "We must keep moving until—"

A shape dropped down in front of him, and He Who Wanders froze. Behind me I heard a horrible whimper escape Broskow and glanced back to find him huddling behind Darik.

"She Who Feasts, how odd to find you here."

"Not odd at all, brother. Your clan has killed Mother; one of us was going to find you eventually."

She carried no weapons, but He Who Wanders stood as if ready to leap into action if she tried anything. I wished we still had a torch, but Dameon's last one had burned out during the climb.

"What do you want?" he asked.

"I want to be part of your new town, what little there is of it."

That seemed to intrigue him, and he relaxed. "Oh?"

"Mother may have reveled in the destruction of Carra, but that left little food for us. Many of us are happy to be rid of her. She wasted some excellent minds with her gluttony."

She glanced to Broskow and gave him a little wave, bringing forth another series of whimpers.

"My terms with these humans are going to be very different from Mother's. I've made a far sounder arrangement with them that should last longer than anything she put together."

"Mmm, as long as I get a steady meal, I'm fine with whatever plan you've made. Only...where will you house them?" She looked at each of us, clearly sizing us up as meals rather than people. "Humans can't live in the trees, can they? Running around out here, you'll only put them in more danger." He glanced back to us, uncertain. "You've begun a great war, brother, one that has been a long time coming. They're calling you the great one: He Who Dreams."

"What?" He recoiled. "That's not my name!"

"I know," she said with a smirk. "But I certainly won't stop them from using it." She went around him to approach us, but he stepped in front of her.

"What are you doing?"

"I'm going to help you take them to a safe place. You have them walking on foot; it'll take days to get anywhere. You don't want them dying on you."

He stepped aside warily. "Somehow I don't think you're a very good judge of that. Your human hates the very sight of you."

She shrugged. "Regardless of my shortcomings, you and I know they won't make it on foot to wherever you plan to house them. That one's not even wearing shoes!" She pointed at Darik's bloody feet. He had tried to wrap them with cloth at one point, but there was no way to completely avoid walking on them and deepening his wounds.

He Who Wanders sighed. "Fine. We'll have to carry them. But where?"

"Back to Carra," I stated.

Dameon turned to me with a frown. "Are you sure? It's overrun with bugs."

"To the Exalted House," I replied.

There was no telling what the Exalted House would be like, but I had to see it. Just from the mob's damage - had that really only been days ago? - I knew there was a lot to do, but we had to try.

The idea of Carra being left to rot put my stomach in knots. Then there was Broskow, Darik, and Marcus; the rest of us were battered, but those three might seriously injure themselves if they didn't rest soon.

"Take us home. Back to the Exalted House," I said, firmer this time. "You two will be given the task of making sure it's safe, though." I wasn't sure where the authority had come from, but I took hold of it like a lifeline.

He Who Wanders nodded, but She Who Feasts merely looked at me as though I had two heads.

"You're taking *orders* from a human? A child, no less?"

"She's the one that killed Mother, not me. I think it's time we started giving these humans a bit more respect. After all, they survived long enough to rope me into their plans."

"Yes, but you're a fool. Everyone knows that."

"Perhaps I am, but here you are." With that he came forward and offered to pick up Bisa, who was still holding Marcus. "May I carry you?"

She glanced back to me as though asking if it was a good idea. I gave her a reassuring smile. "Let's get this over with," she muttered. He picked her up slowly and she had to adjust her grip so as not to drop her brother.

Leaping off, he disappeared and left us alone with the other Gray Person.

"Oh, I hope you get to go last, Alexander." She got close enough to stroke Broskow's hair and he wheezed like he might burst into tears any second. "My goodness, but you do throw a fit."

She laughed and I couldn't help but shudder. "Leave him be," I said. She looked shocked, but then did as I asked and stepped away.

I was grateful for her respect. In all honesty, I was in no mood to threaten or kill another Gray Person today. I felt like I had spent too much time doing that already.

I stepped closer to Darik and Dameon: my brothers, who had somehow survived with me through all of this. We were bloody, bruised and exhausted, but somehow the remnants of the Priest family had stayed together, and I was happy for that.

Yes, we would be forced to live among Gray People, but at least we wouldn't be providing them with entertainment each year. And we would have to tread carefully when making decisions, especially considering those decisions would affect future generations and not just ourselves.

I refused to let our people fall into the same situation as our parents. I refused to allow them to slaughter us out of pure enjoyment.

Putting an arm around my brothers, I whispered, "I'm proud of us," before giving them a squeeze and stepping back. "Dameon, I couldn't have made it here without your help."

He gave me a weak smile. "I honestly won't feel like we've escaped until we're behind locked doors. Nothing feels safe. I wonder if we'll ever feel safe again."

I rubbed his back, a part of me breaking at the thought of the real fears I knew he would carry for years to come, fears that we would all carry with us. I just hoped it wasn't for the rest of our lives. Dameon was too young for that to begin now.

I turned to Darik. "As for you, I thought you were dead."

Darik broke into a half-hearted smile. "I thought so, too. I would have been a fool to turn her down, though. Staying there with Broskow on my own was bad enough." He lowered his voice to add, "I thought he was going to kill me, and I figured Mother would have, too, so I guessed that my options couldn't get any worse." His voice wavered on the last word, and he didn't have to say any more for me to understand.

"We can't call it Carra anymore, you know," Dameon said beside me. "It's not Carra anymore. It never will be again."

"Good riddance," Darik said under his breath.

"I don't know what to call it," I admitted. "I'm not good at that sort of thing."

"You're not," Darik teased and smiled - this time it was genuine. "You're terrible at it. If I ever have kids, you are not allowed to name any of them."

"What about Ivory?" Dameon suggested in his small voice. Darik and I both looked at him, but he wasn't looking at us. He was focused on the sky, where white puffy clouds moved slowly through the sea of blue. "I want to name it after Mother - *our* mother."

I nodded. "I like that."

"Me, too," Darik said.

He Who Wanders returned, leaping down from a tree and landing without a sound in front of the three of us.

"Who's next?"

PART SIX
IVORY

CHAPTER 15

THE ANNIVERSARY

The anniversary of the final Seeking came faster than I expected. I opened the shutters to my bedroom and breathed in the scent of the cold morning, wrapping my cloak around me. Bisa's careful, decorative stitching made it one of my favorites that she had made for me. She dyed it a beautiful light green from the Black-eyed Susans that dotted the land around the Exalted House over the summer.

I breathed in the chilly air. It smelled of dying leaves - not apple pie. My brothers and I were quick to avoid the dish, on this day especially.

Only a few houses had been built on what used to be just the property of the Exalted House, each flanking the long dirt path along which the five of us lived. In the distance, the remains of Carra stood: a reminder of what we had lost, a ghost town that we needed to reclaim. It was a slow and difficult process. Although we buried the bodies that we had found upon our return, the homes themselves were scavenged for supplies as needed. We had grown slowly in the past months, though, adding several families to our town.

He Who Wanders promised that he would not kidnap anyone from their homes, but he would make an offer to them. So far, of the ten towns he visited, only a few had families willing to start afresh. When I asked what the arrangements were in those other towns, he refused to answer, stating that those were led by rulers other than Mother.

I didn't entirely believe that Mother had only ruled over Carra. I saw the forest filled with their birthing trees. I knew we alone weren't sustaining that many Gray People.

What I did believe, though, was that Mother's death had left a power vacuum, and others were quick to take her place. He Who Wanders probably didn't want to mention it because he didn't want me to go on a crusade to free all of them. Honestly, I didn't think I had it in me to try. Not yet, anyway. We simply didn't have the numbers.

I saw He Who Wanders walking along our Boundary Line in the morning light. The circle of glowing dandelions only surrounded the Exalted House and the few modest houses we'd built. He didn't just create one defense when we came home; he created three layers of dandelions. I supposed it was different this time, since we were willing stock. We were probably considered rare next to the other humans they kept.

I put a hand up to the side of my head where Dameon

had cut my braid to free us the day of the Ritual. As much as He Who Wanders and She Who Feasts had gone out of their way to protect us, I couldn't forget what happened to us all that night. The protection of the Gray People was not guaranteed, and they could turn on us again at any moment. Even though we were willing stock, we were still prisoners in a world they entirely controlled, from the creatures of the woods to the magic of the Boundary Line.

Lost in thought, I barely felt Bisa's warm arms wrap around my waist until her lips pressed against my shoulder. "Don't start getting down. There's nobody to hide from this year."

I laughed and put a hand on her arm, rubbing gently. "I know. I'm just worried about us. We're so few right now."

"Yes, but we're alive." She squeezed and I forced a smile to my lips despite everything. I turned around and kissed her deeply. After we pulled apart, she whispered, "I'm excited about today, though. Broskow said he had a mean stew brewing all day yesterday."

"Meatless, I hope! I told him those sheep aren't ready for the slaughter yet. They need another year to get their numbers up."

"No, he knows that. I think he's just excited to be dating again."

One of our new townsfolk was Mrs. Green, a woman who had been widowed in her early forties. All she had were the two sheep her husband used to keep, and they were welcomed into Ivory's small flock. She and Broskow hit it off quite well and had been almost inseparable over the last month. Word had it they'd bonded over their mutual love of cooking.

I took Bisa's hand and we headed downstairs, following the laughter coming from below. The walls still showed some of the damage done by the mob. We were pretty sure one deep gouge along the staircase came from a bug at one point, but there was no telling since the place was utterly abandoned when we arrived.

When we reached the base of the stairs, I knew to stay back from the sound of pounding footsteps. Seconds later, Dameon ran past, followed by Marcus, and finally Darik. My big brother came to a halt at the sight of us.

"Good morning! I hope we didn't wake you. They're both excited for the fun tonight."

I was already shaking my head. "You're fine. It'll be nice to actually get to enjoy the day today."

He gave me a commiserating smile as a bittersweet sadness penetrated his gaze. I knew what he was thinking. *Our parents would have loved this.*

There was hardly a day that went by that I didn't think of them, but it didn't do any good to dwell on grief. We had to focus on survival.

"I don't know if you saw the gathering outside," he said then with a twitch of his lips.

"What? I didn't see any—"

He motioned to the back door. "They wanted it to be a surprise."

Bisa took her hand from mine and planted a kiss on my cheek. "Congrats, sugar."

"You were in on it, too?"

She giggled, a sound I hadn't heard in ages. "Of course I was! Now come on, we've kept them waiting long enough."

I made my way to the back door, hearing the rushed footsteps of Dameon and Marcus as they caught up with us. Dameon ran ahead to push the door open, and we stepped out into the blinding morning sunlight. The sun came up on the back end of the house and it was a moment before I could see properly.

Then I heard the cheer and felt Ivory's only dog lick at my fingertips as my eyes adjusted. Once they did, I spotted the slab of wood being held up a dozen feet away. It looked like it was one of those that had been replaced on the side of the Exalted House after the mob assaulted it. The wood was painted in a variety of colors, the old words there lost to time just as much as the people who had originally painted it.

Written in fresh black paint were the words, *Thank You, Dahlia!*

I gasped, staring at the board. Young couples smiled and cheered for me, all of which had only arrived after we founded Ivory. A few children who had joined in the impromptu celebration were running around in circles. Even Broskow was clapping for me beside Mrs. Green.

Beyond them, I saw He Who Wanders watching from the glowing yellow dandelions. From this distance I couldn't make out his face, but he seemed just as surprised by this show of appreciation as I was.

Then I heard his voice as clear as a bell in my mind. *Your people have strange customs.*

I sighed, glaring in his direction, but he'd conveniently looked away to study the crowd.

Bisa wrapped her hand around my arm and led me further outside.

"What is all this about?" I asked.

"You saved us." Dameon stared up at me from the ground, where he sat petting the dog.

"We would have died without you, sugar," Bisa said, her voice as warm and comforting as her hand around my arm.

"And you helped resurrect Carra." Darik stepped forward, raising his voice and quieting the cheers as he continued. "In years past, this was the day that my siblings and I would plot out survival methods so we could make it through the night. Our fellow townsfolk were forced to believe that the only way they could make a difference was if they hunted down certain children one long day every year." He looked to Broskow as he said this. From where I stood, I saw Broskow turn red in the face and avert his eyes as he nodded.

"We used to live in fear of the Gray People, but today, here in this new town we call Ivory, we live alongside them." He motioned to She Who Feasts off to the side, waving excitedly with her black-clawed hands. "We don't fear the woods, we don't fear our neighbors, and we don't fear our protectors. Instead we live in harmony with all of them. But who can we thank for this?" The crowd grew quiet as he paused. "At the end of the darkness, who let us toward the light, despite how difficult it was?"

He put a hand out toward me and my eyes went wide.

"My dear sister, Dahlia. On this day, we celebrate our lives, our freedom, and our understanding thanks to her leadership. As such, I propose that on this anniversary of what used to be called The Seeking, we now call it Dahlia Day. I pose this decision to every member of Ivory, though. I don't want anyone to feel that we're overlooking anyone else. All those in favor, please raise your hand."

Almost in unison, each person raised their hand to the sky. Tears started to flow down my cheeks.

"Broskow?" There was annoyance in Darik's voice, and I turned to see that Broskow was the only one not raising his hand. A hush fell over the group as all eyes fell on him. I steeled myself for the inevitable insults that he'd hurl my way.

He leveled me with hard eyes as he chewed on a piece of straw. "I wanted to add something to Darik's little speech. It's not something I think many of you will want to hear, but it needs to be said."

I felt Bisa's hand on my arm tighten ever so slightly. She wasn't verbalizing her anger, but I could feel it. The hush broke into murmurs.

"Come on, man!" exclaimed Mr. Baker, a young man who came here with his equally young husband. "Don't ruin a good moment like this!"

Broskow held out his hand, "Easy now, I mean no

offense. I just want to say that I've had the misfortune of hunting many kids on The Seeking with my pack of dogs in tow. I've tried to catch them in traps and chased them on horseback. I've hunted them like animals.

"I never thought of it as terrible or wrong, I thought of it as necessary. I thought that it was the only way to be respected in Carra. I thought that living in the Exalted House would somehow make all my troubles go away." His shoulders dropped. "I was damn wrong. Losing my dear wife Pearl and my beautiful boys taught me that. Dahlia showed me that there are better ways to lead."

His eyes softened as he stared at me and then Darik. "I didn't listen to her at first, but I should have. I was stubborn and set in my ways, but I want folks to learn from my mistakes. I want you all to enjoy Dahlia Day, not as just a celebration of what we've accomplished, but as a day to reflect on what we've lost. Don't get so caught up in what you want that you lose sight of what you have."

What started out as murmurs of dissent turned into nods and cheers. When Broskow was done, Mrs. Green wrapped her arm around his, as though afraid he would topple to the ground after saying so much.

"So... you don't have an objection?" Darik pressed.

"Of course not! I just didn't want you hogging the floor for speeches!" He broke into a grin at the laughs that followed. "Go ahead and make it official already."

Darik put a scroll in my hands and I unrolled it. Written in his finest penmanship was the declaration of Dahlia Day, with a place for all of the Priest children to sign. My brothers had taken the liberty of signing already, and Bisa offered her back for me to add my signature.

It was hard to see the page. My eyes were blurry from the sunlight and all the tears.

Standalone

Short stories, horror, dark fantasy

The Impostor and Other Dark Tales

Weird western, werewolves, vampires, short story

Night Feeders

Mystery, film noir, humor, short story

The Mysterious Disappearance of Charlene Kerringer

The Blade Filled with Stars

A kingdom is under siege from a familiar enemy. Families and friends are pitted against each other without reason. Slaughter is imminent while the winged Queen Khafil soars overhead. Desperate and terrified, Anna works with her sister, Lilah, to summon aid from their mother's ancient spell book.

Determined to save their people, the sisters summon Death to help them, but Death is not easily swayed. Neither of the sisters are prepared for the consequences.

Want a peek behind the scenes?
Want to preview my books before they get released?

Get exclusive access to book goodies, giveaways, and cover reveals by joining my mailing list. Not only will you get notified of all my new releases, you'll get an exclusive copy of The Blade Filled with Stars.

Subscribe to the Mailing List at:
http://marlenafrank.com/mailinglist/

Follow me on Ko-Fi for regular updates on my writing progress.

Monthly subscribers get access to sneak peeks at stories way before anyone else. They also get access to cover reveals, monthly shout-outs on social media, and thanked by name in the acknowledgements in my books.

http://ko-fi.com/MarlenaFrank

ACKNOWLEDGMENTS

The Seeking was a labor of love. After writing Stolen, I had the urge to dive into a very dark world. I wrote down so many notes in notebooks, sorting out the plot and the characters, and soon the book was in progress. It was wonderful to get it down on paper. But writing it was only part of the process. Books are crafted through encouragement, determination, and teamwork.

Thank you to my parents, John and Connie, for believing in my author career. A big thank you to my older sister, Kelley, who guided me to develop a taste for darker tales. Thank you to my Aunt Charmaine for always being such a big cheerleader. Thank you to my cosplay friends who have always believed in creative expression of every stripe. Thank you to Jeff and Kim who helped me explore storytelling with Dungeons and Dragons years ago, and perhaps one day my nephew and niece, Patrick and Amelia, will enjoy my words.

I'm grateful to my editors. This story would be nothing without Rae's incredible eye as an editor. Finally a big thank you to my Ko-Fi supporter Donna for supporting my writing month after month.You always motivate me.

If you enjoyed this dark tale and would like to see

more, please leave a review and share this book with your friends. I love exploring dark worlds and themes, but reviews from my amazing readers are what keep me going. You make books truly thrive. Thank you for reading!

ABOUT THE AUTHOR

Marlena Frank is the author of young adult fantasy and horror novels, short stories, novellas, and book series. Many of her books have hit the bestseller charts, including her debut novel, Stolen. Her work has been praised by Readers' Favorite and featured in De Mode of Literature Magazine. Her stories have appeared in anthologies such as Emporium of Superstition, Catstruck!, Heroic Fantasy Quarterly, Georgia Gothic, and The Sirens Call ezine.

Although born in Tennessee, Marlena has spent most of her life in Georgia. She lives with her sister and two spoiled adopted cats. She serves as the Vice President of the Atlanta Chapter of the Horror Writers Association, is an active member of the Science Fiction and Fantasy Writers Association, and is an avid member of the Atlanta cosplay community.

She is also an INFJ, a tea drinker, and a wildlife enthusiast.

Support her on Ko-Fi: <u>ko-fi.com/MarlenaFrank</u>